Dear Reader,

The editors at Harlequin and Silhouette are thrilled to be able to bring you a brand-new featured author program beginning in 2005! Signature Select aims to single out outstanding stories, contemporary themes and oft-requested classics by some of your favorite series authors and present them to you in a variety of formats bound by truly striking covers.

We plan to provide several different types of reading experiences in the new Signature Select program. The Spotlight books will offer a single "big read" by a talented series author, the Collections will present three novellas on a selected theme in one volume, the Sagas will contain sprawling, sometimes multi-generational family tales (often related to a favorite family first introduced in series) and the Miniseries will feature requested, previously published books, with two or, occasionally, three complete stories in one volume. The Signature Select program will offer one book in each of these categories per month, and fans of limited continuity series will also find these continuing stories under the Signature Select umbrella.

In addition, these volumes will bring you bonus features...different in every single book! You may learn more about the author in an extended interview, more about the setting or inspiration for the book, more about subjects related to the theme and, often, a bonus short read will be included.

Watch for new stories from Vicki Lewis Thompson, Lori Foster, Donna Kauffman, Marie Ferrarella, Merline Lovelace, Roberta Gellis, Suzanne Forster, Stephanie Bond and scores more of the brightest talents in romance fiction!

We have an exciting year ahead!

Warm wishes for happy reading,

Marsha Zinberg

Marsha Zinberg
Executive Editor
The Signature Select Program

SIGNATURE SELECT™

SAGA

Tori Carrington

A REAL McCOY

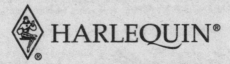

HARLEQUIN®

TORONTO • NEW YORK • LONDON
AMSTERDAM • PARIS • SYDNEY • HAMBURG
STOCKHOLM • ATHENS • TOKYO • MILAN • MADRID
PRAGUE • WARSAW • BUDAPEST • AUCKLAND

ISBN 0-373-83647-3

A REAL McCOY

www.eHarlequin.com

Printed in U.S.A.

Dear Reader,

What is it that sets us apart from others? The characteristics that label some as ordinary, others as heroes and heroines worthy of note? These are but two of many questions we asked ourselves as we sat down to write this sequel to our award-winning miniseries, THE MAGNIFICENT McCOY MEN. And we hope we answered them in *A Real McCoy*.

Criminal defense attorney Kay Buckingham is the antithesis of the McCoy men in that she protects the very people they apprehend in their careers in law enforcement. She's soft and smooth, while they're strong and a little rough around the edges. But when every aspect of her life is turned upside down within a twenty-four hour period, her survival depends on these same men, along with sexy U.S. marshal Harry Kincaid, to protect *her*.

We hope you enjoy revisiting the McCoys as much as we did. We'd love to hear what you think. Write us at P.O. Box 12271, Toledo, Ohio 43612, e-mail us at toricarrington@aol.com, and visit our Web site at www.toricarrington.com for more information on us and those magnificent McCoys!

Wishing you happy—and hot!—reading,

Lori & Tony Karayianni
aka Tori Carrington

THE MAGNIFICENT McCOY MEN
HARLEQUIN TEMPTATION

We dedicate this book to the memory of fellow author and friend Cheryl Anne Porter, who was taken from us all way too soon. She was the ultimate Real McCoy in both spirit and deed. Here's a final signature wave, sweetheart. You will be sorely missed.

PROLOGUE

THE ONE-HUNDRED-YEAR-OLD farmhouse in Manchester, Virginia was built for a big family. Aside from a few Victorian frills, it was simple and large and airy, the wood stairs creaky from years of boys running up and down them, the kitchen sink large enough to bath in, the mudroom wide enough to accommodate a dozen pairs of muddy shoes. Only McCoy family patriarch Sean McCoy didn't think his grandfather had quite this scene in mind when he'd built the place slat by torturous slat. His gaze took in his five grown sons, their five wives and their children seated around the mammoth round kitchen table for Sunday dinner on a fine spring day. Then again, maybe this was exactly what he'd had in mind.

What a difference six women could make in six men's lives.

Sean leaned casually to the side to miss a spoonful of potatoes sailing in his direction, the two-year-old culprit oblivious to the possible consequences to others of launching a mashed missile.

This house was where all five of his sons had grown up, though it was home to Mitch and his wife now, Sean and the others all within the DC area. Watching each of his sons juggle conversation, their wives and, where applicable, their children while making history of the table full of food, Sean found it a wonder they had survived at all much less grown into strong, good men any father would be proud of. All of them had followed him into law enforcement, although no two of them carried the same badge. Only the youngest, David, had followed in Sean's footsteps, having attended the DCPD Academy.

It had once been joked that McCoy men were incapable of producing female children. But looking at his one male grandchild, and four female grandchildren, Sean knew that the belief was dead wrong.

But he didn't need them to prove it to him. Proof existed outside this room that once again rang with the sound of laughter. Proof that often robbed him of breath and plunged him into a dark place where not even his wife Wilhemenia could reach him. He looked at her now, holding Jake's toddler, feeling both like he was looking at the woman he loved, and at a complete stranger.

Of course that was his fault, not hers. That's what happened when a man kept a secret for over twenty-seven years.

That's what happened when a man made a mistake he could never take back.

CHAPTER ONE

A GREAT MAN is measured not by his assets or his accomplishments but rather by his ability to deliver a kiss while his target is walking on a treadmill, listening to a taped deposition and leafing through legal briefs.

Kat Buckingham smiled as her fiancé, James Smith, managed to plant a kiss on her cheek without breaking her stride.

He held up Chinese takeout. "I got your favorite."

Kat tugged the right muff of the headphone away from her ear. "I'll meet you in the kitchen in twenty."

She watched as James headed down the hall of the historic Georgetown townhouse she'd bought last year. He disappeared through the foyer on his way to the back of the first floor. She refastened the headphones then pressed the rewind button to listen to the part she'd missed.

Somehow in law school Kat had never imagined herself being this busy at twenty-seven. As a junior criminal defense attorney at the law offices of

Kennedy, Salizar and Jewison, her calendar easily eclipsed the grueling schedule she'd kept at GWU. Multi-tasking had always been the name of the game, but now... Now she found herself running circles around her own circles.

Of course, it hadn't always been that way. Three years ago, fresh out of law school, she'd been happy making a fraction of her salary as a staff attorney at The Legal Aid Society of The District of Columbia. She'd been just as busy during the day, but more often than not her work day had stopped at five or six, and her case load had involved handling landlord-tenant disputes and helping clients enroll in programs that would help them through tough times, in contrast to the dark, punishing capital crime cases she took on now. While she was still strongly associated with Legal Aid—the case she was working on now had unofficially been recommended to her by a supervising attorney with Legal Aid—her workday never seemed to end.

If her new focus, her drive to make a difference, had anything to do with her parents' death three years ago...well, she wasn't ready to face that possibility, even if she'd had the time to give it the intense scrutiny it deserved.

Her feet automatically slowed, matching the heaviness in her heart, and the treadmill's computer beeped at her. She moved to reset the pace when she caught something on the tape she was listening to.

"...the patient displays all the classic signs of post-traumatic stress disorder. If caught in time, he would never have committed the crimes..."

Kat pressed the rewind button and listened to the passage again while jotting a note on her pad. The pen slipped from her hand. She reached to catch it, accidentally pulling her earphones from the player and catching the edge of her Skechers on the moving treadmill. She was mildly surprised when the abrupt spurt of bad luck didn't end with her butt first on the floor. Instead she stood next to the whirring treadmill, silent earphones still attached to her head, the pen she'd dropped lying at her feet.

That's all right. It was nearly nine o'clock on a Sunday night and she hadn't had a minute to herself all weekend. Maybe this was fate's way of giving her a kick in the behind.

She switched off the exercise equipment and the cassette player then gathered her notes and legal briefs together and dumped them unceremoniously into her briefcase. Only after she rubbed the towel around her neck against her damp face did she notice a sharp scent filling her nose. It smelled like something burning.

That's odd. James had brought takeout. Why would he be cooking anything?

She longingly eyed the stairs to the second floor desperately wanting a shower but instead headed for the kitchen. "James? What's that smell?"

The crystalline sound of breaking glass made her pick up her pace, and then a loud thump drew her up short. What was that?

She pushed the swinging door open and stood staring at James's bloodied, inert body on the otherwise spotless yellow kitchen tile. She rushed to his side and dropped to her knees. "James? James? What's happened…"

Her brain attempted to process the sight of blood covering his face and the front of his crisp white shirt when movement caught her attention from the corner of her eye. She gasped as a shadow darted out the open back door.

Kat pressed her shaking fingertips to James's carotid artery. No pulse.

Oh, God…

She scrambled for the cordless telephone on the wall barely aware she was crawling over broken glass as the sharp shards tore through her leggings. The 911 operator picked up immediately.

"Help! He's dead! James is dead!"

U.S. MARSHAL Harry Kincaid sat in his plain agency sedan down the block from the Georgetown townhouse and glanced at his watch. He might as well go home. He'd seen James Smith enter Kat Buckingham's house a few minutes earlier and routine dictated that Smith would probably stay the night.

Harry's stomach turned. He told himself it was

because of the two chili dogs he'd picked up on his way over to the exclusive DC neighborhood, but he knew the condition was caused by more than just greasy food. The idea that someone like Kathryn Buckingham would be engaged to a sociopath like James Smith left him feeling sick to his stomach.

Of course, there were two things he knew that she didn't: one, her fiancé's real identity; two, her own true family roots.

Harry dry-washed his face with his hands, the movement motivated by more than exhaustion. He was agitated about information he'd learned of Kat Buckingham that not even Kat Buckingham knew about. Information that he still wasn't sure what to do with. Information that touched him personally because his best friend and fellow marshal happened to be Connor McCoy.

As to James's being a participant in the federal witness protection and relocation program, Harry couldn't say whether that fact would have much impact on Kat's relationship with him. Given her "save the world and everything in it" upbringing, he could very well see her being sympathetic, though he couldn't imagine she would appreciate not being told the truth.

Kat… Funny he should be thinking of Kathryn Buckingham as if they were acquainted. They hadn't even met.

Hell, truth be told, he shouldn't even be there, sitting up the block from her house. He'd filed his quarterly report on Smith's status yesterday. Still, something kept him there even though he had a report due later next week on another protected witness. Something that had nothing to do with Smith and everything to do with his pretty fiancée.

Pretty, hell. The criminal attorney was drop dead gorgeous. And probably didn't have a clue that her tall, slender frame, natural almost white blond hair and green eyes turned heads, both male and female, when she walked down a street.

But what got him were those moments when her thoughts appeared to wander—usually in the middle of doing three things at once—and she'd get a wistful, almost lonely look on her strikingly beautiful face as if she was staring at something she wanted but knew she'd never have.

It was then he wondered how she might react to the information, which he'd uncovered while doing a routine check on her. Information that not only proved how small the world was, but how strange and curious. He'd grappled with the knowledge for the past five days, trying to decide what, if anything, he should do with it. Not on a professional level. No. This information was very personal indeed.

Harry grimaced and stared at where he could make out Kat's silhouette through the townhouse's sheer curtains. What did it say about him that he was sitting outside a witness's house on a Sunday night in May watching other people living their lives rather than living his own? Worse, he was infatuated with the fiancée of a relocated witness who should, by all rights, be behind bars along with the people he'd helped convict three years ago—if not for his past crimes, then for his present.

But that wasn't for Harry to judge. He'd filed his report on James Smith's questionable activities. Now it was up to his superior to decide what to do with the file. Either turn the other cheek or forward it to the proper authorities for further investigation.

Harry was adjusting his rearview mirror and reaching to switch on the ignition when he spotted a DCPD car speeding up behind him, sirens blaring. It screeched to a stop in front of Buckingham's place.

Harry reached for the door handle and started to climb out as an EMS vehicle roared up from the opposite end of the street drawing to a halt mere inches away from the front bumper of the cruiser.

Oh, hell.

Remembering the uneasy feeling he'd had over the past week, Harry rushed for the townhouse, his badge in hand.

AN HOUR LATER Kat sat perched on the edge of the couch in the living room, the blanket someone had draped over her shoulders doing little to subdue her uncontrollable shivering.

James was dead.

The three words wound around and around her numbed brain like an unbroken chain, becoming one long sentence rather than countless separate ones.

It seemed impossible that she should lose someone so close to her again in such a violent manner. It was only a few years ago that she'd lost her parents in a car crash. And they'd been visiting *her* when they'd driven home in that freak ice storm.

Her shivers coalesced into a long, bone-racking shudder.

A silent, watchful policewoman sat opposite her while voices sounded in the foyer, closer than the talk she'd been hearing vague snatches of from the kitchen where James's body lay. Kat looked up, staring almost sightlessly at a man who looked vaguely familiar. She might not have registered him at all but for the intense way he was looking at her.

"Mrs. Buckingham?"

She looked up into the face of another man dressed in a plain brown suit that had seen better days. "It's Miss…" Her gaze made it as far as the palm-sized notepad he held. "We…James and I…we are…were engaged. The wedding is…was scheduled for this August."

He flipped through the notepad again and made a note with one of those pens you picked up at the dry cleaners. "And the full name of the deceased?"

Kat pushed her hair back with a shaking hand. "Smith. James." She finally looked up into his face. "Who did you say you were again?"

"Detective Leary."

She glanced around. "I've already told one of your associates the information."

"Actually, Miss Buckingham, I was the one you told it to."

She squinted at him. "Then why are you asking me again?"

"Just to make sure I have the information straight." More flipping. Kat discovered it was easier to look at the pad than at him. "Did you and Mr. Smith have an argument tonight?"

"No…I told you no." This wasn't happening. The blanket slipped from her shoulder and she repositioned it with little success. Her own hand caught her attention and she stared at the blood smeared there. James's blood.

"I…I was on the treadmill going over a deposition when James came in with dinner…"

"The Chinese food carton that started the fire in the microwave."

Kat nodded. "Yes. I had just finished and was going to join him in the kitchen when I smelled something burning and heard breaking glass." Her voice caught and her trembling increased double fold.

"And this?"

She stared at a Ziploc bag that held what looked like a savings passbook.

"We found this near the body, Miss Buckingham. Your name is printed in the front. Were you and the deceased arguing over finances?"

Why would she and James argue about money? While they weren't wealthy by any stretch, they were doing well.

She caught the present tense of her thoughts and felt a fresh bout of tears threaten.

It didn't make any sense. Nothing made any sense.

"Miss Buckingham? Why was this next to the body?"

"I don't know," she said, her voice cracking. "I have no idea why my savings passbook was in the kitchen."

"Detective, can you pursue this line of questioning once Miss Buckingham has had a chance to compose herself?"

Kat felt the urge to laugh hysterically. She didn't think she'd ever feel composed again.

She glanced at the man who had asked the question to find it was the one who had been watching her from the foyer.

"I'm the detective conducting this investigation, Kincaid," said Leary, "so if you'd be good enough to stay to the side."

Emotion welled up in Kat's throat. "Please…

please. My fiancé's dead. Can I have a few moments alone?"

The pad flipped closed.

"Actually, I have all the information I need, Miss Buckingham." He looked to the policewoman across from her. "Officer, please place Miss Buckingham under arrest for the murder of one James Smith."

The world tipped under Kat. "Pardon me? I don't…"

The policewoman jerked her to her feet and swiveled her around to handcuff her. It took all Kat had not to succumb to the black shadow creeping over her confused mind.

"You have the right to remain silent," the policewoman began, reciting words Kat had heard countless times previously.

Only before they had been said to her clients, not to her.

CHAPTER TWO

THE COUNTY JAIL smelled different when you were on the inside.

Kat sat on the lower bunk in her assigned cell and stared at where she'd wrung her hands so hard all night her skin was red and raw. She'd been to the jail more times than she could count as a criminal defense attorney. But she'd never expected to be actually locked up in one of the cells. She had a cellmate, but the other woman seemed as preoccupied as she was and aside from the occasional squeaking of the bedsprings of the upper bunk, Kat was barely aware the other woman was there.

What she was painfully aware of was the direness of her situation and the grief that enveloped her as surely as the cell surrounding her.

James was gone.

The fact was so incredible as to be almost impossible. He couldn't be dead. One minute he'd been so full of life and smiling, the next...

But she had irrefutable proof that he was gone, didn't she? She'd been arrested for his murder.

Kat's mind went blank, as if incapable of accepting the information. When it finally started working again what seemed like a long time later, it homed in on practicalities, which were all that she could deal with right now.

She had no cell phone. No computer. Not even a pad and paper with which to record her thoughts and work out how she'd gotten where she was and the various possible outcomes. Nothing. *Every* privilege she normally took for granted had been stolen from her.

Kat's muscles were tight and sore. She'd gotten precious little sleep last night and her eyes felt coated with sand despite that she'd been crying. And she'd been crying a lot. For James. For herself. For every client she'd represented and thought she'd understood.

Roger Cartright from Kennedy, Salizar and Jewison had been to visit her first thing this morning. She'd felt like she was caught in some sort of ill-cast episode of *The Twilight Zone* as she listened to him go through the steps she, herself, covered with her own clients. First, tell the accused she didn't have anything to worry about. You were on the case and would do everything in your power to help her. Next, get important details, being careful not to actually ask whether the client was guilty or not.

Of course she'd told him she wasn't guilty. But even as she'd said the words she'd known how futile they were. Guilt or innocence held absolutely no relevance In cases of this nature. The key lay in the details. And so she gave them to him, her shoulders slumping lower and lower as she realized how very few of them she had. No, she didn't have any idea who would want to kill James. No, nothing was taken, no sign of robbery. No, there were no eye-witnesses to attest to her innocence. No, she hadn't gotten a good look at the assailant.

Roger had packed up his stuff and told her he was hurrying along the scheduling of the arraignment, but he'd been hesitant when the subject of bail had come up. Kat wasn't stupid. She knew that bail was rarely granted in murder cases. Depending on the circumstances, the accused often stood a better chance on the run than facing a jury of his or her peers.

The bedsprings above her squeaked. Her cell-mate, Lupe Martinez, peered over the mattress at her. "It true you're a lawyer?"

Kat blinked at her. They hadn't said more than their names to each other when she'd come in the night before. She suspected the jail grapevine had been working overtime during her forty-five minute meeting with Roger.

"Yes," she said.

"They say you rep Gina Polanski."

Kat nodded.

"I roomed with Gina at Riker's last year." The

springs squeaked again and Lupe's head disappeared. "You think she didn't do it?"

Gina Polanski had murdered her husband in self-defense two years ago and Kat had had a hard time convincing the original jury that she'd been a battered wife because Gina had only reported one of the battery incidents to the authorities. And since her husband had pled no contest rather than guilty, well, Gina had been sent up the river for life without the possibility of parole.

"I believe she's innocent of first degree murder, yes." That's why she was still working the appellate courts trying to get a new trial set in a different venue. Recently she'd become aware that one of Gina's late husband's distant relatives had actually been seated on the original jury, definite grounds for a new trial.

"You think you can get her off?"

"That all depends."

"Yeah. Probably it depends on whether you're gonna get off for snuffing your own old man."

Kat's breath stopped.

The sound of clinking keys caught their attention and they watched a guard come to the cell door. "You got another visitor, Buckingham."

Kat blinked. Roger back for more information?

Whoever it was, she was glad for the reprieve. The cell seemed mere inches away from closing in on her altogether.

YESTERDAY, if you'd told Sean McCoy where he would be today, he'd have laughed you out of the room. Now he sat on the other side of the bolted down table in the county jail conference room and tugged on his tie. He had no idea why he'd worn the choking article of clothing, but for some reason it had been important to him that he make a good first impression. He patted his jacket pocket, feeling for the photograph there, then cleared his throat and folded his hands on top of the cold table.

He'd rehearsed this moment at least a thousand times in his mind over the years. Not because he'd expected it to come to pass, but because he had secretly hoped that it might.

Only he would never have expected it to happen in quite this way.

A key turned in the metal security door and he pushed to his feet. He blinked at the blond woman with her hands cuffed in front of her, barely recognizing her. The oversize orange jumpsuit didn't help, but he'd never seen her hair in such disarray, her skin so pale. If he'd passed her on the street, he wouldn't have recognized her.

She looked at him, confusion in her green eyes as the guard helped her sit on the stool across from him.

"You have ten minutes," the guard said then exited and locked the door.

Silence settled over the small room as Sean stared at Kathryn and she stared back.

Finally, he cleared his throat, trying to dislodge all the words that he had rehearsed for so long but that now stuck there, refusing to come out.

Kathryn's cuffs clanked as she shifted on her stool. "Are you with the police department? If so, I don't think I should be talking to you without my attorney present."

He'd never heard her voice before up close and personal. Nonetheless, the familiarity of it made his stomach pitch to his feet.

"No, I'm not with the department—not in an official capacity, anyway. I do consult, but that's not why I'm here." He shifted uncomfortably. "It would probably help if I introduced myself. I'm Sean McCoy."

She squinted, apparently waiting for more.

Sean forced himself to sit down, trying to make the action appear normal when it emerged anything but. "Kathryn, I…"

"Kat."

He eyed her.

"Nobody calls me Kathryn."

He knew that. He knew a lot of things about her that he couldn't reveal. Like that her favorite color was purple. Like that when she was eight she'd taken a spill on her bike and still had a scar on her right back shoulder. Like that she dipped her biscuit into gravy but didn't like the gravy on top.

He knew a lot of details about her and her life, both big and small. Some had been provided by her parents, some by his colleagues on the force—who'd always helped him look after her, but had thankfully never asked why—but even more through his own consistent watching of her. Sometimes close enough to hear her speak, but mostly from a safe distance so he wouldn't upset her life.

Yes, he knew that she preferred to be called Kat. But he'd always thought of her as Kathryn and that's what he'd automatically called her.

"Are you a reporter?"

He shook his head. "No."

Sean noticed the slump of her shoulders, the shadow of apathy beginning to edge in around her. He knew jail did strange things to people and affected everyone differently. He'd seen bullies come out weeping like babies. He'd seen patsies come out harder than granite.

And he now saw that just a day in jail had turned Kathryn from a smart, confident young lawyer into a wary, defeated young woman.

Of course, it probably didn't help that her fiancé had been killed virtually in front of her eyes—Sean scoffed at the possibility that she was guilty of the crime.

"So who are you then?"

For a moment Sean had almost forgotten why he was there. For a moment he'd slipped into the role he'd played for the past twenty-seven years. The role of observer, outsider, watching her from afar but never interacting with her.

For a moment he'd forgotten what he needed to tell her.

He cleared his throat again and smoothed down his tie. He followed the movement with his gaze. "I don't know why I wore this." He loosened it and pulled it off, folding up the tie he'd worn for his and Wilhemenia's wedding and putting it into his pocket. His fingers brushed against the photo there. He took the picture out, placed it face down on the table between them, then rested his hand over it. "You don't know who I am, Kathryn…Kat. But I know who you are." He fought to hold her gaze when he might have looked away. "I've watched from afar as you skinned your knee during your first solo bike ride. I was there when you graduated middle school, then again when you graduated law school with honors."

He hated the wariness in her eyes.

"Did you know my parents?"

He shook his head, then nodded. "I met them." He cleared his throat again. "And perhaps after the accident three years ago, I should have approached you then…"

She thankfully remained silent and he could see her clever mind working a million miles a minute trying to figure out who he was and what he was trying to say.

"Look, I never thought this moment would come so I'm having a hard time trying to word this in a way that won't come as too much of a shock."

A knock at the door and the guard said, "Five minutes."

Sean stared at him, then shifted his gaze back to Kathryn's pale features. He offered up a ghost of a smile. "But no matter how I put it, you're going to be shocked, aren't you?"

She squinted at him again.

"What I'm trying to say, Kathryn…Kat. I mean, what I need to tell you is…"

Sean's heart was beating so hard he was afraid it might pound straight through his chest. He slid his hand with the photograph underneath it across the table, leaving it there in front of her facedown. "Maybe this will help."

She stared at the plain, unmarked back of the picture.

"Go ahead. Turn it over."

She hesitantly lifted her cuffed hands to the table and slowly flipped the picture. She was quiet for long moments.

"This is a picture of me, but I…but I don't recognize the clothes or the surroundings."

"That's because it isn't you. It's a photo of Kathryn Connor McCoy."

She blinked at him several times.

"Your biological mother." He could no longer hold her gaze so he looked at the picture instead. "And I'm your father."

CHAPTER THREE

HIS NEWS HAD GONE OVER like a lead balloon.

And he'd bet his DCPD pension that the coming meeting wasn't going to go any better.

Sean may have been wearing more comfortable clothes since returning to the McCoy house hours ago, but he wasn't feeling any more comfortable. The late afternoon sun shone through the back kitchen window, seeming to spotlight the kitchen table—and bring into too bright relief the memory of Kathryn's face when he'd told her the news.

"Look, I don't know what you want from me, what you're hoping to accomplish, but I had two parents. And they're both dead. What you're doing is nothing short of cruel."

Sean blanched as he relived how she'd gotten up, cuffs clinking, and demanded to be taken back to her cell. Away from him. Away from the news he'd shared. Leaving him staring at the picture of his late wife on the table in front of him.

"I think it's a girl."

The table faded into the background as the sunlight illuminated another memory. A memory from the long ago past. The scene was his bedroom. His wife Kathryn was smoothing her hand over her swollen belly. She'd looked so beautiful lying there. Her blond hair was nearly white in the morning light, her lacy nightgown slipping down unheeded over one smooth shoulder. He'd crossed to sit next to her on the bed and put his hand over hers on her belly.

"What makes you say that?"

It had amazed him how Kathryn could flatten him with a single, dancing-eyed look. "I don't know. This time it's different. There's no kicking like with the boys. And sometimes I swear I can feel her singing."

Sean had chuckled at that.

"Don't laugh. I'm serious. Here, feel." She slid her hand out from under his then pressed his fingers against her solid flesh. "There. Can you feel it? The kind of humming?"

What Sean had felt was overwhelmed by his love for this woman, his wife, the mother of his five boys and the little girl she carried.

"What's up, Pops?"

Sean blinked to find David, his youngest son, leaning against the kitchen doorway, the first to arrive although he lived the farthest away in downtown DC with his wife, Kelly. Both worked with the DCPD. And both were so caught up in their careers they didn't have any children yet. But they were young. They had plenty of time.

Sean got up and stepped toward the refrigerator. He took out two beers, opened them then handed one to David.

"Sit down. Looks like we're going to have to wait a bit before the others get here."

He'd purposely asked the boys to come over at a time when all of them would have knocked off work.

"Where's Billie?"

Sean cracked a partial smile. They had taken to calling Wilhemenia that but only when she wasn't around. Truth was, the masculine name didn't fit the ultrafeminine woman.

"I asked that we have some time alone so she went over to visit with Melanie."

Melanie was his middle son Marc's wife and Wilhemenia's daughter. She'd been the reason he'd met Wilhemenia at all. But not the reason he'd married her. If his sons had had their way, they would never have married at all, even though that was now water that had passed under a very distant bridge.

David nodded and took a slug from his beer.

"Hey, starting without us?" Marc and Mitch came in together even though Mitch lived in this very house and Marc had to drive in from Bedford, the same town outside DC Sean and Wilhemenia called home. David leaned back on his chair legs and grabbed another couple of beers from the fridge, reaching for another as they heard the loud beep of a car horn and moments later Jake came in.

Only Connor had yet to show. And Sean knew not only that Connor was the one who would take the news the hardest, but that this might just be the one thing for which he could never forgive his father.

HARRY KINCAID sat in a downtown Capitol diner across the booth from fellow U.S. Marshal and longtime bud Connor McCoy, his coffee cup empty, his blueberry pie half eaten. And he still hadn't said what he'd invited Connor here to say.

Connor talked to another marshal, the coffee shop a popular one with the agents. Harry was glad for the reprieve. It gave him more time to try to match together the words he was grappling for. But just how, exactly, did one go about telling one's best friend, "Hey, you know you have a sister, don't you? Oh, and by the way, she's just been arrested for murder"?

Falsely.

His fingers tightened on his cup. He didn't know that. Couldn't know that. Hell, he'd been sitting right out front of the house when the crime had gone down and hadn't seen any unusual cars or goings on. For all intents and purposes Kat Buckingham had been in that townhouse, alone, with her fiancé, James Smith, and easily could have done him in.

But somehow Harry knew she hadn't. He couldn't say why. He merely knew that she wasn't made that way. She might boot the poor excuse for a human being out of her house, or call 911 to have him forcibly removed. But she would never murder him. He'd known that before he'd seen the squad cars pull up to her house. And if he needed any verification, the memory of her sitting on the couch, shaken to the core as she was being interrogated was all it had taken.

Forget that he was attracted to her. Forget that he'd just found that she was related to his best friend. His gut told him Kathryn Buckingham was innocent of the crime she'd been accused of.

"You've got natural instinct, kid. A real nose for the job."

The memory of his mentor's words came back to him. The words had been enough for him to take the New York City Police Officer's Examination when he was seventeen, then enroll in the military for a three-year stint of active duty where he'd served in Desert Storm before becoming a fulltime officer with the NYC police department at twenty-one. By twenty-five he'd been one of the most decorated officers in Brooklyn. He'd also been one of the most investigated, and suspended because he'd been a little hard on the accused parties when responding to domestic disturbance calls. It was then he'd left the city where he'd grown up and used his experience to gain entrance to a rigorous 10-week basic training program at the U.S. Marshals Service Training Academy in Glynco, Georgia.

His job as a marshal was no less intense than his former position as a NYC police officer. But without domestic disturbance calls his ability to separate the personal from the professional was no longer tested.

"So what did you want to talk to me about?" Connor asked, his full attention back on Harry.

The other agent had moved on to a table nearby, leaving them alone again. Harry stared at his retreating figure then shifted his gaze back to Connor.

He and Con went back a ways. Back to Harry's first days on the job. They'd hit it off immediately although they'd had absolutely nothing in common but their desire to be the best. They'd been partnered together many times and had met up outside the department many times beyond that.

Probably that was the reason he was having a hard time telling Connor what he needed to. Because he knew how the hotheaded McCoy would take the news. Which wasn't well. Not well at all. In fact, he wouldn't be surprised if the first person Connor took his anger out on was Harry. After all, he had known Kathryn Buckingham had been born one Kathryn Jane McCoy for nearly a week and he hadn't said anything. Never thought he'd have cause to say anything. Hey, if Connor didn't want to mention that he had a sister, far be it from him to challenge him on the decision.

Only he'd instantly sensed Connor had no idea that another McCoy sibling outside him and his four brothers walked the earth. He'd heard enough about all of them to know that.

Besides, if there had been a female McCoy anywhere in the McCoy picture while they'd been growing up, Harry liked to think that maybe the guys would be more grounded. As it was, they each seemed to have had their demons to deal with.

Demons. That was funny. Like he didn't have his own personal demons. Put a wife-beater in front of him and it was more likely than not the guy would suffer a severe beating of his own.

"You going to cough it up or stare into your coffee cup all night?"

Harry looked at Connor, pushing images of his mother aside. "I'm still thinking about it."

There was a buzz and Connor took out his cell phone and read the display. "Shit. I completely forgot I was supposed to go out to Pops's tonight."

"For what?"

Connor shrugged as he refastened his cell phone. "I don't know. Some kind of family meeting, he'd said. Which isn't good." He grinned. "If Billie weren't too old to have children, I'd be half afraid he was going to tell us she was pregnant. Hell, seems like everybody else is expecting a baby."

Harry waved away the waitress when she tried to refill his coffee cup. "Hey, you never know about those things anymore. I read the other day where a sixty-year-old woman had a healthy baby boy. Her first child."

Connor gave a visible shudder. "There should be a law. I mean, by the time the kid graduates from high school she's going to be nearly eighty years old." He shook his head. "I mean, what is she going to do by way of discipline? Chase him around with her walker when he breaks curfew?" He pushed away his own half full coffee cup. "So are you going to spill or should we call it a night?"

Harry unfolded a couple of dollars and put them next to his coffee cup.

"You could ride out to Manchester with me. It's been a while since you've seen the guys. I'm sure they wouldn't mind your coming. And I could use the company."

Harry grimaced. He didn't think he would be welcome now. Not considering what Sean McCoy was probably going to say. Harry knew he'd visited his daughter earlier in the day.

"Nah, I'll pass. I'll catch up with you on the other side."

"You sure?"

Harry found Connor looking at him a little too closely. "Yeah. I'm sure."

He was sure that Connor was going to coldcock

him once he found out that Harry had known about his sister and hadn't said anything. But hey, you couldn't say he hadn't tried.

Yeah. Fat lot of good that was going to do him.

THE HOUR AND A HALF drive out to Manchester, Virginia, had been one Connor had made a million times. Manchester was where he'd grown up. It was where he'd settled with his wife, Bronte, in the old McCoy farm adjacent to Pops's place where he and his four brothers had been raised. He could probably drive the route with his eyes closed.

He pulled to a stop at a crossroads, wishing he had time to sneak a few minutes in with Bronte and their twin girls. But considering he was already over an hour late for the meeting his father had called, he figured he'd better see what was up there first so he turned left instead of right. Within moments he'd parked his truck between Jake's Caprice and David's sports car. He pulled open the side screen door, listening to the same old squeak that had always welcomed him.

"There he is."

"It's about time you got here."

"Jesus, man, you keep your wife waiting this way?"

Everybody but Pops and Jake—who'd always been on the quiet side—commented on his entrance. The guys began collecting the cards they were playing while Pops stood at the window staring at the backyard. Or at least appearing to be staring at the backyard. Somehow given his expression Connor didn't think he was seeing much of anything outside his own thoughts.

A strange foreboding assaulted him. He'd be the first to admit that he and his father had never been close. Close? Hell, it had been enough for them to be in the same room without Connor wanting to light into him. Until the truce, called a few years ago. The ensuing peace had seemed strange for a while, but he'd come to accept it. Even enjoy it.

Why did he feel that peace was going to be stolen away?

"Hey, some of us do have work to do," he said by way of a response to his brothers.

Pops had yet to turn around and Connor wondered if he'd even registered his arrival.

David finished gathering the cards they'd obviously been playing, then handed him a brew. Connor took a deep pull from the bottle then turned a chair around and straddled it. "So what's up?"

Jake said quietly, "We don't know yet. He wouldn't say anything until you got here."

Connor's discomfort level shot up by degrees.

"Pops?" David said.

Sean McCoy turned then, blinking, looking every one of his sixty-odd years.

"Where's Billie?"

The guys chuckled. "Banished. Appears this is guy business." Marc sat back and hooked his thumbs through the belt loops on his jeans.

"Speaking of which, Bronte's not too pleased that she and the rest of the women have been banished along with Billie."

"Bronte? You should hear Liz." Mitch looked toward the screen door. "Actually, considering she lives here, too, she's probably lurking around somewhere determined to get an earful."

Sean joined them at the table. "She's with Bronte."

All five McCoy brothers looked at him.

Connor squinted at the old man. He wasn't looking too good. In fact, his pale complexion made Connor remember a time when the only thing Sean McCoy would converse with was a bottle of vodka.

His every muscle tensed.

"So what's the big deal?" David asked, twirling his nearly empty beer bottle on the table. "What did you want to see us about?"

So, it appeared he wasn't the only one who had picked up on the soberness of the occasion. While Jake was never a jabber jaws, it was rare for the rest of his brothers to stay quiet for so long in each other's company, much less look toward their father like they were half afraid of what he was going to say.

"Look, I know I haven't always had the best of relations with you boys…"

Connor didn't move an inch, his every muscle cemented in place.

"And I can't tell you how much it's meant for me, these past few years." He gave a grin that looked a little too shaky for Connor's liking. And he wasn't meeting any of their eyes, instead focusing on the cards in front of David. "It's almost seemed like a real family."

Almost? Connor throat tightened. For all intents and purposes they had been a real family—prissy Wilhemenia aside. But considering how down to earth his real mother had been, he probably wouldn't have accepted anyone too much like their beloved matriarch either. In truth, Billie was the perfect second wife for their father, and stepmother to them. She was feminine to a fault, still blushed when other women her age had long moved beyond that stage, but she tried her damnedest to make sure she was there for each of them. The instant she'd instituted dinner every other Sunday, they'd all come and continued to come, no questions asked. Partly because none of them wanted to face Billie's wrath. Mostly because she created a family atmosphere in the old McCoy place that had been missing for far too long.

"Pops?" Jake said quietly.

"Oh. Yes." Sean looked like he had zoned out. Connor would have questioned whether or not he'd been drinking, but the beer bottle he'd moved from the counter to the table when he'd sat down was still full "What I have to say, well, it's not easy."

An uncomfortable silence again settled over the room.

"Just say it already and get it over with," Connor was surprised to find himself saying through clenched teeth.

Sean stared at him where he sat directly across the table. He nodded. "You're right. There really is no other way to say this than to just say it."

He cleared his throat and sat back. "You remember when your mom passed…"

Connor's heart thudded against his ribcage so hard he thought it might crack a bone or two. This went back twenty-seven years? To when their mother had died?

"Well, you all know she was pregnant…"

Connor's eyes went blank as he recalled that time so long ago. When he'd been nine. His mother's belly rounded with child. Her falling to the kitchen floor, unconscious.

Dead.

"Pops?" David said. The youngest of the family, he had none of the memories Connor had.

Sean's gaze remained glued to Connor's even though a tar-like anger at what he suspected his father was going to say had begun to coat Connor's insides.

"The baby survived. A girl. And her name's Kathryn Buckingham."

CHAPTER FOUR

"I'M YOUR FATHER."

Kat rolled over on the too thin mattress, the metal springs poking into her back, and what felt like razor wire twisting in her stomach, combining to ensure that she found not a measure of comfort. Sean McCoy's words spun through her mind, nicking the walls of truth she'd spent a lifetime building around her. Heaped on top of all that was already happening, she felt a breath away from a nervous breakdown.

Memories of her childhood swept through her mind. Of Christmas mornings with her parents enjoying a special holiday breakfast together and exchanging gifts, then spending the remainder of the day at a downtown homeless shelter serving food and cleaning up... Of her father giving her a full-grown dog when she was ten that had been physically and emotionally traumatized by years of illegal dog fighting but had been sweet-natured with her, always sleeping at the foot of her bed... Of her mother taking her along to teach illiterate adults how to read so they could do simple things like understand their apartment leases and register to vote...

Of her parents' funeral, attended by so many of the people they had helped. But her parents had been unable to help her when she'd needed them most...

Kat jerked fully awake and jackknifed to a sitting position, nearly hitting her head on the top bunk.

"Hey, keep it down," came from her cellmate. "Some people are trying to get some sleep."

Kat quietly moved until her feet were on the cold floor. She stared into the darkness, nothing but a dim blue light chasing shadows into relief. The world before her was so different from the one she knew. Her eyes felt dry and gritty from all the crying. The jumpsuit felt strange against her skin. Her hair spiked out from her head at all angles. Her feet, now bare, felt dirty. And no matter what she did, she couldn't find her way back to normalcy. Mostly because there was no normalcy to be found here in the darkness of a county jail cell. No normalcy to be found in a heart or mind that mourned the loss of James and the loss of her own freedom.

There was a distant clinking of keys. She looked toward the bars and the walkway beyond.

The springs above her squeaked. "You'd better lie back down before that guard gets here."

Kat swallowed hard. Could she really be reprimanded for sitting upright on her bed?

The footsteps and keys drew closer. She quickly did as her cellmate suggested and stared at the bunk above.

A beam from a flashlight slashed across her face. She blinked, wondering if she should have her eyes closed.

"Buckingham?"

Her throat refused to release the response she tried to produce so she moved her head to look into the beam and the faceless voice beyond.

"Get your stuff. You're out of here."

HARRY WOULD RECOGNIZE those eyes anywhere, although it had taken him a minute to realize it was indeed Kathryn Buckingham who'd been led through the door. More than the garish orange jumpsuit that seemed to drain her skin of all color, it was the way her shoulders slumped, as if someone had stolen everything out from under her.

And, in a sense, he figured that's what someone had done. And he was making it his job to figure out who.

He noticed the spark of recognition in her gaze as she blinked up at him.

"Take off the shackles," he demanded of the guard.

There was nothing but the sound of clanking metal and chains as Kathryn was freed. Usually the first thing a prisoner did was rub at their wrists, but not her. She merely stood looking at him as if waiting for him to speak.

"Come on," was all he said.

And she did.

Ten minutes later they were inside his SUV, the bright lights surrounding the jail illuminating the car's interior. It was after two in the morning and all was quiet. Too quiet.

He handed her items sealed in a clear plastic bag, her personal items taken from her when she was arrested. He started the engine and pulled out of the parking lot. Anything that would keep him from looking at her, from comparing her broken appearance with that of so many women he'd seen before. But the women he'd be comparing her to would be like his mother, women who suffered at the hands of men.

"How…how did you just do that?" her voice reached out to him.

Harry glanced over at her although she seemed overly interested in their surroundings. Probably because the only surroundings she'd seen for the past two days had been gray and sterile.

"I know people."

She stared at him, the dark circles under her eyes telling of little sleep and even less peace of mind. "Yes, but I don't know you."

He gave her a small smile. Maybe not all of the spunk had left her. "No, you're right. You don't."

She remained unblinking. "Who are you?"

Where did he start?

Did he tell her he was her oldest brother's best friend? A U.S. Marshal in charge of her late fiancé's case? That he had photograph after photograph of her when it had been James Smith that he was supposed to be watching?

"My name's Harry Kincaid."

She continued looking at him.

"That's all you're going to tell me?"

"For now."

She shifted in her seat, farther away from him, further into herself.

The car remained silent for a long time as he made his way from the county lockup to the north side of the city.

Harry contemplated the woman next to him. What he knew about her. What he didn't know about her. He'd watched her from afar for so long it was strange having her this close. Yet somehow it felt right.

She seemed smaller now. Shorter. Perhaps it was because up until now he'd had only compact-sized Smith to compare her to. But now that she was next to Harry, his own taller than average height served to lessen hers. Alongside Smith she was an Amazon. Alongside Harry she was half a head shorter. At least.

"I know there are things I should be asking you,"

Kathryn's voice reached him although she had her head turned toward her window. "But I can't think of what."

"There will be plenty of time for that."

A rustle of her clothes as she pulled her knees to her chest, making her look smaller yet. Almost childlike. "Will there?"

He nodded, keeping his gaze trained on the road although the empty street needed no extra attention from him.

A soft, broken sigh then, "I can't believe all this is happening. I can't believe James is...gone."

There was really nothing to say so Harry said nothing. Although the man in question lay dead in the morgue, Harry couldn't bring himself to defend the man. A man who couldn't have been more different from Harry. A man who'd made his living— indeed, seemed to enjoy making his living—from the heartbreak of others.

Including the woman next to him.

A long time passed, how long he couldn't be sure. But it seemed like a lifetime as he listened to her soft crying, her slender shoulders trembling as if they held the weight of the world. He drove around aimlessly, giving her the space she needed to grieve a man she had been about to marry. Giving himself the time he needed to adjust to his new role as this woman's protector.

"I can't believe you sprung me so easily and I

don't even know who you are." Her voice sounded hoarse from her crying. She wiped her nose with the heel of her hand. "I'm a criminal defense attorney. I know the system well. And I've never known of something like this to happen."

"Maybe you've been representing the wrong people."

She didn't say anything immediately, then, "Maybe. But…"

"Maybe you haven't represented someone in the witness relocation program before." Harry aimed his loaded words hoping they wouldn't be too much for her to handle.

She uncurled her legs and sat up straighter. "What?" The word was little more than a whisper that he could easily have imagined if he hadn't watched her say it.

They stopped at a red light although there was no traffic at the intersection to regulate. He took in her white-faced expression, her tear-streaked face, her wide, red-rimmed eyes.

James hadn't told her.

He hadn't known how much James had confided to the beautiful but broken woman in his car but he'd suspected that James wouldn't have shared the truth because the truth would have knocked him right out of her life.

Not because Kathryn would judge anyone by their past. Hell, her career focused on helping defendants others had long since given up on, often with no money involved.

No, James would have failed to make the grade with Kat because the one lie would have given her cause to look for more. And James Smith aka Darin Ichatious had been one walking, talking lie. A man who not only should have gone to prison with those he'd helped convict, but should have served the longest term.

But, as Harry's superiors frequently reminded him, that wasn't his decision to make.

"James was in the witness protection program?"

"Relocation. He testified three years ago. Afterward, we relocated him to St. Paul under a new identity. He resurfaced in DC last year."

She remained silent for a long time. Probably searching her memory for any sign that what he was saying was true. Probably wondering if she could trust him over a man she'd known, or thought she'd known, for just over a year. A man she had been going to marry until he was killed.

He glanced over to find she had her eyes firmly shut, her fingertips pressed tightly against her brow line. "That can't be true. This is just a nightmare and any minute I'm going to wake up…"

Without realizing that's what he was going to do, Harry reached out and cupped a slender knee with his hand. The tenderness that burst inside him was shocking in its intensity. He knew only the need to reassure her as best he could. "I'm sorry. I wish I could say this is just all some sort of bad dream."

His touch seemed to have some kind of domino effect on them both. Kathryn melted deeper into the seat, seeming to give herself over to the emotions she was trying so hard to hold sway over. He felt like something intangible bound them together with the simple, physical touch.

He heard her voice crack. "Please…please just take me home."

Harry withdrew his hand, hoping that he'd imagined the connection between them. Unfortunately his empathy for her only increased. "I can't."

She fell silent until he was aware of her breathing growing more even. She shifted. "You can't or you won't?"

"Both."

He felt her gaze on his profile. "Is that going to be one of the things you explain later?"

He nodded.

"I don't…I don't understand…" She began shaking her head. "First my fiancé's murdered right in my own house. Next I'm arrested for his murder…"

Her soft words trailed off as something apparently occurred to her.

As she stared through the windshield her haunted eyes looked very far away. "This…man. This very nice but strange man visited me yesterday morning and he…and he told me I'm not who I think I am.

That he's my biological father and his late wife is my mother."

Sean.

Harry had watched the elder McCoy gain access to the jail complex this morning. He'd guessed it was to try to help the daughter he'd apparently kept an eye on for the past twenty-seven years. But now that she was in trouble…

"He, Sean McCoy, is your father."

Harry didn't dare look at Kat. Didn't dare open himself up to whatever expression she'd be wearing as she stared at him.

"Who *are* you?" she asked in little more than a broken whisper.

"Somebody who just wants to help."

"Please…please stop the car. I can't do this. I need to get out. I need to go home."

HOME…

Once Kat got there, everything would be okay. The world would start turning the right way again. Everything would start making sense.

She wasn't aware how fast the car was going until she stared down at asphalt speeding by when she opened the door. The only thing keeping her from falling completely out was Harry's metal-like grasp on her left wrist.

He yanked her fully back inside then pulled to a stop at the curb.

Kat's chest was tight, making her feel more like she'd just run a 200m race than opened a car door. Somewhere in the clouds that crowded her mind she knew it was the rush of adrenaline, but that didn't make it any easier to get control over it.

No matter how much she cried, a sob seemed forever lodged in her heart, growing, choking off her breath, nearly suffocating her.

"Not very swift." The words were rough but the way he said them was packed with sympathy.

She stared at where he still held tightly onto her wrist. He seemed to realize he still held her and released his grip slowly as if almost reluctant to do so. "Listen, Kat, it's not my intention to hold you captive." He looked tortured in a way that went beyond his actions. "I did not spring you from one jail to put you into another."

She believed him. She didn't know why, but she did. "Where are you taking me then?"

She watched him swallow hard. "I've made reservations at a downtown hotel for tonight. Tomorrow...I don't know. We'll figure it out then."

She considered him long and hard, trying to merge her knowledge of the law with his actions now. "Is this...official? What you're doing?"

He looked away from her. "As official as it can be."

In many ways the law was black and white. There was little room for a gray area in between. "Please...explain to me how official it is."

He didn't say anything for a long moment.

Kat began to get out of the car without realizing that's what she was going to do.

"Wait," he said simply.

She waited. She couldn't be sure exactly why. Maybe because she was a good five miles from her townhouse without a dollar in her pocket. Maybe because she had no idea what was going on in her life and this man could be holding the missing puzzle pieces. Or at least could point her to where she might find them.

Or maybe it was the way he looked at her.

Kat gave an involuntary shiver.

There was something about Harry Kincaid that made her feel safe. That made her feel that so long as he was in charge, she would be okay. That he would lay his life on the line to make sure no harm came to her.

Law enforcement officers. She didn't have much opportunity to interact with the species aside from cross-examining police staff members involved in the arrest of her clients, but she immediately recognized the characteristics of strength and integrity.

She'd certainly never had reason to rely on one before.

"I'm waiting," she said although her words came out as a whisper. Many of her words seemed to come out far less powerfully than she'd intended in the past couple of days.

He let out a deep breath. "Let's go to the hotel. Call it a night. At least what's left of it. We can work out the rest in the morning."

She searched the wide planes of his face. A face she suspected had seen much more than she could understand, even given her present circumstances.

He added, "Separate rooms, but connecting."

"Why connecting?"

"So I can keep you safe."

The shiver she'd experienced a couple of moments ago turned into a bone-deep shudder.

Kat slowly put her legs back in the car and closed the door. Harry put the car in gear and drove the rest of the way to the hotel.

CHAPTER FIVE

A DOOR WASN'T the only thing the two hotel rooms shared. They also shared a bathroom.

Kat locked herself inside of the large, well-appointed room and switched on the shower. She didn't pause until she was standing under the scalding spray scrubbing her skin with hotel soap and a washcloth. Some long minutes later her skin was rubbed raw. All the while, the shower mingled with the tears streaming out of her eyes.

James was dead.

She leaned against the side of the shower for support then slowly slid down to sit, knees squeezed to her chest, barely aware of the water yet thankful for it. James. Dear James who had never questioned her obsession with her career. Who had never complained about her canceling a date because she had an emergency motion to file.

James who had loved her for her instead of what he wanted her to be.

James whom she had found bloodied and still on her kitchen floor. Gone.

Until now she'd been paralyzed by shock. Numbed by the reality of her situation. Now grief gripped her so tightly she didn't know how to find her way out of its grasp.

She'd felt that way only one other time. The stormy night three years ago she'd received the call from the sheriff's office informing her that her parents had been involved in an accident. An accident that had taken both of their lives in one swift shift of fate.

And now she had lost James.

Kat couldn't be sure how long she'd been in the tub. Couldn't really in that one moment tell you whether it was night or day. But she slowly became aware of a pounding on the door that connected to Harry's room.

She limply reached out to turn off the water when the door swung inward and hit the opposite wall and Harry stood staring at where she was still sitting, her hand ineffectually working at the faucet.

AN HOUR AND A HALF. That's how long Kathryn had been in the bathroom. And after ninety long minutes Harry had suddenly thought to wonder if there was anything sharp enough in there with which she could take her life.

Panic. That's what he'd felt first.

But now that he stood staring at her huddled, naked, on the floor of the bathtub, looking like a cold, wet cat, anger suffused his every cell.

He reached out and shut off the water then pulled a towel from the rack and draped it over her, being extra careful she didn't slip when he grasped her shoulders through the towel and helped her to stand. She was shaking all over but barely seemed aware of her condition. With the corner of the towel he wiped the tears from her face, ignoring how red her eyes were.

"He's not worth your tears," he said.

She blinked at him as if he'd spoken a language other than English.

He wasn't sure which bothered him more: that she was mourning a man like Darin Ichatious, or that she was doing so without regard for her own health. All he knew was that if he could be assured putting his fist through the wall would release some of the black emotion filling him he would have done it.

He thrust another towel at her. "Dry off. I ordered room service."

He turned toward the door.

"James was worth a sea of tears," she said quietly.

Harry hesitated. "Darin wasn't worth a single one."

HARRY STOOD in the doorway to her connecting room. The light in his room shone behind him casting shadows against the king-size bed that made

Kathryn's still, slender body look smaller yet. The sheet was pulled up to her chin. Her blond hair was smooth against the pillow but uncombed giving her a cherubic appearance that was in stark contrast to her innate sexiness. From the fullness of her breasts to the neat vee of dark blond hair at the top of her long legs the image of her naked body was burned into his mind.

He quietly drew the door almost shut, leaving it open only an inch so he could hear her if she tried to leave, although he didn't think she'd be going anywhere in the immediate future. Ever since he'd helped her out of the shower two hours ago he'd watched the dark circles under her eyes deepen and her shoulders slump even further until she'd been asleep practically the instant she'd lain down. He was sure a couple of days in the county jail could drain the strength out of most anyone, but combine her brief incarceration with the murder of her fiancé, well, he didn't kid himself into thinking grief didn't factor in there somewhere.

That she should be grieving a slimeball like Darin Ichatious made him angry all over again.

He turned toward the table and the food left there. He'd ordered a couple of club sandwiches from the limited menu but neither of them had eaten much. They hadn't spoken much either. Whatever questions Kathryn must have had appeared to have been washed away with the shower water. At least for now. He didn't fool himself that there wouldn't be plenty of questions later in the morning.

He stepped to the window. Dawn smeared the eastern horizon with purple, the same color that ringed Kathryn's beautiful green eyes. He shoved his hands deep into his pants pockets. It had taken a great deal of convincing to get his immediate superior to appeal to the attorney general for the release of Kathryn into Harry's custody. Thompson had looked over the evidence against her and commented on the appearance of guilt. Harry had asked him when guilt or innocence had factored into the protection of any witness.

Witness. That's what she was. Nothing more, nothing less. She was witness to the murder of James Smith aka Darin Ichatious whom the justice department hadn't hesitated to protect.

That she also happened to be the sister of his best friend—albeit unknowingly—and a woman who had touched his life before he'd even exchanged words with her...well, who was he to admit that?

THE CLANGING OF KEYS. The slamming of cell doors. The smell of fire. Kat's senses were overwhelmed with the stimuli. She twisted and turned, trying to find escape from the dream until finally she sat upright in bed struggling for breath, blinking against the bright sunlight, and taking in the unfamiliar hotel room around her.

"Damn it, Kincaid, let me in!"

She became aware of a pounding on her door, likely the reason she'd awakened. She clutched the sheet to her chest and watched Harry, apparently fresh from a shower, cut through her room with barely a glance in her direction, nothing but a towel around his hips. He opened the door and stumbled back when a dark-haired man she wasn't familiar with burst into the room looking first to her then to Harry…and obviously coming to a very wrong conclusion.

"You son of a bitch…"

He raised a fist to Harry but the agent easily moved out of range of the punch. Kat hurriedly put on the hotel robe she'd laid across the bed and inserted herself between the two men, holding the robe closed with one hand. They ignored her.

"What in the hell were you thinking keeping something like this from me?" the stranger asked, his gaze on Harry over Kat's head.

"Would you just cool your heels, McCoy," Harry shot back.

"Did you sleep with her?"

Kat felt like she had yet to wake up, her dream going from bad to worse in front of her eyes. She felt like she was in the middle of a fight for her honor. But that didn't make any sense.

However, the name McCoy caught her attention…

"It's not what it looks like. You knocked on the wrong damn door," Harry told the other man. "I was taking a shower and cut through Kathryn's room to answer your knock."

Kat shoved at both their chests. "You two are making me dizzy. Would someone please tell me what's going on here?"

The latest addition to her nightmare in progress seemed to register her close proximity and looked down at her. Confusion was evident on his rough-hewn, handsome face. His anger seemed to drain from his body in the time it took her to pull her robe tighter and tie it.

Harry ran his hand through his damp hair. "Kathryn, I'd like you to meet Connor McCoy."

It was her turn to be confused.

She stared at the man in front of her, studying each of his features. It was too much of a coincidence for her not to assume he was related to the other McCoy, Sean, the man who had told her he was her biological father. And since Harry had confirmed that Sean was indeed her blood relative—though she wasn't ready to accept that herself yet—then that meant...

"Jesus," Connor said. "You look just like her."

The picture of the woman. He had to be referring to that.

The picture she'd left sitting on the table in the jail conference room.

"Connor, look," Harry said, pulling the other man aside. "I've only just sprung her. I don't think this is a good time for this. Not yet. Give her a chance to get her feet back under her."

"Good time? When would you say it would be a good time, Kincaid? I've had a sister out there for twenty-seven years and I just find out last night she exists and you say now isn't a good time?" His jaw worked. "How long would you have me wait? Another twenty-something years?"

Kat slowly backed up until the bed impeded her progress. She collapsed onto it.

Sister…

Whatever footing she may have gained in the past few hours she lost.

"Let's go into the other room…my room," Harry told Connor, then looked at her. "I've ordered breakfast. I'll bring the tray in here for you."

Kat could do little more than stare at Connor McCoy—her brother, if everyone surrounding her lately was to be believed.

Her brother…

"How many?" she found herself asking. At least she thought it was her. At any rate the words had been said by a female voice and since she was the only female in the room…

"How many what?" Harry asked.

"How many McCoys are there?"

Harry didn't say anything. Rather Connor was

the one to speak. "After Pops there are five of us. Five brothers."

Five brothers...

She had gone to sleep last night the only child of Joan and John Buckingham and had woken up this morning with five brothers.

She thought she was going to be sick.

She rushed for the bathroom, found the door locked on her side, then dashed through Harry's room and the other door there where she firmly locked herself in.

THERE WERE MANY QUALITIES Harry liked about Connor McCoy. He was strong and intelligent and had a clear understanding of what was wrong and right.

He only wished he had a stronger grip on his temper.

He'd called down to the concierge that morning and requested a change of clothes and necessities to be sent up for Kathryn, ordered breakfast from room service, then climbed in for a quick shower before waking her so they could discuss where they went from there.

Only he hadn't factored one very hotheaded Connor McCoy into equation.

"How long have you known?" Connor asked him after Harry had moved a food tray into Kathryn's room, put the clothes on her bed, then shut the connecting door after him.

"Long enough." He pulled on his jeans and T-shirt and turned to face his old friend, wondering if his response would earn him another swipe at his nose.

"That's not an answer."

Harry rubbed his face, thinking he needed a shave. "One week, three hours and some odd minutes."

Connor's face hardened to stone. "And you didn't say anything to me?"

Harry sighed as he sat down on the bed and put on his shoes. "I did try to tell you. Yesterday."

"Yesterday was six days too late."

Harry stared at him. "When would you have liked me to tell you, Con? Right after I found out? Oh, I can just see that conversation now. 'Hey, buddy, I'm working this really lousy case and, oh, by the way, the jerk's fiancée just happens to be the sister you didn't know you had." He shook his head. "You probably would have landed that punch you just tried in the other room."

Connor stood staring at him for what seemed like a long time then sat down next to him on the bed, leaving a good foot separating them. "Jesus. Tell me this isn't happening."

"This isn't happening."

Connor chuckled softly but there was no humor in the sound. "Pops told us last night. At that family meeting I told you about."

Harry nodded. "I suspected he might."

"That's why you refused to come with me."

"That and I already had plans in the works to spring Kathryn."

Connor took a deep breath. "Kathryn. She's even named after my mother."

Harry knew that. Harry also knew that Kathryn had been close to her adoptive parents. As an only child in an upper-middle class setting, she'd been showered with love and attention, her every need seen to, her every wish granted. He knew in high school she'd played basketball and soccer and had run track. In college she'd switched her major three times before finally settling on law.

But everything he had learned about her, had seen, indicated she hadn't been spoiled or coddled. Rather she'd been nurtured into a remarkable young woman.

Unlike Connor and most of his brothers. From what he knew of them—and he knew a lot—all of them had been so deeply scarred by the unfortunate events that littered their lives that they'd probably never achieve a peace they could fully embrace.

Connor looked at him. Harry had seen the expression several times. First, back when they'd originally been partnered together and Connor had experienced his first loss of a witness. Second, when Connor had first met Bronte O'Brien, the amazing woman who would become his wife. And more recently when his twin three-year-old daughters did something that moved Connor so much he looked about ready to bolt from his own intense feelings.

"How would you feel if this was happening to you?" Connor asked quietly.

Harry slapped his hand against his friend's shoulder. "Probably pretty much the way you're feeling right now, man." He looked toward the door to Kathryn's room. "But right now I think whatever Kathryn's feeling has to take precedence. If I'm right, and you know I'm always right," this earned him a semi-grin from his friend, "then I don't think what went down the other night is as it appears. And Kathryn very well may be in danger."

Connor nodded.

The room fell silent, no telltale signs that Kathryn was still in the bathroom. In fact, it occurred to Harry that she could be on the other side on the door listening to their conversation.

"If I could put anyone in charge of my...sister's safety it would be you, Kincaid."

That made Harry feel good.

"Well, outside myself that is."

Harry chuckled then told him to get the hell out of there before he kicked him out.

CHAPTER SIX

THREE HOURS LATER Kat sat across from Harry in a diner nudging her coffee cup around and around on its saucer until Harry stared at her.

"Sorry," she said, forcing herself to stop.

Harry referred to something in one of the files at his left elbow, put it aside then pulled another official-looking document in front of him.

"You know, you really should eat something," he said.

Kat frowned at her barely touched soup and sandwich, remembered the breakfast she hadn't been able to swallow and the trail of food over the past couple of days she hadn't been able to stomach. She knew he was right.

"Take me home and I'll eat."

He didn't respond right away. Instead he appeared not to have heard her. Until he turned those deep brown eyes on her.

She sighed heavily. "You can't just expect me to sit here and do nothing. I have clients. I have somebody on death row right now and I'm his only hope for survival."

I have a fiancé to bury...

He turned a page. "I think it's a good idea for you to focus on your own survival right now."

Kat felt faint, as much as a result of her last thought as by his comment. But for some reason she couldn't bring herself to say the words aloud. Not to Harry Kincaid who she now knew was a U.S. Marshal. If she'd harbored any doubts about how he felt about James, she didn't any more. Every time she brought him up, Harry felt compelled to bring up something to smear James's name.

She couldn't bear that.

She quietly cleared her throat. "Comments like that one aren't helping matters any, you know."

Harry sat back, considered her for a long moment, then reached for a file under the stack of others. He held it up. "Eat and I'll let you see what's inside this."

Kat leaned forward and read the file tab.

James Smith aka Darin Ichatious.

She'd been looking for something to do but this wasn't it. She didn't feel ready to confront her fiancé's past just now. Wasn't prepared to look at her life through the filter that had been forced onto her in the past few days.

Lies. So many lies.

She shook her head.

He squinted at her then slowly put down the file he was holding and held up another one.

It read Kathryn Buckingham.

Kat slowly pulled her soup and sandwich back in front of her.

Harry grinned and leaned his hands against the folder, watching her.

She said, "You know, this would go a lot better if you didn't stare at me that way."

"What way?"

"Any way."

"Mmm. Probably you're right."

She barely tasted the lukewarm soup but the sandwich wasn't bad. The bread was fresh, the cold cuts tasty. After a couple of bites, she opened one half and wiped off the mayonnaise with her knife.

"I thought you ordered it with mayo."

"I did. But try telling a waitress you only want a thin layer."

"So you always wipe off most of it?"

She chewed. "Always."

He shook his head and went back to the file he was reviewing.

Kat eyed the dessert card. "Let me have five minutes at my house and I'll even eat some apple pie."

Harry looked at her without moving his head. "I expected more from a defense attorney." He closed the file. "You have to have something to bargain with in order to barter, sweetheart. What you've outlined benefits you one hundred percent." He lifted a brow. "What's in it for me?"

Kat's chewing slowed. "I won't fight you anymore."

What went unsaid was that after her attempted escape from a moving vehicle last night she hadn't put up even a token fight. Maybe his cryptic referrals to her being in danger were the reason. Or perhaps his emerging as a solid rock in the middle of a violently churning sea got the credit. Whatever it was she'd accepted that her immediate future was going to include him.

She couldn't bring herself to look at him for fear of what she might see there. So she focused on her food, watching peripherally as he closed the file and slid the others into a large accordion file, keeping the one with her name on it aside.

"Five minutes."

Kat grabbed her napkin and began to get up. He grasped her arm.

"Oh, no. You finish eating first."

"That wasn't part of this deal."

"No, this," he held up the folder, "is part of that deal." He motioned for the waitress. "The apple pie is part of this deal." He ordered two pieces. She hoped one was for him.

HARRY HAD SPENT so much time on the outside of the Georgetown townhouse it felt strange to have gone into it twice in three days. The skinny structure reminded him so much of the Brooklyn neighborhood he'd grown up in, and yet not at all. Yes, it was sandwiched between other brick houses. But this place, Kat's place, more resembled the townhouses in the Upper East Side of Manhattan that he hadn't grown up in. That he hadn't seen more than a passing glimpse of. And that he had accepted he probably wouldn't see any more of either. Ever.

Yet here he was standing in the expensive house, some of the most expensive real estate to be had in DC, and he was feeling like he couldn't get out of there fast enough.

He leaned against the front doorjamb. He'd have thought the first thing Kathryn would have gone for was her bedroom and the designer clothing she seemed partial to no matter how good she looked in the simple black slacks and white blouse she had on. Rather she headed into the library where she picked up papers from a table next to a treadmill, along with a Walkman. She placed the items in a well-worn leather briefcase, then put it on a table next to the front door. Finally she headed upstairs.

Harry ran a hand over his face, thinking he'd never gotten a chance to get that shave earlier. Which only served to make him feel more out of place in the townhouse. Had Kathryn not been with him one of the neighbors would probably have called 911 to report a burglary.

He smirked then went sober as he thought how well James Smith had fitted into these surroundings.

He didn't realize Kathryn had returned with a suitcase until he found her standing directly in front of him. Only she wasn't looking at him. She was looking toward the kitchen.

Harry took the suitcase from her and placed it near the door. "You, um, want me to collect anything back there for you?" he asked quietly.

She appeared not to hear, then shook her head. "No."

Still she stared at the closed kitchen door.

Harry had witnessed the scene. Watched as the DCPD forensics team had collected samples while a crime photographer had snapped pictures of the body. He'd been prevented from stepping too far into the room but he'd been able to see the body, noticing that James's face had been battered beyond recognition, the cause of death not immediately apparent but presumably due to the blows to the head.

"Okay, let's get out of here."

Harry couldn't have agreed more.

He reached for the door handle just as the sound of crashing glass came from the library, then more breaking glass sounded across the hall in the sitting room. An old wine bottle with a burning rag stuffed into the top spun into the foyer. It shattered against the bottom of the staircase releasing the accelerant inside. A Molotov cocktail, he realized as he watched another slam against the wall next to them and yet another roll across the floor. Kathryn gasped and Harry grabbed her, shoving her behind him as he opened the door and stepped outside. A nondescript black sedan with tinted plates sped away.

HOW MUCH COULD one person take?

Kat stood across the street from her cherished townhouse watching as flames licked out of the windows the fire department had broken in order to aim their hoses at the fire within. Given the historical significance of the area, there was a solid firewall between her townhouse and her neighbors, but that didn't prevent the conflagration from destroying her place.

First James was murdered. Next she was arrested for the crime. Then she'd been confronted by a man who claimed to be her biological father. And now she was watching her house, her home, be destroyed.

It was a chilly May night and the white blouse that had been laid out on the bed for her this morning was little defense against the cold. She looked over at where Harry was deep in discussion with a fireman, then beyond him to where a familiar man was standing looking at her.

Sean McCoy.

Kat swallowed hard.

"You okay?"

She blinked up to find Harry had finished his business and was again at her side.

"What do you think?"

He frowned. "Ask a stupid question…" He took his suit jacket off and draped it over her shoulders. The smell of soap and a hint of citrus filled her nose.

"Thanks."

He shoved his hands into his pockets. "Don't mention it."

He followed her line of sight then looked at her. "I'll be right back," he said.

She watched as he made his way toward Sean McCoy.

Even though the house she had called home for the past year was going up in flames across the street, Kat couldn't seem to drag her gaze away from the man who had claimed to be her father. She could connect none of his features to her own. But she could connect his physical traits to the other man she'd met this morning, Connor McCoy. The two men could have been twins if not for the years that separated them.

She pulled Harry's jacket a little closer to her body, not because she needed the warmth but because she needed the reassurance. And strangely Harry seemed to provide that even if it was only through his jacket.

"Come on," Harry said.

Kat looked to find Sean McCoy was gone.

"Where are we going?"

"Probably the safest place in the world for you to be right now."

HIS DAUGHTER was coming home.

Sean McCoy wasn't sure how word had gotten around, but it had. He'd called the house to tell Mitch to get the guest room ready, Harry would be bringing Kathryn, and by the time he'd pulled into the driveway every last one of his sons' cars and trucks was already there.

He parked his own car next to Mitch's then sat for long moments staring at the side door, the one that would take him into the kitchen, the regular family gathering place. He didn't have to ask Harry if Kathryn knew where he was taking her. He could see on the younger man's face that he probably wouldn't tell her until he pulled up.

Sean wasn't sure he was ready for this. It was too soon. He was still reeling from the responses he'd received when he'd shared the news with his sons of Kathryn's existence. He didn't think he could bear another look of pain and disappointment and anger from Connor following on the heels of a lifetime of them.

Somehow he'd never seemed able to do right by the boy. But he wasn't a boy anymore, was he? He was a grown man now with a wife and children of his own.

But last night for a moment Sean had been thrown back in time to face that nine-year-old boy who had found his mother unconscious and dying on the kitchen floor. When Sean had been a grieving husband, a father incapable of reaching out to his son.

He'd be the first to admit that he'd made his share of mistakes in his life. He'd been devastated when he'd lost Kathryn, his wife, his love, his partner, his best friend, his very heart. So devastated that he hadn't been able to face the five boys they'd created together, the family that had been forever fragmented by the loss.

So devastated that when the doctor had told him the baby girl had survived despite his wife's death, he'd decided to give her up for adoption— on the condition that she be given the name Kathryn and that he know who the adoptive parents were.

He'd known he'd live to regret the move. Decisions like that weren't made without the maker knowing that well in advance. What he had been unprepared for was seeing his wife every time he looked into his daughter's face.

Correction, his late wife. He had a new wife now. Wilhemenia.

He climbed out of the car, hesitating at the door to the house. Then he took a deep breath and let himself in, expecting to see the entire clan gathered. Instead he faced his five sons.

He blinked. He couldn't imagine the women not wanting to be there, which could only mean…

"None of you told your wives," he said simply.

The way they looked everywhere but at him told him he was right.

"Did you tell Billie?" Mitch asked.

It was Sean's turn to look at his shoes.

What a ragtag bunch they were though, weren't they? Such an important moment and none of them had shared it with their wives.

And at Sunday dinner he'd been thinking how well they had all turned out, all things considered.

It happened they hadn't turned out so well after all.

A car's headlights cut across the open door indicating someone had just turned into the driveway. Since they were all there, that only left one other person for it to be.

"Is that her?" David said, bolting for the door.

Connor caught him by the shoulders. "Whoa. I already learned the hard way that ambushing her is probably not a good idea."

Sean shared a look with his oldest son as both of them braced for what was to come.

CHAPTER SEVEN

HARRY HAD BEEN QUIET during the drive to wherever he was taking her. Kat figured it was just as well. The sight of her house in flames seemed burned into her retinas and into her heart, and she could do little more than stare out the window grappling with a reality that refused to take hold. She wasn't sure how long they had driven, but she did know that it had been a while since they'd seen more than a house light here, a house light there. And it was a relief to find that with every mile that passed, she felt safer somehow. More at ease.

And she had more time on her hands to think.

The more she tried not to think about Harry, the more her thoughts turned to the man who seemed to have put his own life on hold in order to help her with hers.

Who was this man who had rescued her from county jail, who looked after her in a way few ever had? In so many ways he'd become the metal in her spine that kept her upright. That propped her up when she might collapse into a puddle of unspent emotion. And he seemed to ask for nothing in return.

She studied his profile. So strong. So capable. But she sensed a darkness about him that drew her curiosity even more. Something that told her he was able to understand her and what she was going through because he'd gone through something equally tragic at some point in his life. Something that compelled him to go beyond the line of duty. Because if there was one thing she could be sure of, it was that Harry's actions far surpassed what was expected of him as a U.S. Marshal.

She'd also begun to notice how handsome he was…

She blinked several times, not wanting to look, but helpless not to. There was a roughness about his face, no feature in complete harmony with the rest. His hair was a sandy brown, his eyes a mocha brown; his look resembled that of the actor Harrison Ford when he'd played in the Indiana Jones films. A man not traditionally handsome but appealing nonetheless. Charismatic, larger than life. A man who once he was on your side, always would be.

He was a big man, one a woman wouldn't have to worry about wearing heels around because he would always tower over her. But he also possessed a tenderness that made her feel…well, not so much alone.

She pulled his jacket closer around her.

"Cold?"

"Hmm? No," she said, realizing she wasn't. She shifted, both comforted by and concerned about the direction of her thoughts. "Where are you taking me? To some kind of safe house?"

She watched as he rubbed the back of his neck. "Something like that."

He had the radio tuned to NPR and the signal seemed to be weakening a bit this far outside the city. Harry switched it off. She didn't mind. She hadn't been listening anyway. There were too many thoughts, too many questions demanding her attention for her to absorb anything else.

"Are you hungry?"

She turned her head to look at Harry, thinking how he'd just reinforced all she'd just thought about him. "No."

She didn't miss his grimace and smiled. Not even her parents had made her eat. Their stance had always been she'd eat when she was hungry. And, of course, she always had.

But Harry…Harry seemed intent on making sure she cleaned her plate.

"Are you going to make me barter with you every time I want you to eat?" he asked.

"I was thinking about it," she quietly teased, although she had no intention of making his life difficult. They both had enough to worry about without playing such silly games.

She pulled her knees up to her chest and readjusted her seatbelt. "Actually I could go for something light, maybe a salad or something."

She really wasn't hungry but she'd taken his point earlier when he'd suggested she try to eat to keep her strength up. She needed her faculties about her if she hoped to work through the maelstrom of emotions she was feeling, not to mention adjust to the many changes her life had undergone in such a short time.

"You never did give me that file," she said quietly.

She felt his gaze on her in the dark. "No, I didn't."

"Will you?"

Again with the rubbing of the neck. A nervous action? She guessed it was even as she hoped it wasn't. Because the one thing she was counting on was that she could have faith in Harry.

The thought gave her pause. Three days ago she hadn't even known he'd existed. Now she seemed to be depending on him too much for comfort. But given that everything was relative, she figured Harry Kincaid was the least of her worries. He'd sprung her from that cold, stark jail cell. He encouraged her to eat, even bribed her. In fact, everything that he'd done so far came across as so paternal as to be almost insulting. "Almost" because that's what she needed. "Insulting" because she didn't want him to look at her like she was a little kid in need of parenting.

"So stop acting like one," she said quietly.

"What's that?" Harry asked.

Kat hadn't been aware she'd made the statement aloud. "I'm just marveling at my behavior since you picked me up last night. It's been—I don't know—bad at best."

"You've been through a lot."

"Sure, but…"

She absently bit her lip then forced her feet back on the floor, figuring that it would probably be a good idea if she stopped curling up into herself, as if trying to ward off the world.

Of course that's what she *was* doing. But she was an adult. A twenty-seven-year-old woman. An attorney.

"It's just… I think it's time I started standing a little more solidly on my own two feet rather than leaning on you so much."

"I don't mind."

She gave a small smile.

"But it probably wouldn't be a bad idea if you drew a little more on that strength. Because you're going to need it."

She sat up and looked through the back window. "Why, is somebody following us?"

"No. We're here."

She watched as he pulled into a driveway. "Here where?"

"The McCoy place."

HARRY HAD TO GIVE her credit. Whatever mental machinations she'd gone through during the drive out about being stronger made her get out of the car with very little urging and face the door a few feet away like they were checking into a hotel room. He looked around and grimaced. And the way it looked, every member of that family was in the house waiting for her.

He grasped her hand when she would have passed him, half tempted to tell her to get back into the car so he really could check them into a hotel room instead of making her go into that house and face every last overbearing, stubborn McCoy male.

She searched his expression, apparently waiting for him to speak.

"It's okay." She turned back toward the door, taking in what she could of the old farmhouse. "I'll be all right." He heard her thick swallow. "I think."

"I'm sorry. When I spoke to Sean earlier and he suggested I bring you out here, it sounded like a good idea at the time." She glanced at where he was still gripping her arm. "It's only for tonight. First thing in the morning I'll make other arrangements."

She nodded. "How many of them are in there?"

He grimaced and looked at the cars. "All of them, I think."

Panic briefly flashed in her eyes. "All five?"

"And your fath…I mean, Sean."

Okay, they were leaving.

He turned toward the car and opened his mouth to tell her to do the same.

"Tell me about each of them. Who they are. What they do."

He looked over his shoulder. "What?"

She stared at him.

And so he did…

Kathryn listened quietly as he outlined each of the McCoys, starting with Sean and making his way down the list: Connor, Jake, Marc, Mitch and David. He told her how old they were, which badges they carried, and gave her a brief sketch of their temperament.

When he was done she didn't say anything immediately. Apparently she was running everything he'd said through her mind, absorbing it.

She finally asked, "All in law enforcement?"

He nodded. "Pretty much."

He'd caught onto the irony of the situation himself when he'd first discovered Kathryn was a McCoy, the fact that she was a criminal defense attorney who made a career out of getting the people her brothers arrested off.

Well, getting them off. That sounded shady and he couldn't imagine her doing anything like that. Rather she represented the people the McCoys arrested, making sure they got a fair trial.

He watched as she squared her shoulders, shrugged out of his jacket and handed it to him. "Thanks."

He absently accepted it. "Don't mention it."

Rather than leading her to the house as he suspected he would have to do, he ended up following her, watching as she reached for the knocker only to have Sean open the door for her.

"Kathryn. Welcome."

KAT HALF EXPECTED "home" to follow the welcome but instead watched as Sean choked it back. She smiled her thanks.

Then she walked into the kitchen and faced what had to be five of the biggest men she'd ever seen in her life.

Tall. Brawny. Silent.

And all of them were standing staring at her as if she'd just landed her flying saucer in the field in back and had come in to perform an anal probe on each of them.

Her brothers…

She blinked, not having realized until that moment that she'd accepted that these five men, six counting Sean, were, indeed, her family. It wasn't anything she'd mentally worked out. Instead the shock after Sean had made his pronouncement had dissipated in light of other, more pressing details, leaving her now to stare at what was quite possibly the truth.

And once that happened, little details about her childhood, about what she knew about her parents,

Joan and John Buckingham, began stringing together like shiny beads leading to where she stood now.

She remembered when her mother had given her "the sex talk." She'd been uncomfortable with the exchange, as she suspected most twelve-year-olds were, but she'd caught on to something odd her mother had said and called her on it.

"Why did you just say you don't know what being pregnant's like? You were pregnant with me."

Her mother had clearly been caught off guard. "Of course, sweetie. Of course I was pregnant with you."

There were other times, other odd comments, but nothing she'd spent a great deal of time thinking about because in the end Joan and John were her parents. And if she occasionally entertained the idea that she had been adopted, and that her real parents were royalty from some rich European country, well, she knew most little girls did that. She knew because her friends had done the same thing. They used to lounge around her room at night concocting stories of glass slippers and dashing princes.

But nowhere in those meanderings had been a wish for her to be the long lost daughter of a widower and the sister to five huge older brothers.

"Hello, Connor," she said quietly, nodding at the one she'd met that morning. "Good to see you again."

He coughed and said something along the same lines.

She focused on the only other blond one in the family outside herself. "And you must be David." She smiled as he extended his hand and pulled her closer.

"It's nice not to be the baby of the family anymore," he said into her ear. "Now you get to be the one who's picked on mercilessly."

Kat had never been "picked on" in her life. Strangely enough she was looking forward to finding out what her new role would entail.

"Hi, I'm Mitch," the one with longish dark hair said with an easygoing grin, also taking her hand. "Welcome."

"My, so formal."

One of the last two began taking his hand back and she quickly reached out to take it. "Oh, no. I meant that in the best possible way." His hand was large and warm. "And you would be?"

"Jake."

Quiet. She'd bet that the rest of the guys couldn't say that about themselves.

She turned her gaze on the last McCoy. "So that would make you Marc then."

"Yes, ma'am, it would." He shook her hand slowly as if sizing her up. She wondered if she made the grade.

Kat looked around the large, homey kitchen.

While it appeared to have been recently renovated and held all the latest appliances, signs of use were everywhere, from the scarred spot on the counter next to the sink likely caused by too much scrubbing, to the bit of raised molding on the monster dishwasher, to the worn finish on the dozen wood chairs. It was so unlike what she was used to. She and her parents had taken all their meals in the formal dining room, breakfast included, cleanup left to the housekeeper who came in once a day. In fact, the only times she'd gone into the kitchen was to grab a soda or fix herself a sandwich when she'd missed a sit-down meal.

She'd bet that these guys lived in their kitchen. And she found she liked that.

"Would you like a beer?" David asked.

"Get me one while you're at it."

"It's about time you offered."

"I thought you'd never ask."

And just like that the silence was chased out of the room by men obviously used to interacting with each other as they each grabbed a chair and sat around the table, leaving the two closest to her free while Sean stood near the doorway, a part of the group yet not a part.

Kat realized David was waiting for her answer just as everyone else was.

Six pairs of eyes were trained on her.

Harry cleared his throat next to her. "Kathryn's had a long day..."

"It's Kat," she corrected, then smiled at David. "And I'd love a beer."

CHAPTER EIGHT

LATER THAT NIGHT Kat lay staring at the ceiling of the borrowed room. She breathed in the scent of an oiled leather baseball glove and of the four pizzas they had ordered earlier and devoured within a blink of an eye with Lord knew how many beers.

She smiled and rolled over, rubbing her cheek against the soft pillow. The room was decidedly masculine. Actually, everything about the house was despite that she understood Mitch lived here with his wife, Liz, whom she'd met briefly when she'd returned from visiting…was it Connor's wife? Yes, Bronte.

She pressed her fingertips against her brow as if trying to hold in everything she'd learned that night, her heart thumping a rapid beat as she reminded herself that these guys weren't just any guys, they were her brothers.

And her father.

She straightened the blue, green and white plaid coverlet. Sean McCoy had stayed curiously detached from the rest of them, making sure every-

thing had run smoothly, but otherwise not con-
tributing to the conversation. She'd asked her
brothers questions from the mundane—what their
favorite colors were, not surprisingly they'd all said
blue and acted affronted that she'd assume they'd
say differently—to the complicated—why they'd
chosen their careers, from the DC cop David to the
I.N.S. agent Jake. She was pleased to discover they
all gave as good as they got.

At one point Harry had joked that she sounded
like the trial attorney she was.

But Sean…

She'd felt his gaze on her all night, but he'd remained silent, standing more than sitting, smiling
when the conversation called for it, but mostly
somber. She supposed the death of her fiancé, her arrest and the torching of her house was cause for the
man who called himself her father to be somber. But
somehow she got the impression that his emotions
were more deeply rooted than immediate events dictated.

She felt her own smile fade as she thought of
what existed for her outside this house full of laughter and good-natured ribbing, nonstop action and
conversation.

After the pizza was gone, and the guys had fought
over the last beer—she'd jokingly said she'd wanted
it but when it had been given to her she'd handed it
to David to the groans of everyone else—the entire

atmosphere had dampened when Connor asked Harry to brief them all on what was happening. And so Kat sat and listened to the details of her life, feeling somehow detached, yet very much attached. She noticed that Harry avoided calling James her fiancé and listened with curiosity as he explained the steps he'd taken to spring her and have her classified as a witness in need of the justice department's protection.

He'd ended with the torching of her house and shared that he'd called the DC fire department for an update earlier and they'd said the house would have to be entirely gutted.

Gutted.

Funny, just thinking about it made Kat feel like she'd been gutted.

So much going on. So little she seemed to be able to do about it.

She heard a knock and strained her ears, realizing it wasn't the sound of someone knocking on the door but of something bumping the wall next to her. Harry? She knew he'd been given the room beside hers. Was he even now rolling around trying to find a comfortable spot and had knocked his elbow against the wall?

Kat sat up with the sound of old bedsprings, her feet bare against the polished wood floor. But while she'd been uncomfortable with the feeling in the county jail, here she curled her toes, enjoying the sensation. It seemed strange that something so simple would bring her pleasure.

Carefully getting up with a minimum of squeaking, she straightened the white lacy nightgown Liz had loaned her and stepped to the door, listening for movement before opening it. There was a nightlight at the end of the hall and she used it to navigate a path downstairs and into the kitchen. She was surprised to find Harry clad only in his slacks foraging around in the refrigerator.

"Hey," she said softly.

He looked over his shoulder, his profile thrown into relief by the fridge light. "Hey, yourself."

"You can't possibly be hungry again," she said, flipping on the overhead light.

He shook his head and closed the refrigerator door, a gallon of milk in hand. "Nope."

"You wouldn't happen to be warming that up, would you?" she asked.

"I hadn't planned on it. Would you like some warmed?"

She took the milk from him and found a small saucepan. "You want me to fix one for you, too?"

"Sure…thanks." He leaned against the counter. "Why not use the microwave?"

She glanced at the appliance in question. "I don't know. There's something about milk warmed over an open flame."

He smiled. "Ah. A warm milk connoisseur."

She stirred the milk, noting how at home she felt in a house she'd never known before tonight. How easy she felt talking to Harry when neither of them were wearing much of anything.

She absently noted how attractive Harry was, though not in the traditional Brad Pitt kind of way. Rather his looks were the type that improved the more often you viewed them. Or maybe that wasn't it at all. Perhaps it was the kind of person he was that made him appealing.

Her arm accidentally brushed against his bare abs as she moved to get a couple of mugs. Abs that were ripped to the max.

She caught herself flushing.

"Here, let me," he offered, appearing oblivious to the innocent contact.

"Thanks." She poured the milk then moved both mugs to the monstrous wood table that seemed just this minute to have been built for two. She sat down next to him and put her feet up on an empty chair.

"You handled yourself well tonight," he said quietly.

Kat blew on her milk and stared at an empty pizza box in the middle of the table.

He cleared his throat. "I don't know if it's appropriate but I was—I don't know—does the word proud make sense?"

She smiled. "On the drive out I was thinking about how you were acting like a surrogate parent

with me." She nodded. "Yes, I'd say proud fits."
She motioned toward the kitchen door with her mug.
"They're a great bunch of guys."

Harry took a sip of the milk and made a face.
"Yeah, that they are. A little bullheaded, maybe."

"This your first time drinking warm milk?"

He made a face. "Yeah, does it show?"

She laughed. "Let it cool a little more before trying again."

"Thanks."

She considered the sentiment. "Actually, I should
be thanking you."

"For what?"

She shrugged. "Oh, I don't know. Everything, I
guess."

He sat back, causing the wooden chair to creak.
"Well, I can see why you'd thank me. I whisk you
out of jail in the middle of the night, hold you captive, force you to eat, shove you like a cat into the
middle of a pack of dogs... Yeah, you *should* be
grateful."

She laughed softly. "Funny."

"What is?"

"Like a cat in the middle of a pack of dogs. You
know, Kat."

He cracked a grin.

"Anyway this is how I see things. You rescued me
from county jail where I was a breath away from an
anxiety attack. You looked after me when I was in

no condition to look after myself. And, the greatest gift of all, you introduced me to my brothers."

His gaze raked her face in the semidarkness. "Is that really how you view everything?"

"Mmm. Yes." The milk was cool enough. She nudged his hand that held the mug. "Drink."

He did and his face showed mild surprise. "Not bad." He grinned. "Now who's taking care of whom?"

"Actually, I'm buttering you up."

"Uh-oh. I don't know if I like the sound of that."

Kat stared into her mug rather than at him. "I need access to your cell phone in order to follow up on a couple of pressing cases."

"I don't see a problem with that."

"Good. I, um, also need to see to burial arrangements for James."

He went silent, all humor gone from his handsome face.

"Look, I understand you know things about James that I don't—"

"Darin."

She searched his eyes. "But you have to understand that there are things I know about him that you don't." She took her feet from the chair and sat up. "I need to see to this for him. He deserves at least that."

Harry didn't say anything for a long time. But he hadn't said no either. That was a good sign, wasn't it?

"So you want to go to Maryland then. It might be difficult to swing, but not impossible."

Kat's throat tightened. "Maryland?"

His gaze was steady on hers. He opened his mouth, then closed it. Instead he got up, let himself out the door and came back in with the file he'd offered her earlier at the diner. The file she hadn't been ready to see. The file she still wasn't ready to see.

"His family's in Maryland."

Kat felt the chair teeter under her. "James doesn't have any family."

Harry didn't have to say it. "No, but Darin does."

He laid the file on the table near her elbow, rinsed out his cup and put it in the dishwasher, then moved toward the door where he turned to face her. "Thanks for the milk."

Kat nodded absently, her attention on the closed file on the table. "You're welcome."

AT SOMEWHERE AROUND DAWN Kat heard movement upstairs. She blinked, not realizing until that moment that she'd been up all night. The contents of the file Harry had given her were strewn across the table, each of the reports read once, twice, three times.

She became aware of someone watching her from the doorway.

"Good morning," Sean said quietly.

Kat's heart skipped in her chest as she considered the man who was her biological father. She knew he was married and that he lived in a small town close to DC with his second wife, Wilhemenia, but he'd stayed there last night in order to be closer to her.

That meant a lot to her.

She cleared her throat and began gathering the papers. "Good morning."

"I'd ask if you slept well but I get the impression you didn't sleep at all."

She smiled as she closed the file. "No, I didn't."

He began preparing coffee and moments later was sitting near her. "Nothing I or any of the boys said, I hope."

She blinked at him. "No, no. This has nothing to do with the family."

The family.

She supposed she should have found it strange that she was referring to the McCoys as family already. But somehow she didn't. Especially since attached to the file Harry had given her last night was the other file he'd used to bribe her into eating lunch yesterday, the one he'd compiled on her, likely as an adjunct to James's. In it had been a copy of her original birth certificate and the adoption papers her parents had signed. If she'd had any doubts regarding her parentage, she didn't now. Sean and Kathryn McCoy were definitely her biological parents. And those five men she'd met last night were her older brothers.

Still, she felt a little awkward around Sean, who didn't appear to know what to say to her, what to do. Even now he had his hands clasped so tightly on top of the table that she could hear the scrape of his skin.

"I take it Harry's moving you again today."

She nodded. Harry had said something about a safe house that her brother Connor had access to and that belonged to the justice department.

"I hope you'll come back for a visit every now and again."

The sentence was said so quietly that it touched something deep inside her chest. Warmth spread throughout her body…and a longing to ease whatever discomfort Sean was struggling with.

Kat reached out and worked her hand between his two. She gave a squeeze and smiled, although Sean's face became a fuzzy blur through a thin sheen of tears. "I hope you'll have me back."

"Anytime," he said, appearing not to know what to do with her gesture before squeezing her hand between his. "Always."

Kat searched the face of the man who had told her two days ago that he was her biological father. A man she'd initially rejected. Well, maybe not him personally, but she had been ill-equipped to handle his words so she'd taken it out on the person who'd uttered them.

Now…

Well, now she still didn't know what to make of things, but she did know that she felt comfortable, welcome in this group of gruff, handsome men.

Sean cleared his throat. "I won't pretend to understand what must be going through your head right now. But I need to say…want to tell you…" He increased his grip on her hand. "I just want you to know that you were conceived in love."

She looked down at the table and nodded.

"Is that coffee I smell?" Mitch entered the room then drew to a stop. "Hey, Pops. I didn't know you stayed over last night."

Sean nodded and released his grip on Kat's hand. She slowly pulled it back and smiled at her brother. "Morning."

Mitch's gaze scanned over her and the file next to her. "I notice you didn't group a 'good' with that. Liz said she heard you get up. She wanted to come down but I wouldn't let her. I thought you needed the time alone."

"Thanks. I did."

And boy had she. Only not for the reason they thought.

While her life had changed radically over the past couple of days, it wasn't these men she was having difficulty getting used to. Rather, she was having a hard time understanding that everything she'd thought, everything she'd believed, over the past year about James had been a lie.

And the only two things that were saving her from emotional collapse were Harry and these men who were her family.

CHAPTER NINE

HARRY GLANCED OVER at where Kat was fast asleep in the passenger seat, her cheek pressed against her shoulder. He'd suggested she stretch out in the back but she'd insisted she was fine. Then sleep had snuck up on her, probably brought on by the rhythmic hum of the car, and it was like someone had flipped a switch.

The city growing nearer, he turned NPR back on. He'd known she'd stayed up all night because he'd lain in the narrow twin bed upstairs listening for her to come back upstairs. She never had. After breakfast with the McCoys, he'd asked if she wanted to catch a few zzz's before they hit the road again but she'd said no. So after a few awkward hugs that had made even him feel uncomfortable and yet touched, they'd hit the road, heading for the safe house on the shores of the Potomac. The same safe house where Marc had kept Melanie when he'd kidnapped her out from under her groom's nose two days before her wedding to protect her from a would-be assassin's bullet. Connor had suspected all along that the escaped shooter hadn't been Marc's only motivation for kidnapping the pretty blonde. He'd been proven right when the two had married shortly thereafter, and an even shorter six months after that their first child had been born. A boy they'd named Sean.

Harry reached for his cell phone and checked for messages. His superior looking for a case update. He'd left word for the coroner's office to get back to him right away with Darin's autopsy results, but they had yet to contact him.

He began sliding the cell phone back into his pocket when he remembered Kathryn asking to use it. Of course, she'd probably understand that arranging for James's funeral was no longer something she had to do. But he saw no harm in letting her have use of the phone after all that had happened.

"And the time clock to the electric chair ticks ever closer for Joseph Alan Greer. The warden says that everything is going according to plan and barring a last-minute reprieve from the governor, the execution will take place next Thursday night. Greer was convicted of killing his parents seven years ago at age thirteen."

Kathryn shifted next to him and he noticed her eyes were open, her gaze plastered to the radio.

He switched it off.

She reached out and switched it back on.

"Twenty-year-old Greer's last meal request is in."

"Fried chicken, mashed potatoes and gravy, bacon, pineapple upside-down cake and gummy bears," Kathryn said quietly.

Harry listened as the radio reporter listed the same menu along with a glass of milk.

Kathryn shifted again, staring out the window.

"He's my client."

He'd known she was a criminal defense attorney, and that she'd made reference to having a client on death row. He just hadn't put two and two together to link her to Greer.

"Did he do it?" he asked. "Did he kill his parents?"

Kathryn was still for a long moment then nodded. "Yes, he did."

The onramp to the highway was coming up and he flicked the blinker on to move into the right lane. "But you don't think he deserves to die."

He heard her thick swallow. "No, I don't."

She seemed to notice then that his cell phone lay on the seat between them. She looked in his direction and he nodded. "It's yours to use."

She didn't move for a long moment, then reached out to pick up the phone. "Thanks."

"Just know that you'll be billed for any 900 numbers."

His attempt at humor at such an intense moment

was lame but it earned him a small smile. And, small or big, he was coming to realize that Kathryn Buckingham's smile was enough to knock the breath straight out of him.

HOURS LATER Kat sat on the threadbare sofa, a yellow legal pad open in front of her, the cell phone molded to her ear.

"You need to have the motion sent by messenger to the governor's office, with another copy delivered to his house. Now. I don't care if you have to take it to both places yourself, Roger, get them there by five."

"Greer wants to see you."

Kat swallowed hard. Of course, Joe wanted to see her. He was in the special death row cells that separated him from the rest of the prison population, allowed only an hour a day solitary exercise with nothing but a guard for company, and the only hope he had was Kat.

Not that he held out hope. In fact, he seemed not only resigned to the fact that he was going to die, but accepting of it.

"Tell him I'll see what I can do. Just get those papers to the governor's office."

After Roger agreed, she disconnected then sat for a long moment, the phone pressed to her chin. Her associate didn't have the same kind of emotional investment in Greer's case that she did. Of course, she'd been working on the case for two solid years, trying to find grounds for a new trial to challenge Virginia's twenty-one day law, appealing all the way up to the U.S. Supreme Court. Still, Joe's execution day was edging closer. Kat could almost hear the loud ticking of the clock.

The safe house Harry had taken her to was little more than a three-room shack, the furniture old, the wood floors dusty, the iron bed in the other room stripped of sheets, and the kitchen empty of supplies. Harry had stopped off to pick up some groceries before they'd arrived, but since neither of them knew how long they were going to be there, they hadn't known what to get.

Kat's gaze kept moving to the folder marked "Darin Ichatious" on the corner of the scratched and dented coffee table, but she ignored it, instead moving another legal pad in front of her, the one she'd been using to check off items involving personal matters. She'd contacted the insurance company to report the house fire. Called a construction company to board up her house until she could go through it with them to see what repairs needed to be made (she imagined the delay wasn't going to make her neighbors very happy, but that's all she could do for now). And then she'd begun making the calls needed to cancel the plans for her and James's wedding.

Her gaze drifted again to the folder and she

pulled the phone from where it was making an indent in her chin and dialed information for the number to the wedding reception hall James had reserved. She explained who she was and why she was calling then listened to the sound of pages being turned.

"I'm sorry, Miss Buckingham, but I don't show any reservation for the dates you indicated."

Kat rubbed the area between her brows. "Pardon me?"

"When did you say the call was put in?"

"About two months ago, maybe."

More page turning. "Yes, yes. I do see an inquiry made by…well, by you." A pause. "But I see no follow-up."

"But Mr. Smith came by to pay the deposit shortly thereafter."

"I'm sorry, but I show no record of that."

That didn't make any sense. The check she'd given him to cover the deposit had cleared through her bank account. If the hall hadn't received it, where had the money gone?

"Could you check for me one more time, please?"

"I don't have to. Another party has already taken the dates you indicated. The Jensen wedding."

Kat thought she'd thanked the hall manager but she couldn't be sure as she absently disconnected the call and sat staring across the room.

She was so preoccupied a sound from outside the house barely registered the first time she heard it. But the second time…

Probably Harry checking things out. He'd gone outside some thirty minutes ago and had yet to return.

Her gaze was again drawn to the file she'd spent all last night reviewing. The same file she'd been avoiding all day. Now she pulled it in front of her, looked inside for the contact numbers of James's family members in Maryland. She'd called James's import offices no fewer than a dozen times during the day and received no answer. No voicemail, no secretary, no nothing. She supposed given the circumstances surrounding James's death, it would be necessary to close the small office, but she hadn't thought it would happen so fast. She'd wanted to talk to James's secretary, the only other person she knew with a connection to James outside herself and her friends. But a check with information had pulled up two Janet Talbert's and neither of them had been the one she was looking for.

"Hello?"

Kat drew a deep breath when someone answered her call on the first ring.

"Mrs. Ichatious? This is Kat Buckingham…"

She waited for Dolores Ichatious to indicate whether or not she was familiar with her. When she said, "I'm sorry, do I know you?"

"I'm calling about James…I mean, Darin."

Silence, then, "If you're from the Washington police, I've already told you me and my family want nothing to do with his remains."

Kat felt like her breath had been knocked out of her. "Pardon me?"

"You heard me. We haven't heard from him for three years, but even before that all he brought was bad news, pain and heartache to this family. All I have to say about his death is 'good riddance.'"

The couch seemed to shift under Kat. "Mrs. Ichatious—"

"Don't call me that. My name is MacMillan now. Has been for twenty years."

"I'm sorry, Mrs. MacMillan, it's just that…I am, I was James's fiancée. We were to be married this August."

Silence.

"I'd like your help in seeing to his burial arrangements."

"Are you calling for money?"

Kat couldn't have been more shocked by the frosty question had she been slapped. "No, no. I don't need any money. I just thought if you could tell me where you think…Darin would have liked to be buried—"

"How in the hell would I know? Now I've talked about Darin more than he deserves already so if you'll excuse me…"

She hung up.

Kat sat stunned, not sure what her reaction should be. Sad that James's own family didn't want anything to do with him in death and apparently hadn't wanted any connection while he was alive either? Hurt that his mother hadn't cared they'd been engaged to be married and been at least a little curious about the woman who would have been her daughter-in-law? Insulted that she'd thought Kat's call had been about money?

Her reaction was a lot of all three, plus a little disappointment thrown in for good measure. The file before her indicated that James had suffered brutal physical abuse throughout his childhood as documented by the schools he'd attended, but whenever things got too hot, his mother had moved him to another school. When he was fifteen he'd gotten into all sorts of trouble, everything from forging his mother's name on a check and running away with two thousand from her savings account, to aggravated robbery of a convenience store. He'd been in and out of detention centers and when he was seventeen had even been sent to adult prison for three months for assaulting a police officer.

Another sound outside.

"Harry?"

Kat slowly got up. The rattling metal fan in the corner was doing little to cool off the room so the windows were open, though barred.

"Harry, is that you?"

Clutching the phone to her chest, she waited near the door for an answer. Nothing.

She felt a burst of fear. What if it wasn't Harry? What if someone else was lurking out there? The same someone who had killed James?

But that didn't make sense. No one knew where she was. And there was no way anyone could have traced her.

She opened the door and gave out a shriek as she stared at a man that wasn't Harry.

"Whoa, didn't mean to startle you."

Marc McCoy held up both his hands as if to indicate he wasn't armed.

"Well you did." Kat found herself curiously out of breath. "God, you scared the crap out of me."

"Sorry about that. I was just checking over everything here."

Kat looked outside to find it had grown dark already, amazed she'd been working that long.

"Where's Harry?"

"I ran into him when I pulled up. He said he didn't want to interrupt you so he asked I keep an eye out while he picked up a few things in town." He squinted at her. "You okay?"

Kat considered what she'd just gone through with her client, her wedding arrangements and her would-be mother-in-law and said, "Yes." She made a face. "Actually, no." She opened the door farther. "Come in and keep me company for a while. I could use a little cheering up."

Marc looked doubtful. "I don't know if I'm the

guy who should be doing that. I mean, Mel says I'm as sensitive as a baseball."

Kat wasn't sure what that meant but she was fairly certain it wasn't flattering. "That's all right. I won't expect you to tap dance for me on cue or anything. In fact, sharing a beer with me is all I ask."

His grin was completely disarming. "That, I can do."

He came inside and she moved to close the door.

"Here, let me," he said, giving a thorough look outside before solidly bolting the door after himself. "And I'd advise against opening up like that again without knowing who's out there."

"It was just you."

"This time. Next time…"

Another guy who liked to let his sentences hang. She resisted the urge to give him an eye roll.

Was it fused into guy DNA to be suspicious? Or was it only those in law enforcement?

She got two beers out of the fridge, handed him one then motioned for him to sit next to her on the couch, which was essentially the only other place to sit aside from a rickety rocking chair in the corner.

"So, tell me about your Melanie," she prompted.

"Huh?" Marc ran the back of his hand across his mouth after taking a deep slug of beer. "You wanna know about Mel? What do you want to know about her?"

"Harry said you and she stayed here awhile?"

He looked around and gave a goofy smile. "Yeah. About four years ago. One of the best times, and worst times, of my life."

Kat settled back into the sofa and gazed happily at her brother. Yes, this was exactly what she'd needed. Something to ground her in the present. To remind her that she wasn't the only person on earth. To hear about love and laughter and happiness when the past couple of hours had been so devoid of all three.

CHAPTER TEN

HARRY PICKED UP the sound of someone talking as he neared the house. Kathryn must still be on the phone.

He moved the bag he held to his opposite arm and rubbed the back of his neck with his free hand. She'd been on the phone for pretty much the majority of the day, moving from one item to the next on whatever agenda she'd come up with on the legal pads she'd pulled from her briefcase. She hadn't even noticed the lunch he'd fixed and put next to her, and he was pretty sure she hadn't even realized he had left a little while earlier, leaving Marc in charge.

Of course, it didn't help that Harry hadn't said a word to her. Truth was, she'd looked so damn pretty, so fully engrossed, he hadn't had the heart to interrupt her. So when Marc had shown up from out of the blue—he had the feeling all the McCoys would be doing that at one point or another—he'd relied on the middle McCoy to keep an eye out while he'd gone on a food run.

He'd watched Kathryn eat on countless occa-

sions with James. Still he hadn't paid much attention to what she'd eaten. And while she'd gladly
guzzled beer and eaten pizza last night, he didn't
think that was her normal fare. No. She struck him
as more of a salad and chicken breast kind of girl.

Although why he should care to do anything
more than keep her fed was beyond him.

Okay, so yes, he was attracted to her. Truth be
told, he'd fallen hard the very first time he'd seen
her. But he hadn't known the extent of that attraction until he'd heard her on the phone following up
on items for Darin then sitting for long moments
looking a blink away from tears.

His hand tightened on the bag as he climbed the
two steps to the door. It grated on his nerves to think
of her crying for the likes of Darin. And it was that
emotion that let on how very much he'd come to feel
for a woman he had no business feeling anything for.

He knocked on the door.

"No, wait," he heard a male voice say. "Remember what I said."

Marc. Marc was inside with his sister.

"Who is it?" Kathryn asked as if she were trying
to make it deeper.

Harry cracked a grin and decided not to answer.
A moment later he knocked again.

"They're not saying anything," she stage whispered to Marc.

Harry noticed a shadow at the window to his left

and moved until he was flush against the outer house wall, out of eyeshot.

He knocked again.

Kathryn finally opened the door…and clobbered him with her briefcase, catching him in the corner of the eye with the lock.

"Oh, my God! It's Harry! I'm so sorry."

She rushed forward as Harry rocked back on his heels. What did she have in that thing? An iron weight?

"Are you okay? Can you stand?"

He was standing, wasn't he? At least he thought he was. He was teetering a little bit, but still upright. He could tell because the first thing to come into sight was Marc's grinning face at eye level.

"That's going to leave a mark."

"Shush with the jokes and help me get him to the couch."

Marc took the bag from his hand, tossed it to the floor then did as Kathryn asked.

"You should know better than that, Harry."

"How was I supposed to know she was going to bean me with a two by four?"

Kathryn and her brother shared a look.

"Marc taught me. You see, I went through the same thing with him a little while ago. He knocked, I opened the door and when it wasn't you, he scared the crap out of me."

"Ah." There was no possible way he could have

known that. "Did you whack him with your brief-case, too?"

"No," she said softly.

Something cold was pressed against his head and he realized it was a beer bottle, probably Kathryn's.

"Are you all right? How many fingers am I hold-ing up?"

Marc chuckled. "He's fine. That's what's great about having a head made of rocks."

"Ha, ha. You're a regular comedian, McCoy." Harry gently pushed Kathryn's hands away, not wanting the attention. Frankly, it was doing strange things to his libido having her this near, her breasts brushing against his arm as she tended to his head. Her sweet smell filling his senses. The softness of her skin tempting him to respond with his own touch, which would have nothing to do with innocent car-ing gestures and everything to do with wicked sug-gestive moves.

His gaze met hers and he felt an irresistible pull there, a shared attraction that knocked him back on his heels more than the blow from the briefcase.

He quickly broke eye contact.

"What's wrong?" she asked quietly when he tried to push her away too stringently.

"Nothing. I just don't like being fussed over." *I don't like wanting a woman who's still in love with another man.*

"Well," Marc said, crossing his arms where he

stood on the other side of the coffee table, "since you're back and obviously no longer in need of my services, I think I'd better get home to my wife and kid."

Harry watched Kathryn get up and give Marc a hug that caused the middle McCoy to flush straight through to his ears.

"Thanks for taking my mind off things."

Marc hugged her back. "I just hope I didn't talk your ear off."

"Not hardly."

Harry got up and walked him to the door then minutes later stood staring after his disappearing headlights. He quietly closed the door then turned toward where Kathryn sat on the sofa looking at him openly, curiously.

She patted the cushion next to her, her eyes large and dark. "Now I think it's time you and I had a nice, long talk."

Aw, hell.

SURE KAT had been preoccupied lately, for good reason, but not even she could miss the undeniable spark of attraction she'd witnessed in Harry's eyes a moment ago.

Nor could she deny her own visceral response to that same want.

And she wasn't sure how she felt about that. On the one hand, she was glad to feel alive again. Like a woman capable of positive feeling, not just the grief that plagued her like a shadow.

On the other hand…well, she felt like she was betraying James.

Harry still hadn't moved from where he stood near the door. "I brought dinner. Why don't I go into the kitchen—"

"Dinner can wait." She patted the sofa again.

Harry looked like he'd rather run over hot coals in that one moment. And she couldn't say she could blame him. The urge to ignore what was growing between them was strong, even in her own heart. Pretend it didn't exist and it would go away, right? Wrong.

She'd never been one to avoid anything and she didn't think now was a good time to start. No matter how uncomfortable the topic.

Finally Harry sat near where she'd indicated, but as far away on the sofa as possible.

"There." He squared his shoulders. "Now, what did you want to talk about?"

Kat smiled. The type of men she was used to, James included, was dry-witted and kept nothing hidden. Well, under normal circumstances, anyway. The men who had been introduced into her life over the past few days, however, were the exact opposite. While physically they were strong and gutsy, emotionally they were evasive and awkward. She was coming to appreciate the intriguing juxtaposition even while she was frustrated by it.

"I think you know," she said quietly.

"No, I don't think that I do know." He crossed his arms over his chest in a defensive way she was all too familiar with in the courtroom.

And just like that Kat was pressing her lips gently against his.

Which couldn't have been any further away from her intention.

She didn't know who was more surprised, he or she, as they stared into each other's eyes after the brief kiss. But as much as her mind argued for her to break the connection, she was curiously unable to. And as much as he apparently wanted to pull away, he couldn't seem to either. Their lips met again in a deeper, more passionate kiss.

As pure human need suffused her veins, she distantly pondered what a pair they made.

She'd never done anything so impulsive before. Not with James, not with anybody. Everything had been perfectly timed. Third date, kiss good night. Fifth date, a little scratch and tickle. Seventh date, they'd made their way to the bedroom. Not in a flash of passion, but instead as an almost detached natural progression, like she'd said, "Okay, I like him, he likes me, let's go to the next stage."

This unexpected mouthwatering need she wasn't sure what to do with.

Her eyes began drifting closed and her heart hammered a thick rhythm in her chest. Heat, sure and swift, surged to her delicate parts. At some point she'd lifted her right hand and her fingers splayed against the side of his face, the stubble there scratching the sensitized skin of her palm. He gently coaxed her lips open and she allowed him access to her mouth, exploring his with the same lazy strokes, the sensations hardening her nipples, making her underpants feel suddenly damp.

She heard a groan and realized Harry had made the low, guttural sound. He slid sideways on the couch, his arms going around her, shifting her until she lay almost completely flush against him. His fingers burned a path across her shoulders, down to cup her bottom, then tunneled under the back of her T-shirt and pressed against her too hot skin.

Kat gave an involuntary shiver, loving the feel of his hands on her, his mouth kissing her. It somehow seemed…right. She found herself moving until his thick, hard length pressed against her lower belly, shooting fresh pangs of want and need bulleting through her as she sought even closer contact.

The hands at her back unhooked her bra and then skimmed up her sides. She lifted her shoulders slightly to give him access and just like that his hands caressed her bare breasts. Kat moaned and the intensity of their kiss increased. The full breadth of her desire for this one man was stunning, leaving her spellbound and curious and not a bit scared. Which surprised her. She'd never felt so outside herself. So unable to control her actions. So much at the mercy of her own desires.

She slid her fingers down his chest to his stomach then lower still until she cupped his length in her palm through his jeans.

Harry abruptly pulled away, looking like a kid who'd gotten caught with his hand in the cookie jar. Although it was her who had her hand in a naughty place.

"Whoa," he said, practically leaping from the couch.

Whoa, indeed.

Kat sat up, tugging at her T-shirt and crossing her arms to cover where her bra was still undone under the soft material, her nipples clearly visible. Who knew the no-nonsense U.S. Marshal could kiss like that? Who knew she, considering all that was happening in her life, could respond the way she had?

"I, um, need some air."

Kat quickly got up from the couch. "Actually, I could do with a bit of air myself."

She hadn't been outside the house since their arrival early that morning and she suddenly had a craving for space. If only to get her thoughts together. If only to make herself remember who she was, who Harry was, and why it was they were stuck together in this house for God only knew how long.

If only to figure out why that had just happened…and how to stop it from happening again.

Harry opened the door, running his free hand through his hair again and again as he avoided her gaze. "You go on ahead. But don't go far.

"Yes, right. I won't."

"Okay, sure. I'll be right here if you need anything. Just…yell."

"Fine, all right." And just like that she was standing outside, the only light from the door behind her and from the stars spilled across the navy blue sky. She took a deep gulp of air then another, willing her heart rate to slow but having considerable difficulty. She was filled with the sudden, incredible urge to go for a run. She hadn't gotten any real exercise since Sunday and her muscles screamed for it. Perhaps that had been part of the reason she had reacted so physically to Harry. Her body was seeking a release he could offer in spades.

She began stepping away, squelching the urge to go too far if only because she questioned her ability to find the cabin again in the dark.

What had happened? While she'd come to trust and depend on Harry far more quickly than she would have under normal circumstances, she hadn't been aware of a physical attraction. Her heart was still grieving, her mind still occupied with the chaos that swirled around her. Was their kiss a momentary blip on the emotional radar screen? A moment of weakness brought on by the need to feel loved when everything she'd shared with James was being called into question?

She didn't know. What she did know was that she couldn't handle this one more complication on top of so many others.

She turned around to find she'd walked farther away from the safe house than she'd intended. It was little more than a small shadow some ways down the shore, the waters of the Potomac lapping a couple of feet to her right. She made out some house lights on the other side of the riverbank, probably from other cabins, but they weren't bright enough to illuminate the area where she stood. It was cool here, cooler than it was in the city. Her T-shirt and slacks were ineffective against the dip in temperature and she shivered, glad to feel something other than the thick need she'd experienced in Harry's arms.

She began moving back toward the cabin, her arms crossed over her chest, when two hands reached out from a thatch of bushes and grabbed her.

CHAPTER ELEVEN

HARRY SQUINTED into the darkness in the direction Kathryn had gone, then gave in to the urge to pace again.

What had he been thinking, kissing her like that? Only he wasn't sure who had kissed whom. What he did know was that he hadn't resisted. Resisted? Hell, it had been all he could do to push her away when they'd been moments away from making love right there on that ratty old couch.

Oh, that would go a long ways toward maintaining her trust in him.

As it stood, he wasn't all that convinced they could move beyond what had transpired between them. Now, with the flush of passion gone, would she look at him, wonder if he had purposely taken advantage of her vulnerable emotional state to satisfy his libido?

He couldn't stand even the suggestion that she might entertain the idea.

He stopped again and stared into the darkness. She'd been gone too long. He glanced at his watch, closed the door to the safe house, then started off in the direction she'd gone.

KAT STRUGGLED FOR BREATH, inhaling the smell of new leather, the leather of the gloved hand tightly covering her mouth. An arm like a band of steel was clamped around her rib cage from behind, preventing her from taking in all but the smallest amount of air.

Someone had followed her from the safe house.

She remembered thinking she'd gone too far, but she'd been more concerned about not finding her way back than the possibility she might be at risk.

The arm tightened and she whimpered as her captor kneed her hard in the back of the leg, urging her to move forward.

Think, she ordered herself. *Think, think, think.* What could she do? Screaming for help was out of the question. Not that Harry would necessarily hear her this far away, but she would have tried if she could. Maybe someone else would hear her and come to investigate.

Since yelling was out of the question, she had to come up with something else.

A health fiend, she'd taken classes both in kickboxing and the more intense version, Taebo. But she didn't know how she could utilize the movements while being held from behind. Anyway, she hadn't learned the techniques for self-defense purposes;

she'd merely been looking for a way to spice up her regular workouts.

Her captor had moved her a good twenty feet farther away from the cabin and deeper into the surrounding woods, causing panic to set in. Was he taking her to his car? What would her options be if they reached it? She highly doubted he would be as generous as Harry had been, leaving her free to try and jump out.

The ground beneath her was damp from a recent rain. She firmly dug her heels in, sliding a bit until her feet found purchase, stopping their forward progress.

"Move," a harsh male voice ordered.

Screw you, she screamed mentally.

She didn't know if he was armed, but she did know he wasn't presently holding a weapon in his hands because she would feel it. If she could get him to release one of his hands she could stand a chance of turning toward him and defending herself.

He jammed his knee against the back of her leg again. But rather than stepping forward to keep herself from falling, Kat dropped to her knees, forcing him to loosen his grip.

Her heart beating loudly in her ears, she elbowed him solidly in the solar plexus then struggled the rest of the way free. She rose and dodged away from him toward a stand of trees, yelling out for help at the same time.

If her captor was armed she was in deep trouble.

Her knees felt so watery they almost refused to hold her. She ducked behind the thick trunk of a tree and wildly took in her surroundings. It was dark, too dark to make out much of anything. They must have been walking along a path because here the vegetation was much denser, making a direct escape impossible. She zigzagged around a few more trees, putting a little more distance between them and nearly tripping over a branch. As she was hugging the bark of a tree trunk, her mind caught on the word "branch."

A hand reached around the tree to her left, catching the sleeve of her T-shirt. She gasped and dove around the other side of it, the soft fabric tearing as she did so. She crouched down, feeling for the thick branch she'd nearly tripped over. Just as her assailant came around the tree after her, she swung, catching him across the knees. He dropped and she swung again, this time aiming for his head.

She heard a dull thump, watching as the shadow became one with the ground. Then she ran full out for the shore.

Her lungs burning, her knees hurting where she'd hit the ground hard, her shirt torn, she burst into the clearing—and straight into Harry's wide, capable chest.

Thank God.

THE ASSAILANT was gone by the time Harry found the spot where Kathryn had hit him. Either that or he was watching from the shadows waiting for his next opportunity.

After, Harry had hurried Kathryn back to the safe house, locked it up tight, then stood sentinel at the window in the darkened structure, his firearm armed and ready in his holster. He'd placed a call to his superior and two marshals had been dispatched immediately to the location. He watched as they walked a tight perimeter around the house.

They were safe. For the night, anyway.

He couldn't see Kathryn huddled on the couch, but he could feel her gaze on him and could hear her even breathing and occasional deep inhalation. While she'd been through a lot over the past few days, she hadn't been face-to-face with a menacing presence. Until now. And she was understandably having a tough time with it.

Harry tried to relax his jaw muscles, his teeth beginning to ache. She shouldn't have been at risk to begin with. If he hadn't been so distracted by their kiss, he would never have let her wander so far from the house. Or at the very least he would have followed from a safe distance and seen her snatched.

What if she hadn't broken free? What if she hadn't come exploding out of that clearing when she had? Would she even now be far away from here at the mercy of whomever had killed Darin?

And just who had killed Darin anyway? And what designs did he have on Kathryn now?

It didn't make any sense. If both of them had been targets, why not take Kathryn out when Darin was killed?

He didn't have a clue. What he did know was he'd been resting on his laurels for too long. It was time to put his feelings for the beautiful blonde aside and start taking care of business. While his official job was to protect Kathryn as a witness of the state, his personal job was to see that his best friend's sister remained safe. And that rested on his ability to find the real killer and put him behind bars where he could never threaten anyone's life again.

He wasn't aware Kathryn had moved until she was standing right in front of him, more shadow than person. His throat tightened to the point of pain at the sweet scent of her. His groin tightened at her nearness.

"Harry, I won't pretend I understand what's going on…"

"It should never have happened. He should never have had the opportunity to grab you. I should have stopped it."

He watched her head bow down. "That's not what I'm talking about."

He suddenly couldn't draw a breath.

She was talking about their kiss.

"But right now I need you to hold me so badly I ache."

Oh, hell…

Harry could have refused anything but her softly spoken request, even though he knew touching her in any way wasn't a good idea. He'd already proven his inability to hold in check his growing want of her.

"Come here," he murmured, folding her against his chest and wrapping his arms around her.

She shivered then relaxed. There was nothing sexual in the reaction. Instead, the response was trusting and it touched off something inside him that went deeper than physical need. Something he wasn't sure he wanted to explore.

He smoothed his hands over the soft blouse she'd changed into when they'd returned to the house. She smelled of fresh soap and soft woman. A woman whose faith in him moved him beyond anything he could explain, even to himself. Simply, he'd never felt this way toward another human being. Sure, it was his job to protect people, but he'd never felt this fierce desire, this almost primal need to keep Kathryn from harm.

And, damn it, for the life of him he couldn't stop himself from wanting her in every way there was for a man to want a woman.

KAT WASN'T SURE when the platonic hug had turned into something more. One moment her cheek was pressed against Harry's hard, comforting chest, the next she grew slowly aware of a bottomless sensation in her stomach, a burning between her thighs. She'd experienced a similar response earlier but this wasn't a result of an impulsive kiss. Instead the desire simmering through her veins seemed to come from a place she hadn't known existed. A faraway spot inside her heart that demanded she react on a plateau she'd never visited before now.

She was familiar with the cliché of patients falling for the doctors who saved them. She was also aware of the Stockholm syndrome. And while Harry wasn't a physician or a kidnapper, he'd been unwaveringly close and accessible, caring and protective. And there was a bond developing between them she couldn't hope to explain or fight.

And even more surprising was she didn't want to do either. She merely wanted to feel.

She splayed her hands against his wide chest, reveling in the feel of his hard muscles beneath his shirt. She could feel him tense and heard him mutter something under his breath. But he didn't pull away.

Was he just as spellbound by their predicament as she was? Then again she didn't see Harry as being at the mercy of his desires. He was a man very much in control.

She remembered seeing him Sunday night standing in her foyer, looking at her with those sober brown eyes. He'd tried to call off the pit bull detective who'd had her arrested even then, before it had been his job to protect her.

She looked up at him, though she couldn't see him in the dark. Would she even be a protected witness if not for him? Would she now still be in that county jail cell?

"Kathryn, I…" he said quietly, seriously.

She moved her fingers to his face, exploring the solid planes, running her fingertips along his strong brows, the lined length of his lips.

"What?" she asked, caught off guard by the watering of her mouth, the irresistible urge she had to kiss him.

"I…um, don't think this is a good idea."

"I don't think it is, either." She tilted her head and kissed him. "But I'm coming to believe thinking is overrated."

She gently kissed him again. "Feel with me, Harry."

He groaned and his hands on her back moved to her hips where he pulled her tighter against his hard arousal. Then he was kissing her like it was something he'd wanted to do for hours, days, years. Not with breathless, reckless need as they'd kissed earlier. No, this kiss was slower, more concentrated, as if it wasn't a means toward an end but a reward in itself.

Kat wasn't used to this. This surrender to physical desire. But she half suspected the reason was that she'd never truly experienced this raw, undiluted want for a man before. Oh, sure, she'd enjoyed sex with James. But never had she felt this incredible urge to share herself with someone. Sex before had been a release, almost like exercise. Gravy to go with the mashed potatoes of her intimate relationships. While she'd never really been disappointed, often she would have preferred her own, solo explorations over another's attentions.

But now...

Now she burned so hot with the desire to feel Harry's hands on her bare skin she was afraid she might combust.

He tangled his fingers in her hair and tugged her slightly away from him, their breath mingling between them. "Are you sure this is what you want, Kathryn?"

She searched his eyes in the dark then slowly nodded. "Yes. Yes, it is."

He swooped her up into his arms so quickly she gasped, clutching his shoulders to brace herself.

So gentle...so attentive. Kathryn was fascinated with the way he laid her on the old mattress as if she were crystal and the bed the box where he was placing her for safekeeping. He placed his weapon on the nightstand with a dull click, then returned to unbutton her blouse in an unhurried way at the same time she slowly pushed up his shirt. These items of clothing were dropped to the floor along with jeans and pants until he leaned over her completely naked and she wore only her underpants. She watched as he curved his fingers over the top of the elastic and lifted her hips presumably so he could remove them. Instead he pressed the heel of his hand against her swollen flesh through the silky material. Her breath caught and a soft moan escaped her mouth. If he'd been testing her for readiness, questioning her desire to go forward, she suspected she'd passed.

He sheathed himself with a condom he took from his back pocket then ever so slowly tugged her underpants down. Her coarse wedge of hair sprung up and the elastic pulled against her hips as he dragged her panties down further. When he bent down and pressed a kiss to the damp curls, her hips bucked up off the mattress.

The panties joined the rest of their clothes on the floor as Harry sat back as if taking in her body in the dim light. Kat felt helpless to do anything but watch as he skimmed his fingertips from her shoulders to her collar bone then down between her breasts and over her stomach as if he were memorizing every inch of her. Never had she felt so…cherished, was the word that came to mind. As if he was marveling over the burst of luck that found him right there in that one moment, touching her.

And never had she wanted, needed someone to cherish her so much.

His hands reached her thighs and slid inward to part her legs, baring her to the cool night air. Kat shivered and swallowed thickly. Harry skimmed the back of his knuckles over her hair then slipped a finger lengthwise into her slick channel, parting her swollen flesh further. Then his tongue followed his finger, providing her with a pleasure she hadn't dreamed existed.

Just like that she came apart, exploding at the sweet pressure of his mouth against her tight bud, suckling her. Her breath came in ragged gasps and her hands restlessly sought his shoulders as he drew out her climax, lapping and laving her with precise strokes of his tongue. Only when she felt the pressure building again did he move to lick his way up her stomach, over her straining nipples, then up to her mouth to kiss her.

Kat kissed him deeply, tasting her own musk there. She curved her ankles around his calves and tilted her hips, putting her wetness in direct contact with his hard, latex-sheathed shaft.

Then all at once he was filling her. For a long moment Kat couldn't seem to catch her breath. She lay there, feeling him not only inside her but all around her, overwhelming her senses, driving all thought from her mind, suffusing her body with sheer ecstasy and bliss. He slowly withdrew then stroked her to the hilt, and she finally took a shaky breath. She shivered all over as she slid her hands to his rear, clutching him to her, forcing him to stay there, deeply embedded in her tight, slick flesh.

He withdrew then sank into her again, going even deeper than he had before. Again…and again. Kat grasped him tightly, her heart beating so hard she swore she could hear it in her ears. He bent to kiss her, and her head came up off the pillow to meet his at the same time her hips rose off the bed to join his.

She felt a part of everything and nothing. As substantial as lead and insubstantial as air. She felt cherished and wanton.

And then, as if she were a piece of crystal, she shattered into a thousand tiny shards sent soaring into the night by this incredible man.

CHAPTER TWELVE

LATER THAT NIGHT, Sean pulled into the driveway of the house he shared with Wilhemenia Weber.

He caught his mistake. Her name wasn't Weber anymore. It was McCoy, and had been ever since he'd married her.

He ran his hand over his face, feeling more tired than he had in a long, long time. He wasn't looking forward to the coming conversation. Earlier that evening during a dinner of petite chicken breasts in some kind of white wine sauce and small round potatoes and okra, he'd accidentally mentioned Kathryn.

At first Wilhemenia had thought he was referring to his late wife. But as Sean had quickly realized, the truth wasn't any better. He simply hadn't gotten around to figuring out the best way to tell Wilhemenia about the daughter he'd given up for adoption so long ago. A daughter who had stolen his shattered heart away when she was born twenty-seven years ago and still had the same effect on him today. Not because of who she looked like. But because of who she'd grown up to be.

Never in a million years could he have hoped for the meeting between his boys and Kathryn to go so well. He hadn't known what he'd expected, but whatever mixed feelings they felt toward their father for having kept the truth from them for so long weren't turned toward Kathryn. Rather after some initial awkwardness, the six of them had seemed to get on like they had grown up together in the same house, with the boys teasing her and Kathryn matching them jab for jab.

He'd stayed in the old farmhouse last night after a quick call to Wilhemenia at about one a.m. explaining he wasn't up to the drive back. He had to give her credit for her patience. He'd been more than distracted for the past few days. In all honesty, he had been distracted for much longer than that, but that was a topic he wasn't willing to explore just then.

A light went on in the front window of the small Tudor-style house with its neat shrubs, lawn and planters. Wilhemenia had probably heard him pull up and was waiting for him. Not that he expected otherwise. On any given night when he came in late she was there waiting to serve him a cup of tea with some cookies.

But somehow tonight he didn't think his path straight for the bedroom was going to be interrupted by polite food offerings.

He finally switched off the car and climbed out.

Although he'd been in the house for four years, somehow it had yet to seem like home to him. Not like the McCoy place. Part of the reason might be that Wilhemenia preferred using the same land-scaping company she'd been using for the past thirty-five years and his tinkering with her garden was absolutely forbidden. He remembered bringing home a couple of tomato plants and exchanging them for the tubs of flowers she had on the back patio. She'd nearly gone into cardiac arrest when she'd come home from the flower shop where she worked to discover what he'd done.

He'd thought she'd be pleased, or at the very least amused.

Instead she'd been inconsolable.

Sean grimaced. How was he supposed to know that the flowers were a rare and special hybrid that only bloomed every five years and that he'd yanked them out just when the buds were about to pop?

He wasn't sure if he was remembering correctly, but that was the gist of it.

Then there was the shop.

He climbed the two steps to the door and sorted through his keys.

A few months into their marriage, Wilhemenia had decided to get a part-time job. What with both her daughters now married, and with him out of the house so much of the time, she'd needed something to distract herself, she'd said. The position she chose was at a flower shop about a mile down the road in what could be considered downtown Bedford. To him the place was a small, plant-clogged nightmare. To Wilhemenia it was heaven.

The moment he'd met the widower owner Walter Purdy, he hadn't liked the guy. But Wilhemenia did and that's all that mattered since she was the one going to be working there. And when the part-time job turned into a full-time one, Sean was more relieved still because it meant she wouldn't be harping on him to be home on time so dinner wouldn't be ruined, or asking him about every single detail of his day and actually expecting him to share them with her.

He put the key in the lock. That wasn't fair. From the get-go, Wilhemenia had been generous to a fault, going out of her way to make him comfortable in the house, her house. It was he who'd had a hard time adjusting. So he'd lived in the same house his entire life. What was wrong with that? But since Mitch and Liz had taken over the farm and turned it into a horse ranch, he couldn't very well have moved Wilhemenia in. Anyway, now that Mitch and Liz had built the new place, he couldn't imagine Wilhemenia living in the McCoy place. The mere thought made him smile slightly at all the trouble she could get into in a single day.

He entered the house, listening for sounds. Nothing but the *tick-tick* of the enormous grandfather clock at the end of the hall. He hated that clock. Thought sometimes it would drive him insane when he couldn't sleep and it seemed to mock him with the loud reminder of the passage of time.

"Wilhemenia?" he called out.

He heard her delicately clear her throat. "In the sitting room."

She could have just said "in here." But not Wilhemenia. The living room was the sitting room. Their bedroom, the master bedroom. And the backyard, the garden.

He put his keys in a basket on the antique foyer table then stepped into the living room. There she sat perched on the edge of her flower-patterned couch, a real china cup on the coffee table in front of her.

"You didn't have to wait up," he said, standing in the doorway.

"That's all right. Walter stopped by to keep me company and just left a little while ago so I was up anyway."

Too bad Walter hadn't stuck around. Sean could have gotten away with a few minutes of pleasantries then gone up to bed and left them alone to go on talking incomprehensibly about flowers.

"Would you like some tea?"

"No, no," he said, resigning himself to this conversation and taking the seat on the couch next to her.

He still hadn't quite figured out how to sit on it without disturbing the cushions, but at least he'd insisted she take off the awful plastic she'd had covering it when he'd first moved in. She reached behind him to straighten a cushion. It wasn't so long ago that he would have used the excuse to steal a kiss. Now he shifted so she could have easier access.

"We need to talk," she said quietly.

"I know. I'm sorry about running out of here earlier. I wasn't ready to discuss this then."

He wasn't ready now, either, but he didn't think Mitch and Liz would be up for another guest, especially so late.

Besides, he reminded himself, this was his wife. If there was anyone in the world he should be able to talk to, it should be her.

Although, to be truthful, talking had never been their strong suit. And that had never seemed to cause any problems before now. Their strong attraction for each other had been enough to see them through four good years of marriage.

For Pete's sake, he was thinking like things were over between the two of them.

Wilhemenia took a dainty sip from her cup. "I think it only fair to warn you that I called Melanie as soon as you left earlier."

Sean winced. Mitch had told Liz, mostly because he'd had to since Liz lived at the farmhouse where

Kathryn had stayed last night. And he strongly suspected Liz had told Connor's wife, Bronte, since that was whom she'd gone to visit while the guys had met their sister for the first time. And he was pretty sure David had probably told Kelly. But Marc and Jake…well, like him, it would probably take them a good, long while to get around to bringing the subject up with their wives.

He could just imagine the five women burning up the phone lines getting the scoop and venting and discussing ways to make their husbands lives miserable for not having told them right away.

Sean tried to play off his uneasiness. "I suppose she was going to find out sooner or later anyway."

"I suppose."

He waited for her to say something more, but she didn't. There was only the sound of that incessant grandfather clock and the clink of her cup against her saucer as she took small sips from her tea.

"So…" he said, forgetting about the cushions he wasn't supposed to be mussing up and stretching his arm across the back and near her. "I guess an apology is in order."

He just then realized she had yet to look him in the eyes. She gazed at him indirectly, more specifically the area of his chin or the front of his shirt, but not his eyes.

"You didn't track mud into the house, Sean. You neglected to tell me a very important detail of your life."

He nodded. "Yes, I know. And I'm sorry for that. Really, I am. It's just…well, until the other day I couldn't tell anybody. And I probably wouldn't have at all had Kathryn not run into trouble."

"Somehow that brings me little comfort."

What did she want him to do? Get on his knees and beg for forgiveness?

He instead shifted his arm forward until his hand rested on her opposite shoulder. The silk of her blouse was cool, the skin underneath hot. While a lot of the ultra feminine stuff bugged him no end, he loved this part. Loved her silky clothes and the way she always smelled so damn good. Loved how with one kiss she would toss aside her inhibitions like her shirt and turn into a wild woman.

She shrugged off his touch. "I think you should stay with one of your sons for a while."

Sean blinked. "What?"

He couldn't possibly have heard right. "I don't think I'm following you here…did you just ask me to move out?"

She finally looked at him and in her steel-blue eyes he read determination. He also realized that she'd been crying.

Damn.

"I think it would be for the best. For a little while anyway." She sniffed slightly and reached for the handkerchief that was forever tucked into the sleeve of her blouse. "Until I can come to terms with your betrayal."

Betrayal? Betrayal would be his flirting with the waitress at the town coffee shop.

It was then he realized that a suitcase, his suitcase, sat near the doorway to the foyer.

"I think betrayal's the wrong word," he said quietly.

"Walter thinks it's the right one, and frankly so do I."

She'd talked to Walter about their personal lives? And he'd used the word "betrayal"?

"Now *that,* your talking to someone outside the family about such personal business, is what I would call betrayal," he said.

He searched her face, looking for a crack, waiting for a sign that she might take her words back and they might have the conversation they needed to have.

Instead she lifted her chin higher and her eyes grew more stubborn.

Sean held up his hands and got up from the couch, half tempted to throw the damn pillow that toppled to the floor.

"When you think I've been gone long enough, you can find me at Mitch's."

AN HOUR AND SOME MINUTES later Sean pulled into the driveway of the McCoy house, surprised to find that the lights were still burning, and that he wasn't the only one looking to borrow the couch for the night. He walked in to find Marc reading what looked like a self-help book in the kitchen.

"Hey, Pops," he said, putting the book on the chair next to him where Sean couldn't read the title. "You're in the doghouse, too, huh?"

"Yeah, you could say that."

Mitch came into the room wearing pajama bottoms and asked if Sean wanted a beer.

"No, I'm fine."

"Women," the three of them said in unison, then shared a chuckle.

"What's your wife mad at you about?" Marc asked.

"Liz? Nothing. She's just pissed that neither one of you told your wives."

Marc grimaced. "That's because she wishes she'd known they hadn't heard the news so she could have told them."

Mitch laughed. "No, that's not it and you know it."

Marc shrugged and nodded. "Yeah, I know. Out of all the women, I have to admit Liz is one of the most laid-back."

Sean knew that was because she'd had so much happen to her growing up that little now fazed her.

"When are you two going to move in to the new house, anyway?"

"Yeah, well, that is a problem." Mitch put his feet up on the chair across from him. "Liz seems to keep finding reasons not to go. First she didn't like the tile in the master bathroom, so we had to wait for it to be replaced. Then she thought the paint in the living room wasn't working so that had to be redone." He shook his head. "I'm beginning to think we're never going to move in to it."

Marc lifted his bottle of beer. "Yeah, well, try talking to your son about why it's not okay for him to go around the playground lifting little girls' dresses so he can see their underwear."

Sean laughed at that one.

Mitch took a swig of beer. "We think we have it bad. Poor Connor…"

All of them began nodding their heads in unison.

By far, Connor had it the worst. He didn't have one kid to deal with, he had two, and twins at that. Which, all told, made three women he had to contend with on a daily basis.

"Then again, Jake doesn't have it any better. And he's got another one on the way. What do you think Michelle will have this time?" Mitch asked.

Jake's wife, Michelle, was six months along with their second child together. They already had Lili from Michelle's first marriage, and another little girl who was three.

"It will probably be another girl."

"Women," they all said again.

The room fell comfortably silent despite Marc's and Sean's reason for being there.

"Except for Kat. She's pretty cool."

Sean and Mitch looked at Marc.

"You know, for a woman and a sister and all."

Mitch smiled. "Yes, she is pretty cool, isn't she? I mean, we don't know her all that well yet, but…"

"I stopped by the safe house to check up on her earlier," Marc said. "Told her Melanie had kicked me out for the night and you know what she did?" He shook his head. "She laughed. Then offered to let me bunk there for the night. I almost took her up on it, too, but I thought I could still patch things up at home."

"Your being here kind of tells us that didn't work."

Marc grimaced. "Mel threw my overnight bag out the bedroom window into the bushes." He lifted a finger. "But you know what Kat said when I told her I didn't know how to communicate with my wife, or any other woman for that matter?"

Neither Sean nor Mitch answered but they were listening.

"She told me the key is to stop looking at them like women and start thinking of them as one of the guys."

Mitch picked up the book on the chair next to his brother. "That why you still reading this crap?"

Marc snatched it away and Sean got a look at the

title—*Crossed Wires: Open Up New Lines of Communication with Your Spouse.* He smiled.

"Yes, well, when are you and Liz going to get started on those five kids you want?"

Sean stared at his middle son. Politically correct was not a trait Marc had ever mastered. And he had a feeling he never would.

Sean had long since suspected that Mitch was having a hard time talking Liz into having kids. The large new house and her reluctance to move into it told him Mitch would have his hands full convincing Liz to have one child much less the five he wanted.

Mitch was saved from answering when the side door opened, letting in a burst of cool air that got even cooler when Sean realized who it was.

"Hey, Con," Marc said. "Don't tell me you're in the doghouse, too."

Sean looked at his oldest son.

"Doghouse?" he said warily, looking everywhere but at Sean.

"Yeah, you know, booted out for the night because you didn't tell Bronte about Kat."

"I told Bronte about it the first night."

More likely Bronte had pulled the information out of him. Connor had never been very good at hiding his emotions. Like now. It was obvious he was still holding a grudge against Sean for not having told them about their sister before now.

Another thing his eldest wasn't good at was realizing there was nothing he could do to go back and change things.

"I was out for a walk and saw the lights on and cars in the drive and came over to see what's going on."

Connor had always been fascinated with one of the older tracts of McCoy farmland adjacent to the piece Mitch used as a horse ranch. It had been a working farm for years before it had been left to fall into decay like everything else over twenty-five years ago. But Connor had taken the farm and the connected house over and had just recently planted soybeans. Oh, he was still very much a U.S. Marshal. But he said working the soil helped keep his head screwed on straight.

Everything considered, Sean believed he was right.

He only wished there were something he could do to keep his son from judging him more harshly than Sean already judged himself.

CHAPTER THIRTEEN

KAT KNEW HARRY was going take her back to Manchester at some point today. Simply because the safe house was anything but safe. But this morning he'd indicated he had some things to see to and he would prefer if she stayed near him at all times. A prospect that felt right to her on complicated levels she wasn't ready to explore just then.

Now she was sitting in the same diner he'd taken her to two days ago and watched her oatmeal congeal while he paced outside the front window, one eye on her, and talking on his cell phone.

It was almost hard to believe that so much passion had passed between them the night before. Almost. Truth was, her body hummed from the sexual workout she'd given it. And her heart thrummed in a way she couldn't help but notice even if she wasn't ready to study the reasons why. Somehow colors emerged brighter, sounds louder, and her take on the world was a great deal more generous.

She couldn't be sure why she still felt so sunny. After all, she'd woken up that morning alone in the bed she and Harry had shared, longing to share even more and found Harry apparently reluctant to admit they'd shared anything as he'd prepared the car to leave.

Kat eyed the phone he held, thinking about how much she'd like to have that phone right about now. She stuck her finger into her cold, buttered toast. Her gaze caught on a guy in the next booth talking on his cell phone and she resisted the urge to tap him on the shoulder to ask if she could use it when he was done.

They'd been there for two hours and her butt was starting to hurt.

Besides, the more she sat, the more difficult it was to ignore that she had been grabbed last night and that her assailant had Lord only knew what on his agenda.

Oh, she didn't kid herself into thinking it had been a random attack. Some rapist who just happened to be hiding in those woods on the off chance that she would stroll by. She wasn't much into coincidence, but even if she were, that would be stretching it.

Rather she suspected the guy who had grabbed her was the same shadow she'd seen in her kitchen the night James had been killed.

She pressed her fingertips against her collarbone, much happier remembering how Harry had touched her. How for a few precious moments he had chased all the darkness around her away and shown her light.

Passion was something she'd read about in books. Had seen in television shows and, yes, every now and again on the soaps when she was working from home and the news channel was running the same old stories over and over.

Passion was something that tempted people into infidelity, ended marriages, wrecked people's lives.

Passion was something that made you feel alive.

Passion was an irrational emotion that knew no bounds or rules.

And passion was the last thing she needed in her life right now.

Or maybe it was just what the doctor ordered.

She glanced at where her legal pads sat haphazardly at her right elbow. Had it really been only yesterday that she'd cancelled all her wedding plans? Only a mere matter of days since she'd lost her fiancé? It seemed so incredible to think of the passage of time in those terms. Especially since it seemed like years had passed since she'd knelt over James's still body, trying to find a way to bring him back.

She watched as Harry disconnected his call. She sat up, hoping he'd come inside and rejoin her. Save her from her thoughts.

Instead she watched as he dialed another number and resumed pacing.

"Miss, can I take this for you?" the waitress asked, motioning to her barely touched food.

The last time she'd inquired, Kat had told her to leave it for now because she had a feeling she'd be there for a while. Now she motioned for her to take it away and asked for a fresh cup of coffee.

"Oh," Kat said, catching the waitress's arm before she turned. "Is there a payphone I could use anywhere here?"

"Sure, hon. It's in the back near the washrooms."

Kat smiled her thanks then checked her purse and briefcase for spare change. She found none so she replaced the seventy-five cents that was part of Harry's change from their breakfast check with a dollar then went in search of the phones.

"I DON'T UNDERSTAND. You're telling me the body was cremated before an autopsy was performed?"

Harry realized he was a shade away from barking into the phone and grimaced when a couple entering the diner stared at him.

"Who in the hell released the damn body?"

He picked up his pacing thinking how the morning had started on a downhill slope and was only gaining momentum with every call he made.

"I want the order faxed to my office yesterday," he told the coroner's assistant then gave him a number.

He disconnected and stood staring down at the sidewalk.

What was happening here that he wasn't getting?

He looked through the window, expecting to see Kathryn's exasperated face again...only she wasn't at the table.

Holy shit.

Disconnecting the call he'd begun to make, he pushed through the doors and strode toward the booth the waitress was now cleaning.

"Where'd she go?" he demanded, grabbing her arm probably a little too roughly.

"Who?"

"The woman who was sitting here? The woman I came in here with?"

The waitress stared at him, fear coloring her eyes. "She's at the payphone in the back."

"No, I'm right here."

Harry blinked at where Kathryn had stepped up behind the waitress.

He released the woman's arm and tried to look like he wasn't as panicked as he felt. All he could think about was how close she'd come to being taken from him last night. And it was driving him crazy.

"I thought I asked you not to move."

"What am I, a pet?"

The waitress hurried away with the remainder of the dishes.

Harry stared down at Kathryn. At her still bruised lips. Her flushed skin. Her welcoming body. And he was overwhelmed with the urge to crowd her against him and to find his way back to the place he'd forced himself to leave early that morning. A place he might never return to again.

He ran his hand through his hair. Last night had been so unlike anything he'd ever known that he still wasn't sure what to make of it. Didn't know if he'd ever figure it out. While an important part of him had been on the lookout for her assailant, an even more important part had responded to Kathryn Buckingham in a way he never had to another woman. He'd...given her something. And while he wasn't entirely sure what that something was, he was afraid he'd never get it back.

"Are we leaving?" she asked, interrupting his thoughts.

He cleared his throat, wishing it were as easy to clear his mind. "No. Sit back down."

"I don't want to sit down. I've been sitting for the past two hours and my legs are numb."

"Tough. Sit."

He heard the gruffness in his voice and winced. Thankfully either Kathryn didn't notice, or didn't find it anything out of the ordinary, and did as he asked. He slid into the other side of the booth.

"Who did you call?" he asked.

"My office." She added sugar to her coffee and slowly dragged her spoon through the dark liquid. "Who did you call?"

"My office."

She hiked a softly shaped brow. "That all? That's what took all that time?"

He started to motion for the waitress to refill his coffee cup as well, ignoring that she looked reluctant to approach the table.

Instead he got up. "Let's go."

Kathryn immediately followed. "I thought you'd never ask."

He peeled off a couple of more bills, tossed them to the table, then took Kathryn's arm.

"Wait."

He released her so she could get her briefcase and purse.

She seemed particularly taken with the air outside the diner, taking a deep breath the instant they were on the sidewalk. Surely he hadn't left her in there that long? A glance at his watch told him he had.

"So are you going to tell me what's going on or should I guess?" she asked as they walked toward his SUV parked a short ways away.

Now that was a question. What concerned him was his answer.

What did he tell her first? That her fiancé's remains were in a crematorium? Or that his superior had reviewed her case and decided to pull her protection?

He didn't want to tell her either so he remained silent.

"Okay," she said slowly.

Harry opened the passenger door, helped her in, then rounded to the other side, hesitating slightly as he caught a glimpse of his stern expression in the window of his door. Was it really only last night that he'd made love to the woman sitting inside his car with her arms crossed tightly over her chest?

Why couldn't they hit a smooth patch of ground? What was happening between them had so many ups and downs, it was as far from normal as you could get. Not just professionally, but personally. He'd appreciate it if he'd stop getting more and more complications to juggle. There were so many balls, and he was afraid if he dropped one, every-thing would come tumbling down around his ears.

He climbed into the car.

"Where are we going now?" Kathryn asked after he'd started the engine.

"The McCoy place."

She nodded. "At least maybe somebody will talk to me there."

From what he understood, a lot of somebodies would be there to talk to her. Namely most of the female part of the clan who were even now gathered at the old farmhouse waiting for her arrival.

But he didn't want to tell her that either.

He headed for the highway onramp, trying to ig-nore the way she shifted until she was facing him, her arms no longer crossed.

"Harry, I can't do this. You've got to share with me what's going on. This being in the dark stuff is driving me insane."

He glanced to find her looking at him in a way that he suspected few men could ignore. Her green eyes were filled with sadness and pain, and her hair was slightly disheveled where she'd run her fingers through the soft strands.

"Darin's…James's remains were cremated before he was autopsied."

She didn't say anything for a long time as he concentrated on the road.

"Cremated? I don't understand. How could that happen?"

He liked that he didn't have to explain procedure to her. Being a criminal defense attorney, she was well versed on how things went, and understand that what had happened with Darin's remains was not normal.

"I don't know. The coroner's office is faxing a copy of the order to my office now."

"Then why aren't we going there?"

Ah, but that was the rub, wasn't it?

"We can't," he said simply, tightening his grip on the steering wheel.

She sat back in her seat, seemingly preoccupied with what he'd told her. Without an autopsy they didn't have an exact cause of death. Without an autopsy, any evidence not picked up by the forensics team was gone forever.

And without a body, Kathryn no longer had anything to bury.

"Define 'can't,'" she said quietly.

Harry was mildly surprised she'd been thinking about his response to her last question rather than the state of her late fiancé's remains.

He didn't say anything.

He felt her gaze on him. "Is that 'can't' as in 'won't' or..."

"Just drop it, all right?"

He was surprised by the force in his own voice and noted her immediate flinch.

They drove for a while in silence. Then Harry pulled to the side of the road, shoved the transmission into Park and faced her.

"Are you really sure you want to hear this?"

She nodded slowly.

Harry took a deep breath. "We can't go to my office because the minute we do, your protected witness status will be stripped away and you'll be taken back into custody."

SHE COULD GO BACK TO JAIL...

Kat wrapped her arms around herself, not because she was upset or angry but because a violent chill had just taken hold of her.

Jail...dim cell...hard cot...orange jumpsuit... isolation...

She distantly heard Harry curse but could do little more than stare out the windshield as if held in thrall by a horror movie. Only this wasn't any movie. This was her life.

"Why?" she whispered.

Harry put the car back in gear and merged with the traffic. "Upon review of your case, and with the new information—the cremation of Ichatious's remains—my immediate superior decided there was nowhere else to go."

"The most likely suspect had already been arrested," she said absently. "What about the guy who grabbed me last night?"

"A coincidence," Harry said flatly.

A man hiding in the woods waiting on the off chance that she'd stroll by…

She felt Harry's warm hand on her arm and blinked at him.

"Don't worry. I'm not going to let them take you back into custody. Your family won't let them take you back into custody. Officials wouldn't dare go near the McCoy place with all that testosterone in one place."

Kat gave a watery smile. She could imagine that not many people messed around with the McCoys.

"Thank you."

Harry looked at her. "What?"

She swallowed past the emotion threatening to choke her. "Thank you."

He squeezed her arm. "You're welcome."

Silence stretched between them as long as the miles disappearing under the car. She was having a hard time absorbing all that he'd said and even half wished he had remained silent. Better she should think him a jerk for keeping her in the dark because he was the man in control, she was the woman he had to protect. Another to know the truth of the situation and understand how very dire it was—and how little control she had over the outcome.

She looked at him. "Not taking me in…can it get you in trouble?" she asked. "I mean, is your job in jeopardy as a result of this?"

He didn't respond. Which was an answer in itself.

She pressed a shaking hand against her forehead.

He grasped the steering wheel. "That's not something I'm going to worry about right now. What we need to do is put our heads together and see if we can't find a way out of this mess."

CHAPTER FOURTEEN

WOMEN. That's not what Kat was expecting when they stepped inside the McCoy farmhouse over an hour later. But that's exactly what they got.

She stood stunned as her five sisters-in-law introduced themselves, the exception being Liz, Mitch's wife, whom she had met the other night.

She mentally sorted through them, committing them to memory. The easiest one to remember outside Liz was the French-accented Michelle, Jake's wife. Simply because her belly was almost as wide as she was tall. It was obvious she was pregnant, and it was also obvious given the toddler she held and the eight-year-old that this wasn't her first pregnancy.

Then there was Kelly, David's wife, a pretty, athletic blonde who was probably closest to her own age. Kat knew from her brother that she was also DCPD, not that you could tell. Kelly could easily have been a cashier at Nordstrom's. Or one of the models in their fashion shows.

Then there was Bronte, Connor's wife, who was

also an attorney but a U.S. attorney, which meant she worked with the justice department. Well, used to anyway, until she was waylaid by motherhood. While she didn't see them around, Kat knew that Connor and Bronte had a pair of twin girls.

"Hi, I'm Melanie, Marc's wife," another blonde said, thrusting her hand forward.

"Hi, Melanie. Nice to meet you."

Harry grimaced next to her. "What's going on here? An estrogen convention?"

All five women gave him dirty looks in varying degrees. "Watch your step, buster," Melanie said pointblank, "or you'll be in the doghouse just like most of our husbands."

Harry held up his hands and had the decency to look abashed. Either that or he was genuinely afraid of the women facing him.

Kat figured she wouldn't blame him either way. They were an intimidating bunch.

"Now, scoot," Liz said, nudging Harry toward the door. "We can take care of Kathryn from here."

Harry cleared his throat. "Liz, you mind if I use your office in the barn?"

"Go ahead. Just don't move anything."

He met Kat's gaze. "I'll, um, be across the driveway if you need anything."

It was all Kat could do not to yell "help" as he disappeared through the door.

THE OFFICE Liz and Mitch used to run their horse-breeding operation was large and cozy with a nice view of the large piece of McCoy land and the Shenandoah Mountains beyond. To the side could be glimpsed the house they'd built on the other side of the stables. He couldn't imagine having enjoyed such a view as he'd grown up. The outside view through his childhood bedroom window had been of the brick building next door two feet away. While here in Virginia everything was green, in the part of Brooklyn he'd grown up green had to battle with cement gray and brick red.

Here nature provided the color. In Brooklyn, people and their different cultures created a fascinating kaleidoscope.

He wasn't sure which he preferred. In DC, his place didn't differ all that much from his mother's apartment in Brooklyn, until he went outside anyway. But still D.C. had all the city trappings.

Here it was so quiet it made you think you were the only person in the world. And made you think about who you'd most like to have with you.

Dangerous territory that, he thought. And definitely better left for another time.

He squinted at the new house to his right, wondering why Liz and Mitch hadn't moved in yet. For all intents and purposes it was done. Why were they still living in the old place?

He glanced down at the notepad he'd borrowed

that held the Red Shoe Ranch's logo. He'd placed
about half a dozen calls, checking into the two men
Darin had helped convict. He'd learned that Newton Granger had actually been released about three
months ago.

Coincidence? Or did Granger tie into what was
going on?

At any rate, some digging had unearthed that
Granger was back on the beltway in Washington,
working his way back up the political ladder. The
way the city operated never failed to amaze Harry.
Committed of a felony? Don't worry. The only office off limits to you was that of the president. No
matter, that wasn't the most powerful position to
be had. It was the men behind the president, the
ones no one read about, the ones that weren't in-
terviewed by Ted Koppel, who really ran the
country.

And one of them was wealthy financier Newton
Granger.

Few things in life surprised Harry. He supposed
it was due to his New York upbringing. Granger's
association with a snake like Darin Ichatious didn't
surprise him, either. People of his caliber tended to
quietly keep expendable men like Darin around to
see to their dirty work. And when the hammer fell,
they counted on missing being hit by it while the
Darins of the world were flattened.

Not this time, however. This time the scapegoat

had scampered away and Granger and his partner had taken the hammer hit full on.

But like a kids' cartoon, it didn't take men like that long to re-inflate themselves and move on as if nothing had happened, their stretches in the federal pen nothing more than a momentary bump in the road. Not unlike the way the Italian mob operated in New York.

Harry tapped a pen on the pad wondering how straight-and-narrow Kathryn had gotten involved with someone like Darin.

Then again, she repped death row inmates without a hope of survival, so who was he to say what she did and didn't know about her late fiancé?

The thought caught him up short. Was it possible she'd known of Darin's past and had accepted him anyway?

He remembered her look of shock when he'd told her his real name. And she'd refused to look at his case file early on as though afraid to learn the truth.

The sound of gravel crunching under car tires caught his attention. He got up and walked to the bank of windows facing the front of the house.

Thank God, a male.

THERE WAS SOMETHING therapeutic about helping making dinner for such a large group. Kat pitched in with everything from peeling a massive amount

of potatoes to cutting vegetables for a salad, to setting the table to entertaining a brood of knee-hug-
ging kids that were always in need of something.

She liked her sisters-in-law and could see
where each of them could hold their own with her
brothers. But while she had the most in common
with Bronte in terms of upbringing and career, for
some reason it was Michelle she was drawn to.
She couldn't be sure why, but she suspected it was
because that while she enjoyed the company of
each of them, Michelle seemed to share her view-
point on more subjects than the others. While her
adoptive parents hadn't been flower children or
pacifists, they had been liberal-minded and she
wasn't used to being around a houseful of con-
servative people.

"It can be a little overwhelming, no?" Michelle
brushed against her arm as she reached for a gallon
of milk in the fridge while Kat was taking out the
salad dressing.

"A little."

"I know. It takes a while to get used to all the
noise. In France it's not unusual to have this many
people in one place, but they are significantly quieter."

Kat laughed.

Of course, she understood her feeling of being
overwhelmed had more to do with the news Harry
had shared with her earlier. Namely that the attorney
general's office no longer thought her deserving of

witness protection. The thought of…to even consider…

"You think that's enough?"

She jumped at the sound of Harry's voice behind her.

She noticed the way his eyes narrowed as he took in her jittery behavior.

"If it's not I can always make more."

"It was a joke. That salad could feed a small country."

"Oh."

And "oh" about covered it, too.

Was she so preoccupied she couldn't recognize a joke?

One by one her brothers joined them in the kitchen, each of them coming off work or driving in from the city because their wives and children were there. She understood that Sunday was usually the day they came together for dinner but that given the circumstances they were making an exception.

And like that everything was on the table. Everyone was sitting down. And everyone seemed to be talking at once.

And Kat felt so…how had Michelle put it? Overwhelmed. Yes, she felt completely, utterly overwhelmed by everything surrounding her.

"If you'll excuse me…" she said quietly after a few minutes of staring at her fried chicken, mashed potatoes and corn.

She thought about going into the other room, at least pretending she had to use the washroom or something, but at the last minute headed for the door instead.

She burst outside, the air feeling cool and refreshing against her skin, and pulled in deep lungfuls of the sweet resource.

She wasn't aware Harry had followed her until he spoke.

"You okay?" he asked.

She nodded. "Yes. I just, um, need a few moments."

Silence.

"You can go back in."

"Not without you I can't."

Last night. She remembered that last night she'd also gone outside for some air and someone had tried to make sure she wouldn't make it back inside.

"I'll stay with her. Maybe we'll go for a walk. I can show her around the place."

Kat looked over Harry's shoulder at where Sean was standing on the top step.

Harry's gaze was locked with hers. She gave a small nod.

"Okay," he said after a long moment. "But don't go too far."

"Are you implying I don't know how to protect myself and my daughter, Kincaid?"

"No, sir. Of course not."

"I didn't think so. Kathryn and I will go as far as we like for as long as we like."

"Yes, sir."

Kat smiled at the boyish look on Harry's face as he went back inside the house.

"That was effective. I'll have to remember it."

Sean drew even with her and offered her his arm. "I don't think it will have the same impact."

"Why?"

"Because you have to be a crusty old ex-police officer for that attitude to work."

He began leading them back between the house and the barn to the paddocks beyond. In a far pen a pair of toffee colored fillies lazily swatted flies from their hindquarters and nibbled on grass. To the north lay freshly plowed fields.

"Connor planted those last week."

"I thought Connor was a U.S. Marshal."

"He is. He says this relaxes him."

She smiled. She could see her wound-up oldest brother saying that. And that it would take exactly the hard work of growing crops to relax him.

"You know, I've met so many people over the past few days," she said quietly. "But there's one I haven't met yet. And I'm a little curious as to why."

He dug his chin into his chest. "Wilhemenia."

"Yes."

Sean got a faraway look on his face. "Unfortunately things aren't going very well with me and

Wilhemenia right now. I don't want to go into details. And the boys don't know yet. But we're...I guess you could say we're unofficially separated."

Kat's heart gave a pang.

He smiled at her. "But that's neither here nor there right now. Things will work out as they were meant to between Wilhemenia and me. Don't you go worrying about us."

She wondered if that was even possible.

"Look, Kathryn, I know we haven't had a chance to talk much yet."

She squeezed his arm. "I really don't need to talk. Not now, anyway. There's so much going on that I can barely keep my head on straight."

He nodded. "That's what I thought." He cleared his throat. "I just wanted to let you know that I'm here if you need anything."

He brought them to a stop. Kat realized they'd walked at least a good half mile.

"Also, while I have you out here, I wanted to show you what now also belongs to you."

She squinted at him against the setting sun. "I don't understand."

He motioned toward the land surrounding them. "All this, the McCoy spread, is part of your heritage. And you're welcome here, always."

Warmth burst through Kat's bloodstream.

Her parents had never failed to always provide well for her. She had never wanted for anything.

They had been her emotional rock. But what Sean was laying at her feet was a real rock where she could always find purchase.

Again she was overwhelmed by emotion. But this time it was emotion she more than welcomed.

She turned toward the man who had just told her exactly what she'd needed to hear at exactly the time she'd needed to hear it and hugged him.

He appeared shocked at first and unsure what to do. Then he wrapped his arms around her and held her close. Held her in the way a father would hold his daughter.

"Thanks," she whispered, and kissed him on the cheek.

CHAPTER FIFTEEN

KAT FELT SOMETHING wet and cold on her right toe. She shifted in her sleep and turned over. Again the sensation, this time on the heel of her other foot.

She bolted upright in bed, staring at the scraggly monster responsible for waking her up.

Goliath. It had to be. She'd heard about the German shepherd–husky cross that belonged to Liz and Mitch, but this was the first she'd seen of him. Presumably they kept him outside in the stables while they had company. She pushed her hair from her face. This wasn't exactly a stellar intro. She plucked the wind-up clock from the nightstand and squinted at the glow in the dark numbers. Just after five-thirty.

She groaned.

"Goliath! Get out of there this minute," Liz ordered from the door in a hushed voice.

Kat cleared the sleep from her throat. "That's all right. The damage is already done."

Liz opened the door farther and stepped in to grab the hulking dog by his collar. "Sorry about that. When Mitch and I started closing our door at night he made it his business to learn how to open doors. I should have warned you."

"That's okay." Kat smiled. "I can think of worse ways to start the day."

She swung her feet over the side of the bed and scrubbed the mammoth animal behind the ears. He made an agreeable sound and his tongue lolled out the side of his mouth.

"What are you doing up already?" she asked her sister-in-law.

"This is the time we get up every morning."

Kat stared at her. "Every morning?"

"Mmm. We like to get an early start. A lot of animals to feed and take care of."

Kat thought of all the members of the extended family and trusted she wasn't referring to them.

It was much too early for coherent thought. Especially without coffee.

Liz half dragged the dog toward the door. "Why don't you try to get in a couple of more hours? You were up late last night."

"Thanks. I think I will."

"Just make yourself at home if no one's in the house. If you need anything, Mitch and I will be in the barn office."

"Thanks. I will." Kat heard her and the dog's retreating footsteps as she snuggled back under the covers.

Then it hit her. Why would no one else be in the house?

"Kathryn?"

She nearly hit the ceiling when she heard Harry's voice so close. She levered to a sitting position again.

"Oh. I thought you were up," he said from the door.

She hadn't been, but she was now.

"I just wanted to tell you I was going to drive into the city today. I won't be back until later."

She lifted her brows although he probably couldn't see her expression in the semidarkness, the only light a sliver provided by the hall fixture through the open door.

She started to climb out of bed. "Give me a minute."

"No, that's all right. You don't have to see me off."

"See you off? I plan to come with you."

His silence caused her to stop.

He said, "I don't think that's a good idea."

"Yes, well, it's not your ass on the line."

It was the first time she'd used profanity in his presence and she caught the shadow of his surprise.

"Besides, I thought we already had this discussion." Ignoring that the nightgown she wore only brushed the top of her thighs and was probably transparent given the current lighting conditions, she grabbed her slacks and put them on, turning from him in order to do them up.

"You'll be safer here."

"I'll be just as safe with you."

"I can't guarantee that."

Kat finished dressing and laid the nightgown across the bed before facing him. "I'll take my chances."

He remained unconvinced.

"Look, Kincaid, I can't just sit by as someone else makes my decisions for me. I need to be a part of figuring this out. And I'd just as soon do it with you."

"I have to stop by my office."

Kat's lungs froze. The same office where he'd said they very well may take her back into custody.

"But I think I have a solution." He turned toward the door. "Go wash up and I'll meet you down in the kitchen."

"Sure." Kat watched him go.

HARRY'S SOLUTION was to create a tiered schedule so that when he couldn't be with her because of safety's sake, one of her brothers could. It meant a lot of impressive maneuvering seeing as all of them worked during the day. The fact that they didn't seem to mind making a few exceptions for her touched her more than she could utter.

The first brother up on rotation was David. He

pulled up in his DCPD squad card and popped the door open for her.

Kat looked at Harry then her brother. "Are you on duty?" she asked.

"Yep. But I won't tell anybody if you don't."

As Kat hesitantly climbed into the car, she pondered the irony that she was in a police car in order to avoid being taken into custody by police.

Well, it was probably the last place they would look for her.

And, Harry had shared during the drive in, they would definitely be looking for her.

Harry grasped the door. "I'll see you this afternoon."

Kat nodded. "Okay."

He closed the door and David grinned at her. "Consider me your personal driver. Where to?"

IT SEEMED ODD being at HQ after everything that had happened in the past week. Harry greeted people he'd worked with for years, got himself a cup of coffee from the conference room, then collected his messages and rotating case files from the assistant that handled a number of the marshals.

Since so much of their job was spent outside the office, the need for an actual office with a desk and chair was unnecessary. Instead there were about ten marshals to an assistant who kept track of their whereabouts, the status of their cases, and ran interference between them and their supervisor when need be.

And recently the need had been often for Harry.

Tamara Severn looked relieved to see him. Probably her feet were hurting from all the running she'd had to do for him lately. "Thank God. I was actually wording my resignation letter."

"You wrote one?" Harry asked, familiar with the assistant's humor although usually it was directed toward somebody else.

"No, I was wording it. In my head. You know, something along the lines of the Paycheck song."

"Take This Job and Shove It," as performed by the aptly named Johnny Paycheck. Harry was familiar with it. Not because it had been played in the Kincaid household in Brooklyn, but because when you were in DC, you were essentially in the south, and southern culture dictated everyone know the song by heart by age five.

"Good thing I showed up when I did then," he said, playing along. "I mean, I wouldn't want to be the one responsible for the department's demise."

"Demise?" Tamara asked even as she signed off on some documentation.

"Yes, you know. Without you, we cease to exist."

The smile she gave him was nothing short of a thousand watt.

"Who knew you were charming?"

Harry chuckled. "The big dog in?"

She motioned over her shoulder. "Not only is he in, he's waiting for you. Spotted you the minute you walked in the front doors." She lifted a finger. "I still think he has the security cameras wired so he can access them on his laptop."

Scary thought. But apropos given Bud Thompson's position. What did it say about a department assigned to protect people if it didn't know what was happening within its own doors?

"I'd give him another minute or two though," Tamara said.

"Why?"

"Just to piss him off more."

"Thanks, but no thanks."

Tamara laughed as he put his coffee on her desk and walked toward the closed door behind her. A brief rap and he walked into the corner office.

"About damn time you got in here. I thought you and Tamara were having a family reunion."

"Just catching up on what I've missed."

"If you'd have gotten your ass in here yesterday morning as I requested you wouldn't have missed nearly as much."

"Point taken."

Bud Thompson swiveled his chair from where he was facing a computer against his left wall. Harry couldn't see the screen from this vantage point and figured Bud had probably designed it that way.

He'd never had much use for technology. Oh, he wore the earpieces and transceivers. He relied on

Tamara to research all sorts of interesting stuff for him, ranging from how often a witness accessed porn sites to how many times he'd been to the dentist in the past year, but he'd never done an electronic search himself.

No, his job required he rely more on his gut instincts. Which was okay with him. The way he saw it technology only complicated things. Because when all was said in done, it was those instincts you'd have to rely on anyway.

And his instincts were telling him that he had to do everything possible to protect Kathryn Buckingham.

"Where is she?" Bud asked.

"Safe."

His superior narrowed his gaze. "That's not what I asked."

"I know."

"You sure you want to be putting your job on the line here for a nice piece of ass, Kincaid?"

Hearing Kathryn classified in such a crude way made his muscles bunch in automatic reflex. He figured it was a pretty good thing Bud was seated across a large desk.

Again, he suspected his superior had designed the setup that way. It probably allowed him to say a lot of things he wouldn't normally get away with.

Bud picked up a file and tossed it to the corner of his desk. "I've got another assignment for you."

Harry left it where it was. "I already have an assignment."

"No, you don't."

"Then I officially request vacation time."

"And the one-month advance notice?"

"Lost in the mail."

Bud leaned back in his chair, causing the springs to squeak. Seeing that everything else in the large office was brand new, he figured that the old, squeaky leather chair was also a part of the package Bud was going for. "You're not going to let go of this, are you?"

"No, sir, I don't plan to."

Bud stared at him for a long moment then sighed. "You remind me of an old dog I used to have. No matter how hard I tried to break him of the habit of chewing on my favorite pair of leather shoes, he'd go right back to them. It wasn't until I gave them to him that he lost interest."

Was he trying to say that with the conflict removed, he'd lose interest in Kathryn?

"Consider the shoes yours."

Without preamble, Bud turned back to his computer.

"That it?"

"Take the new case file with you."

Harry picked it up, noticed it was a long dead case that periodically required a half-assed check, then walked toward the door. "Thank you, sir."

"Yes, well, I hope you still feel like that when this is all over." Bud stared at him over his shoulder. "And speaking of over, you have twenty-four hours."

One day?

Harry's expression must have shown his thought. "Okay, forty-eight. Then I send someone out after you."

"Seventy-two."

"Fine."

KAT WAS ON her third brother rotation and was, frankly, finding the whole exercise amusing and, well, touching. It wasn't so long ago that the only person outside her clients who cared about her well-being was James. Now she had an entire clan that was willing to drive her around at the drop of a hat, no matter if they were on duty, had other items on their agenda or thought what she was doing was questionable if not just plain boring. They merely grinned at her, put the car in gear and patiently waited until she got whatever was in her system out.

In three hours she'd managed to stop by her office and confer with Roger Cartright who had taken over her caseload in her absence. David had snuck her in the back way and stood guard like her own personal sentinel. The women in the office had swooned and gladly done whatever asked if just for a chance to meet the handsome guy in uniform. She'd also visited with one of her clients in county, and made an appointment for later that afternoon with a construction company to go over what renovations her gutted house would need.

She'd gotten more done in three hours than she had in the past three days. And she was feeling better for the experience.

Connor was her fourth driver and she was in such a good mood she gave him a big hug and a kiss when she got into the car.

Marc, who had been on third rotation, held the passenger's door open, grimacing. "I didn't get one of those."

Kat smiled and got out again to do just that.

"Okay," Marc said, looking more than a little red around the ears. "Now explain what it means."

"It's just my way of thanking you."

"For what?"

For what, indeed.

Not only were they helping her out, they didn't seem to think they were doing anything out of the ordinary. She felt blessed, indeed.

"Ask Mel when you get home. She can probably explain better than I can."

And just like that Marc was off and Connor was waiting for her to tell him where to take her.

The problem was she really didn't have anything else on her agenda. Since she'd grabbed a kind of brunch with Jake she wasn't hungry…

Then it occurred to her. The person she wanted to talk to. The one person she had yet to meet.

"Take me to see Wilhemenia."

Was it her or had Connor just given her a frown to rival all male frowns?

"Something wrong?" she asked.

He shook his head. "Long story."

"Would you prefer we not go?"

He shrugged. "If it's where you want to go, I'll take you. Just don't expect me to go in with you."

Curiouser and curiouser…

"Are you sure?"

He looked a little aggravated but somehow managed to flash her a grin. "No, but I'm game if you are."

Kat pondered this. "So you wouldn't be the one to ask about what's happening between Sean and Wilhemenia."

"So I wouldn't."

"Then perhaps you can tell me what's going on between you and Sean…"

CHAPTER SIXTEEN

HARRY WASN'T SURE what he was expecting to uncover when he went to Newton Granger's office, found out he was on the golf course, and met up with him on the eighth hole. Something had been bothering him since he'd found out Granger had been released from prison. And he needed to keep chipping away at the feeling until he found out why.

It was noon, the sun was shining, the course was green, and he couldn't have looked more out of place with his flat shoes and suit had he gone to a soccer match. But still he stood with his hand in his pocket, watching Granger tee up—dressed in his plaid knee pants and cap and yellow oxford shirt—and trying to pretend he wasn't fazed by Harry's impromptu visit.

"What can I do for you, Marshal?" Granger asked, using his club to visually line up where he wanted to hit the ball.

He was with a party of another three men whose faces were familiar if only because Harry knew they were all Washington connected in some way or another. Harry suspected this wasn't merely a round of golf, but a meeting specifically designed to be well away from any possible planted bugs and anyone who might overhear what they were discussing.

And he'd interrupted it like a horse fly buzzing around their ears.

"I'd like to talk to you about Darin Ichatious."

Granger missed his first swing. Something Harry didn't think he was used to doing as the other three men started paying more attention to the exchange.

"There's nothing to discuss," Granger maintained, quickly regaining his bearings.

"I beg to differ, sir."

He lined up his shot again.

"We can either do this with me following you from hole to hole, or you can take a few minutes out of your game and meet up with your associates at the next hole."

Newton Granger squinted at him against the sun. He appeared to be trying to gauge how serious Harry was.

On any other day Granger could probably have him removed from the premises. But he was a U.S. Marshal and Granger was a recently released convict. That left the balance of power solidly on Harry's side. For the time being anyway.

"Very well. Give me a minute."

Harry watched as Granger spoke to his golf partners, slid his club back into a bag on the back of a cart, then moved toward him.

"Why don't we walk this way?" he suggested.

Harry followed, the pace he set casual, probably so that if anyone were looking they wouldn't find the pairing or the conversation they were having too suspicious.

"What do you want to know?" Granger asked.

"When was the last time you heard from him?"

"The day he testified against me."

Harry had suspected as much. When deals like the one Ichatious and Granger worked went sour, they rotted straight through. "Fair enough." He slid his hands into his pockets to continue to perpetuate the illusion of a casual stroll.

"Now, you want to tell me what really went down three years ago, or should I go rent a golf cart?"

THE LITTLE BEDFORD FLORIST SHOP was a quaint little place with powder blue shutters and a profusion of spring blooms positioned everywhere. Kat liked the place on site.

She also liked Wilhemenia McCoy.

Leaving Connor sitting in his car on the street, Kat had entered the shop and pretended to browse, listening as a woman at the counter who was the right age to be Sean's wife talked with another customer, a woman extraordinarily picky about the flowers that would be part of a birthday bouquet for her sister. She didn't want it to be too showy, but she didn't want it to look cheap either.

Wilhemenia handled the customer with patience and skill. And when the fussy customer finally left, she didn't let on that she was in the least bit flustered by having to deal with such difficulty.

"May I help you?"

Kat turned and smiled at her. "Sometimes it seems there's no pleasing some people," she said.

Wilhemenia smiled, as if grateful her ordeal had been recognized but not about to indulge in any negative backbiting. "The customer is always right."

Kat held her hand out. "I hope you don't mind, but I thought it was time you and I finally met. I'm Kat Buckingham."

Wilhemenia didn't appear to register the name as she politely shook her hand.

"Sean calls me by my given name Kathryn."

She watched as the older woman's eyes widened slightly. "Oh. I see. I'm Wilhemenia McCoy as you already know."

"Nice to meet you, Wilhemenia."

An older man came out from the back wearing a white apron and carrying fresh white lilies. "Need any help, Wilhemenia?"

Kat blinked at him, surprised by the wary look in his eyes, the protective way he immediately came to Wilhemenia's side.

"No, Walter, I'm okay. Thank you."

"Can you take a break?" Kat asked quietly.

Wilhemenia looked over her shoulder at where Walter still stood in the doorway.

"I know I probably should have called in advance, and I'm sorry for the inconvenience—"

"Don't be ridiculous," Wilhemenia politely interrupted her. "Actually, it's time for lunch, so why don't we go across the way to the little restaurant there? They have wonderful watercress sandwiches."

"I thought we were going to lunch," the man named Walter said.

Wilhemenia introduced the two of them. While the shop's owner, Walter Purdy, was courteous enough to cross to shake her hand, she got the very distinct impression that she wasn't welcome there.

Did her father know that another man was putting the moves on his wife? She'd chance a no.

She fully intended to let him know.

KATHRYN LOOKED BETTER than he could remember seeing her.

Harry stood as she approached the booth at the back of a downtown pub. Her smile was wide. Her eyes bright. Her step light. All at once his collar felt unbearably tight. He reminded himself that he wasn't to credit for this change in her. At least not in the way he'd like to be. Rather it had been his absence that had apparently had a positive impact on her. A morning spent with someone other than him. Or, more specifically, four other someones: David, Jake, Marc and Connor.

She joined him and kissed him lingeringly on the cheek, causing his collar to tighten further. "You're a sight for sore eyes," she murmured.

Harry's stomach tightened along with his collar. Okay, maybe he was to credit for the changes. She'd missed him. The mere suggestion was enough to do him in.

"You guys all set?" Connor asked from where he was eyeing the exchange behind Kathryn.

She smiled at him and wove her arm through his, giving his hand a visible squeeze. "We're fine, I think."

Harry cleared his throat. "Thanks, man."

"You sure you don't need any more help?" he asked Harry. "I could call in a couple of favors and be at your beck and call."

"I'm fine."

"You know the number."

He did. And he wouldn't hesitate to use it if he thought Kathryn was in danger.

But right now, in the back of the dimly lit pub, all was right as rain.

Connor left them alone and suddenly Harry didn't know what to say. He merely stood staring at Kathryn.

"This your table?"

He looked at the booth as if he'd never seen it before. "Oh, yes. Please. Sit down."

"Actually, I have to make a run to the little girls' room first. Why don't you order one of whatever you're drinking for me?"

"Club soda."

She laughed. "Then club soda it is."

After he watched her disappear down the narrow hall at the far end of the pub, he managed to sit down.

Whoa.

He'd known he'd had a thing for Kathryn. A thing deepened by what had happened between them at the safe house a couple of nights ago. But this…this was far more than a yearning to sleep with a woman. What he was coming to feel for her was much more powerful and all encompassing.

And cause for a great deal of concern.

Simply, there was nowhere for them to go from there. When he figured out what was going on, who had killed James, the immediacy of the situation would be gone…and so would Kathryn. He didn't kid himself into thinking it would work out otherwise. He wasn't into self-delusion.

She didn't see him as permanent lover material. Not really. In her eyes, he was her rescuer. Someone who had stepped in and provided help when she'd needed it. She was confused and nowhere near ready to make any immediate decisions about her life. And because of that, she couldn't really love him.

She rejoined him and sat across from him in the booth, giving him a slow smile. And in that one minute he knew it didn't matter what happened tomorrow. What mattered was right now. This minute.

And the fact that she wanted him.

KAT DIDN'T KNOW what had happened to Harry while she'd been with her brothers that morning. But she did know she liked whatever it was. His gaze seemed to singe her skin. His body gave off a scent she wanted to breathe in.

"I know I asked you this before, but…who are you?" she said somewhat provocatively.

Of course when she'd asked him who he was after he'd sprung her from the county jail, she'd wanted little more than name, rank and serial number. The second time she'd asked, she'd wanted to know if he was some dark angel sent from the underworld to bring hell to her doorstep.

Now she wanted to know everything beyond the surface appearance of the question. She wanted to know what his favorite breakfast cereal was. If he liked a lazy day spent floating in a boat going nowhere on a calm lake, or if he preferred kayaking in Level 1 whitewater rivers. She wanted to know if he had brothers and sisters, if he'd always wanted to be a U.S. Marshal.

She wanted to know everything.

"I'm afraid I don't understand," he said simply.

The waitress came up and asked to take their orders. Kat had eaten a big, late breakfast so she asked for an order of mixed finger foods to pick at while Harry requested a large heart attack on a bun with fries.

As soon as the waitress was gone, Kat folded one leg under her and leaned forward on the pitted table. "First of all, where are you from?"

"What makes you think it's not here?"

"Because you don't talk like anyone from here. In fact, sometimes I think I detect a New York accent."

"Bingo."

"Where in New York?"

"Brooklyn."

"Ah. Just in the way you said it I can tell it's the truth."

"Either that or I'm really good at accents."

She smiled. "Brothers? Sisters?"

"Only child."

"Like me." Then she caught herself. "Though not anymore, I guess."

"Mmm."

"Both parents still alive?"

He chuckled quietly. "What is this? Twenty questions?"

"Maybe," she admitted. "Why? Do you have a problem with it?"

He fussed with his tie again and she realized that he was a little uncomfortable. But why?

"You do have a problem with it."

She unfolded her leg and accepted her glass of iced tea.

"Okay, then since you're finished answering my questions, why don't you take over? Ask me anything you want."

He considered her for a long moment. "Anything?"

"Uh huh."

"What made you fall for a louse like Darin Ichatious?"

He knew the minute the words were out of his mouth that he'd said the wrong thing. The light vanished from her eyes, the animation from her movements. Hell, even her hair seemed to hang a little limper.

Damn.

He wasn't too clear on why he'd said what he had. His conversation with Granger on the golf course was probably partially to blame. He also supposed it had a lot to do with his growing feelings for the woman sitting across from him. His need to understand her. Learn her heart. But how did he go about that if he couldn't clear up what confused him most about her?

"James…filled a need for me when I met him."

He winced. He'd had to ask.

He began to lift his hand, to ward off her words, but she prevented him.

"I've been doing some thinking about this. About the James I knew. And the James…or Darin you knew. And I've come to the conclusion that they were two completely different people." She slowly nudged her large glass around on top of the napkin. "In the midst of this huge cloud that is my life lately, there's one truth that remains with me. One truth I've always held dear. That there really is no truth, only interpretation."

Harry grimaced. This wasn't what he was after. He wasn't up for a class in Philosophy 101.

Then what had he wanted to hear? Did he want Kathryn to say she'd been duped? But wouldn't that by extension make her a victim?

No, it would make her human.

But given all she'd managed to endure of late, he was starting to wonder if she wasn't superhuman.

Which might explain how she could be so philosophical about all this.

Kathryn held his gaze. "Don't you believe that everyone has the capacity for goodness in them?"

"No."

She sat back as if slapped. "Wow. You answered that fast."

"That's because like you I've grown up with

some facts and truths of my own. The biggest one being that a person can't change his stripes."

"I'm not saying anyone can change their stripes. I'm saying that beyond those stripes there's a huge area that's not so black and white—a gray area."

"You're assuming I'm talking about a zebra."

She gave an exasperated eye roll that looked altogether too sexy on her. "Look, we both live in a city famous for creating and mastering spin control. Two different people can take the same basic fact and make it say whatever they want it to." She flipped her hands face up. "I can tell you the sky is blue and you can tell me that the sky, in fact, is not blue, it's black. It's only the sun's reflection off the seas onto our atmosphere that makes it appear that way."

"Is there a point here somewhere?"

"Yes. That nothing is hardly ever the way it appears."

"Does that also apply to yourself?"

She seemed caught off guard by his question.

If what she said was true, then did that mean that what he was seeing in her wasn't what she was truly about?

And how about him?

"I've stumped you," he pointed out.

She twisted her lips. "Only momentarily. I'll figure out how to answer that one. Maybe not right this minute or even tomorrow, but don't be surprised if I bring the subject back up sometime next year."

Sometime next year.

Of course, in order for that to happen, they would actually have to have some sort of contact sometime next year.

Was she saying they would?

Harry took a long slug from his beer. He was reading far too much into this stuff.

"Okay, let's say we stick to a topic we're both familiar with. Criminals."

"Like Darin."

She waved her hands. "Like anyone. What you see when they enter your world is the laws they broke."

"That's all I have to see."

"Yes, but that's not the entire story." She pointed at him. "I mean, if you read a piece in the paper about a thirteen-year-old African-American boy who's stabbed his parents, you automatically assume the thirteen-year-old should be locked away for life if not led straight to the electric chair, do not pass go, do not collect two hundred dollars."

Joseph Alan Greer's case, Harry recognized.

"But if you hear that the same thirteen-year-old suffers from Down syndrome and spent the majority of his life locked in a windowless room while his parents went about their lives and sometimes forgot to let him out for days at a time, then it changes the entire scenario and how people react to it."

"So you think Greer should get off for killing his parents?"

"No. I think he should serve time, probably the rest of his life. Not in prison, but in a facility equipped to deal with someone with his condition." Her voice lowered. "Most states don't even allow a mentally challenged individual to be eligible for the death penalty. But not Virginia. Throw them away with the others is their take."

Harry shifted uncomfortably. He realized he was holding his beer bottle to the point of shattering it and that she had caught onto the movement and his tense demeanor.

"Are you all right?" she asked.

He nodded, not trusting himself to speak just then.

"No, you're not. You're white as a ghost." She reached out and touched his hand, the feel of her warmth against his cold skin almost too much for him to bear. "What is it, Harry? What did I say?"

"Nothing." Everything.

"That's not true. I've upset you. Tell me why."

Harry's every muscle twitched. "Look, let's just drop it, okay?"

He'd said the words far more forcefully than he'd intended. Kathryn winced and sat back from him, her expression one of shock.

"Okay," she said carefully.

Thankfully the waitress picked that moment to deliver their meals.

Unfortunately, Harry didn't think this was the last time he and Kathryn Buckingham were going to have this discussion.

CHAPTER SEVENTEEN

AFTER LUNCH, the frayed connection between Kat and Harry appeared beyond repair. And she hated that. She hated that she'd said something to upset him. She hated even more that there was nothing she could do to make it better because she didn't know what she'd said to begin with.

She'd offered to take a taxi to her place to meet with the contractors who would see to the renovation of her townhouse, but he'd merely given her one of those steely-eyed stares. The ones she'd gotten often in the beginning, but she hadn't seen for the past couple of days.

So they were back to square one.

And she was back to riding in a silent car with a guy she was coming to have some very strong feelings for. A guy who was emotionally just as much of a stranger to her as he'd been in the beginning.

Although physically... She shivered, the mere memory of the way he'd stroked her, touched her, making her feel suddenly vulnerable.

She'd asked that he stop at an ATM so she could

get some cash, something to offer the contractor by way of a deposit for the extensive work that needed to be done to her townhouse. But as she stood at the machine and reentered the amount, only to be told again that there were insufficient funds in her checking and savings accounts, her mind was yanked firmly back to the here and now.

She printed out a balance of each account, barely hearing Harry when he left the car and joined her.

"What's the matter?" he asked.

Kat shook her head. It was impossible. The bank showed that she had less than twenty dollars in her savings and a negative balance in her checking.

"I need to go inside."

Five minutes later the assistant manager told her the same thing.

"But that's impossible. I haven't accessed my accounts in over a week."

The young woman's fingers worked over her computer keyboard then turned the monitor so Kat could see it.

"Withdrawals were made from both accounts first thing Monday morning."

"Monday morning? Monday morning I was—"

Harry grasped her hand tightly, catching her up short. Telling the bank employee that she'd been in jail probably wouldn't get her the assistance she needed.

"Can we see the withdrawal slips?" he asked.

"I'm sorry, sir, but the withdrawals were made at our main branch downtown and are likely now en route to our archives where they'll be microfilmed before being filed."

Kat somehow managed to mimic Harry's moves, thanking the manager then getting up and walking outside as if her luck hadn't just taken another steep nosedive.

"I THINK WE SHOULD STAY in town tonight."

Following the visit to the bank, Harry had taken her to keep her appointment with the contractor at her townhouse. She received an estimate although no work would be done until she put down a deposit. She claimed to have the money in another money market account at another bank. Unfortunately the passbook for that account had been found next to Darin's body and was even now evidence in the capital murder case against her, and therefore the account had been frozen.

He made a mental note to arrange for the contractor to receive the deposit out of his own account when he got back to his place.

Afterward he'd driven around and now they both sat in the car facing the banks of the Potomac. They hadn't said much to each other. There hadn't been much to say.

She nodded. "I don't think I'm up to family right now."

He knew what she meant.

"A hotel?" she asked.

He glanced at her. "I was thinking my place."

She blinked, the dazed look in her eyes vanishing, replaced briefly by curiosity.

Harry resisted the urge to rub the back of his neck, afraid of what the nervous tic would give away.

What she'd said earlier at the pub had hit too close to home. And had made him realize that while he'd given himself to her on a number of levels, he had kept her well in the dark about his past and his present, the very things that went into making him the man he was.

And he suddenly felt a need to show all of it to her, no matter the consequences.

"Okay," she said quietly.

His apartment was in Woodley Park, a small place with a great view of the city. A short drive and they were there, Kathryn following him up the two flights and waiting as he unlocked the door. Harry pushed it open and motioned for her to lead the way in.

Connor had once mumbled that Harry's place would be the perfect candidate for Queer Eye for the Straight Guy. He'd never given much thought to style when he'd moved in, merely added things here and there as he'd needed them. The bookshelves lining the living room walls he'd made himself. Each was stacked to overflowing with novels and political tomes and biographies and history texts he'd collected while browsing library sales and used bookstores. There was no rhyme or reason to the way they were placed, but he had a good idea where everything was.

In the corner was an old leather recliner with a good lamp and a table stacked with newspapers and magazines. He'd added a black leather ottoman later that somehow matched the recliner even though it was burgundy. To the left an open counter separated the small dining room from the kitchen. Since he hadn't needed a full table, he'd bought instead two mismatched bar-style stools to pull up to the counter. It was off one of these that he removed a good week's worth of papers and dropped them to the floor, indicating she could sit if she liked.

But Kathryn hadn't noticed. She had stepped to the bookshelves and seemed to be reading each of the titles on the bindings one by one. When she reached the end of the middle shelf, she found herself near the open door to the bedroom. Her fingers resting against the front of her throat, she moved the little way needed to see into the other room.

Harry grimaced. He wasn't much of a housekeeper. He knew there were three small piles of clothes on the floor in there, sorted by things that needed to be taken to the cleaners, items he could wash himself and stuff that still had another good

wear in them. He passed her to clean up then realized she wasn't looking at the clothes, she was staring at the bed.

He scratched the back of his neck. "I don't know
why I bought it. I was on a book hunt at a flea market and passed an antique place and…"

And, well, the mammoth bed had mesmerized
him. Made of heavy, carved mahogany, it was larger
than a king-sized and he'd had to order special, non-
fitted sheets for it. In most beds his feet stuck out a
good couple of inches beyond the end, but not in this
one. It seemed custom made for him. And it domi-
nated the room, leaving space for little else. Since
a dresser wouldn't fit, he'd installed drawers on the
right side of his closet and mostly hung everything
else up. And what didn't fit there he put in the linen
closet in the hall.

Kathryn had followed him in and gripped the top
of one of the thick foot posts.

"Are you hungry?" he asked.

She looked over her shoulder and blinked as if
she hadn't heard him. "Um…no."

He watched her fingers caress the old wood. "I've
heard of bachelor pads but…" She looked at the
charcoal prints he'd bought from a Brooklyn street
artist of scenes from the borough he'd grown up in.
They contrasted yet complemented the scene outside the large window of the Capitol building and
the Washington monument beyond.

Kathryn picked up a novel lying on top of five other books on the one nightstand he'd been able to squeeze in, then put it back down.

Harry wasn't sure how he felt about her being here. It seemed…strange, somehow. Oh, he'd had other women in this room. He'd lived in the same place for the past ten years. But never had one looked around as if trying to figure him out by his surroundings.

"Have you ever been married?" she asked.

Harry lifted his brows. Normally that would be a question asked and addressed during a first date. But he and Kathryn had never dated, had they? Rather their relationship had been forged through need.

"No."

She slid him a glance over her shoulder. "Ever come close?"

"No."

"Have anything against marriage?"

"No." Harry turned and left the room.

In the small kitchen he went about making coffee with the top-of-the-line industrial stainless-steel coffeemaker. He wasn't aware Kathryn had followed him until he closed the refrigerator door after retrieving his specially ground coffee and found her standing there.

He continued making coffee.

"This…this place isn't what I imagined it would be," she said quietly.

"What were you expecting?"

She leaned against the wall and fingered bulbs of fresh garlic hanging near the wall phone. "I don't know. Something my brothers might have if they were still single. You know. A place to sleep, but nothing more." She took in the canisters lining the counter that were arranged in no specific order. "This is…well, it's a home."

At that he paused for a moment as he scooped coffee grounds into the maker.

Home.

She picked up a copy of the *New York Times* that sat on top of his recycling bin. "You read a lot."

"You thought I was illiterate?"

"That's not what I meant."

He flipped the switch to start the coffee machine then turned to face her. He remembered her George-town house with its rich fabrics and brittle furniture, the rooms looking unused and unlived in.

The battle-scarred cat that had been perched watching their visitor from the top of a bookshelf when they'd come in sauntered into the kitchen, startling Kathryn.

"Oh!" She put a hand to her chest as she considered the gray scrap of uneven fur while the feline sized her up in the same way.

"Kathryn, meet Bob. Bob, meet Kathryn."

She crouched to scratch him behind the ears. "Bob?" she asked.

"Yeah. I had a friend named Bob back in Brooklyn. The cat reminded me of him. Always getting into trouble."

"He looks like he's molting."

"He probably is." Harry got two mismatched coffee cups from the cupboard. "You want some coffee?"

"Hmm? Yes, please." She picked up the large feline. "So you're Brooklyn Bob."

Harry stared at the tom. Bob never let anyone pick him up. Not even him, except when he was transferring him from one place to another to get him out of the way. Otherwise he had the run of the place.

"Who looks after Bob when you're working?"

"Mrs. Steinhaufer across the hall."

She wore an odd expression as she looked at him. "What?"

She shook her head and smiled. "I don't know. You're just full of surprises. You have books out there that any lifelong collector would be envious of. You own a battered old cat named Brooklyn Bob. And you have an old woman looking out after you."

"Mrs. S isn't old. She's only seventy-two."

Her smile widened. "And you remind her of one of her grandsons."

"Would if she had any. She and her husband didn't have a chance at children before he shipped off to Korea and never came home."

"She's been a widow all this time?"

"Oh, I see a male friend come visit about once a month. Same guy. Same time. But she insists they're just old friends."

She was looking at him strangely again.

This time he suppressed the urge to say, "What?"

"Sugar and cream?" he asked instead.

"Hmm? Oh. Black, please."

She put Bob down.

"Thanks," she said as she accepted the cup from him, appearing in no hurry to move from the kitchen.

Harry leaned against the counter opposite her and sipped from his own mug.

"Your parents still alive?" she asked.

He pretended an interest in his coffee. "No. My mother died about five years ago. Never set foot outside of Brooklyn her entire life."

"And your father?"

"He died a long time before that." He cleared his throat, not up to discussing that part of his life. Although his answers to her questions seemed to come far easier here in his apartment than they had at the pub. At the pub…well, she'd hit a little too close to home with the details of Greer's case and his almost angry response had caught even him off guard. You would have thought he'd have got over all that a long time ago.

She was looking at him a little too closely so he changed the subject. "Do we want to talk about who had access to your bank accounts?"

She blinked and the soft expression disappeared from her pretty face, making him regret having posed the question so abruptly, though it needed to be asked.

"James had access. We'd just gone down to sign the necessary papers last week. A couple of days before…"

Before he was killed. Harry nodded. "Anyone else?"

"Who? There isn't anyone else."

He knew that. Aside from a few casual friends she had at work, Kathryn Buckingham McCoy was all about her job. She exercised at some point every day—either a jog in the morning, or a stint at night on her treadmill, or a visit to a downtown gym—but otherwise she had her ear to the phone or her nose in a stack of papers.

"I paid a visit to Newton Granger today."

Her gaze was steady on him. Since she didn't register confusion or ask him who he was referring to, he assumed she remembered the details in Darin's case file. Namely that his testimony had landed two men in jail for accepting illegal campaign contributions from communist countries that had never found their way to any political campaigns but rather into their own pants pockets.

Kathryn swallowed so hard it was audible. "You visited him in prison?"

"No, he made parole three months ago." He

watched her absorb the information. "It seems there was at least one person left out of the case three years ago. It's my guess Darin made an outside deal that included a large amount of cash. And that when that ran out, he resorted to blackmailing him."

The color drained from her face. "A viable suspect."

He nodded. "Yes. I'm going to meet with my superior tomorrow morning and see that your protective witness status is reinstated."

"Who is it?" she asked.

"A banker by the name of Conrad Bowman."

He'd expected her to look relieved by the news. Instead she looked upset.

"What's the matter?"

She slowly shook her head and wandered out to take one of the stools. "I don't know. I'm familiar with Bowman's name. And if I am, that means others will be, too. Which makes him a hard target if he is behind James's murder." Her voice dropped an octave. "Then there's the fact that good news for me seems to mean bad news for James."

Harry stepped next to her and halted her hand where she was nudging her cup around in circles—a nervous habit. "It would probably help if you'd start looking a little more closely at Darin…James's activities prior to his death instead of romanticizing the loss of him."

He hated the smear of pain he saw in her eyes. "I know. It's just…"

Harry was in real danger of kissing her. Of pressing his lips against hers to wipe away the sad frown she wore.

Instead he stepped back from her. "I've got a few calls to make. The place is yours to do whatever you want."

She glanced toward the chair in the other room then back at him. "Okay."

Harry took the stool she vacated, pulled a pad in front of him and made his first call, all the time wishing he could be in the other room with Kathryn doing something much more interesting.

When he finished up an hour later he looked over to find that Kathryn wasn't in the chair.

He got up, nearly tripping over Bob on his way to see if she was in the bathroom. It was the sight in his bedroom that caught him up short.

There in the middle of his gigantic bed she lay snuggled up, a book open on the pillow next to her, her sexy mouth slightly open as she slept.

A need so engulfing, so powerful overtook him at seeing her lying on his bed in his apartment reading his book.

A need he had to suppress if he hoped to get her out of the mess she was in.

A need he was helpless to ignore as he stepped inside the bedroom and softly closed the door behind him....

CHAPTER EIGHTEEN

KAT GREW SLOWLY AWARE of an unbearable heat. Not that caused by an increase in temperature. Rather the gradual tingling awareness that went with sexual desire. It dampened her inner thighs and made her back come off the mattress as she sought the source of a pleasure so sweet, so skilled it seemed more a part of her dream world than reality.

She vaguely remembered that Harry had been making phone calls in the dining room when she'd wandered into the bedroom, finding the gigantic bed all too tempting and the books on the nightstand intriguing. He'd told her she had the run of the place, so she'd allowed herself the luxury of crawling into the middle of the soft bedding, breathing in the scent of the book's leather cover and…and she must have drifted off to sleep.

The fingers stroking her caused a moan to build in her chest. It wound around and around until it came out in one, long quiet sound. She languidly blinked her eyes open to see Harry, his shirt unbuttoned, sitting next to her on the bed, the purple haze of sunset backlighting him. She reached out, pressing her palm against the washboard muscles of his abdomen then dipping lower until she tucked her fingertips inside the waistband of his slacks and his boxers, seeking his silken heat. There, she found the throbbing proof of his arousal and rubbed her fingertip against the knob until moisture coated her fingers.

He groaned and stood to take off his clothes. Kat lay watching him, seeming unable to do more than look. Then he was peeling off her top and pants and bra, leaving nothing but the scrap of lace between her legs. Again he sat on the bed, his left hand between her thighs, touching her but not touching her there. Then he leaned forward and kissed her... once, twice. Such sweet torture. Kat's mouth watered and she reached to pull him closer. He moved out of reach. She moved to protest. A protest that died on her lips when he skimmed his fingertips over the dampness of her panties.

Delicious shivers ran up and down the length of her, making her feel utterly, gloriously alive. Before she could ride out the last of them, he fastened his mouth over her right nipple and suckled. Kat threw her head back and gasped when he released her breast in search of her other.

Harry edged a finger inside the crotch of her panties, slowly stroking her. Kat bore down, trying to force a more solid meeting. He avoided her attempts, instead setting a pace designed to drive her out of her mind with pleasure and need. Up and down his finger went, the back of his knuckle skimming over her clit then down past her dripping portal and back again.

Had she ever experienced this kind of insatiable need for anyone? Felt so out of her mind with ecstasy that if she was asked her name in that moment, she wouldn't be able to remember it? Outside the cloud of sensual pleasure Harry was creating, nothing existed but shadows and vague outlines and ideas. Inside there were him and her, stripped of everything but their most fundamental needs. And their growing connection to each other.

Even as he coaxed her thighs apart, baring her to his gaze, she knew that what they shared was far more than physical need. Being in his apartment, in his bed, was evidence of that. Not merely because of setting, but because her being there, his allowing her inside his life, proved he was opening up to her in ways she had craved.

He slid a condom on his pulsing length. She cradled him between her legs and he filled her in one long stroke, catapulting her into a world reserved strictly for sensation and emotion. A world of intimacy beyond words, where their bodies were free to communicate in ways they themselves could not.

Kat clutched him tightly to her, the closeness

causing a friction between their pelvises that increased the sweet ripples moving through her each time he thrust and she moved to meet him. She ground against him, watching in the dimming light as he stretched his neck and clenched his jaw as if it was taking everything in his power not to come right then and there. The knowledge gave her a sense of wicked power. Confidence. She shifted her hands over his tight behind and held him still even as she moved, increasing the friction between them. Her legs curved around his hips and he caught them with his arms, pushing her knees so they were bent between them. The position allowed for a penetration so deep Kat was helpless to stop the loud moan that ripped from her throat.

So good...so good.

She swore she could feel every ridge of his penis, every vein as he slid out then thrust back into the hilt only to repeat the process until she was out of her mind with pleasure.

"Oh, yes," Harry murmured as he thrust into her deeply one last time and his every muscle seemed to clench as hard as his jaw had moments ago.

Kat blissfully followed after him.

HARRY LAY AGAINST the pillows, lazily caressing Kathryn's bare back, the top sheet half covering them. The sun had long since set, and Bob sat on the corner of the bed giving himself a thorough tongue bath.

For the second time he'd given in to his desire to bed the woman curled against his side. And for the second time she'd absolutely blown his mind. Not with skill, although her lack of inhibition made her a great lover. Rather his growing attachment to her seemed to add an undeniable significance to their lovemaking.

An attachment that frankly was beginning to scare the hell out of him.

He didn't just want to enjoy her body. He wanted to enjoy everything about her. Her deep-throated laugh. Her generosity. Her strength. Her inquisitive mind…

He heard the click of his own swallow.

"You know, you never did tell me what happened to your father," she said quietly, rubbing her cheek against his chest.

Did he just say he liked her inquisitive mind? He quickly amended that.

"That was a drastic change in topic," he murmured, kissing the top of her fragrant pale hair.

"I wasn't aware there was a topic on the table."

Harry closed his eyes. After the sun had set, he'd switched on the light on the bedside table. The warm yellow glow bathed the side of the bed she was on making her look like an angel.

"No, there wasn't," he agreed.

She shifted until she leaned her head on her elbow, her gaze studying him. "Is it something you'd rather not talk about?"

Yes, it was. But strangely enough he found himself wanting to tell her. If only to get if off his chest. If only to see what her reaction would be to the information.

"He was killed when I was fourteen."

Kat caught her breath, her eyes growing large in her face. "Oh, Harry. I'm so sorry. Had I known, I would never have brought it up."

He looked at her unblinkingly. "I'm the one who killed him."

He was as shocked as she was that he'd said the words aloud. That he'd said what he hadn't told another solitary individual in his adult life.

"I…my mother was always a constant presence in my life. She'd never married my father. And even I didn't really view him as my father. Not in the traditional sense. He kind of blew in and out of our lives."

Kat had lain back down, listening.

"Everything would be great for a couple of weeks. We'd be a real family. Or at least what I considered a real family at the time. We'd share dinner every night in the kitchen. Watch television together…"

And then it would start again. The arguments. His mother would ask his father when he planned to get a job. Or would leave the want ads out on the table after she left for work with a few possibilities circled. And his father would grow more and more angry at what he called her trying to control his life. They'd begin shouting at each other. Then the shouting would lead to physical violence, sometimes with his mother starting the bouts by slapping his father.

But it was his father who always finished.

How many times had he come out of his room after his father had left, slamming the door after himself, and helped his mother off the floor and into the bathroom where he would clean her up? And that was before he was seven. After that, when his father would show up again after an absence of a year or two, and the fighting would pick up again, the beatings grew to require emergency room visits. Stitches here, resetting of broken bones there.

Until the summer of his fourteenth year. Until he'd been nearly as tall as his father and had demonstrated his own capacity for anger. His own capacity for violence. A demonstration that had left his father dead after Harry had slugged him repeatedly in the jaw and he'd fallen backward, hitting his head on the coffee table.

A freak accident, the police department had declared.

Harry had thought it ironic that after all the times his mother had gone to the E.R. with various injuries and stated "accidents" as the cause, his own father's death would be ruled the same.

"A neighbor called the police and one of the cops who arrived lived a couple of blocks up the street from us. At first he'd check up on my mom and me every now and again, you know, to make sure we were okay. Then he gradually became like a surrogate father or a big brother to me." Harry rubbed his chin against the top of Kathryn's head. "He's the inspiration for my going into law enforcement. He encouraged me to take the officer's exam, go into the military." He smiled sadly. "I started as a police officer but while I loved my job, well…my track record when it came to domestic disturbance calls wasn't good."

Harry had never shared that with anybody. Not even Connor knew of the details of his fourteenth summer. He only knew his father had died, not the circumstances surrounding his death.

No, Kathryn was the first and the only one he'd ever told. Maybe because he sensed she wouldn't judge him for the past act. Maybe because for too long the information had served as a black spot against his soul. A spot Kathryn shone a warm light on as she looked at him, compassion and understanding on her beautiful face.

"I'm so sorry that happened to you," she whispered, unshed tears making her eyes look all the brighter.

He thought about shrugging, playing that it was no big deal. But there was no need to pretend with Kathryn. No reason to hide what he really felt.

"I am, too," he said.

She leaned in and kissed him. A soft meeting of lips that told him she understood even what he hadn't shared. He threaded his fingers through her hair and drew her closer, drinking deeply from her sweetness. Allowing her light to suffuse the darkness…even as he reached over to switch off the lamp.

CHAPTER NINETEEN

SEAN SAT ACROSS the street from the florist shop, his
car engine shut off, his stomach tight. He'd gone first
to the house he'd shared with Wilhemenia for the
past four years, but she hadn't been home even though
it was past seven. She always came home at five on
the button. So he'd come to the shop to find her still
inside, appearing to do inventory of some sort.

With her was Walter. And he was looking far
friendlier than Sean was comfortable with.

He reached for the door handle, then took his
hand back, torn between two options. One option
was wanting to go in there and set the record straight
with the widower who had designs on his wife—via
a fist to the jaw if need be. Option two was to drive
back out to Manchester for another night and wait
for Wilhemenia to contact him.

Of course, a third option was to go to their house
and wait for her to return so they could talk. But that
wasn't a real choice because nothing had changed
since she'd asked him to leave. Except that he was
coming to see how much he missed her.

"Tell her," Kathryn had said during a phone call earlier. "Tell her you not only want her, that you need her. A woman needs to be needed."

The question was whether he felt that he needed Wilhemenia.

He reached for the handle again and stopped this time not because of some battle inside him, but because Wilhemenia and Walter appeared to be closing up shop.

Good. He would follow her to the house so they could talk this out.

Only it didn't appear Wilhemenia was going home. Rather than getting into her own car, she instead allowed Walter to hold the passenger door open of his late model sedan for her. She got in.

And Sean knew a stab of jealousy so deep his vision blurred with the intensity of it. But before he could act on it, Walter's car drove away.

WAS IT REALLY SATURDAY? Kat sat on the front porch swing of the McCoy farmhouse marveling that so much, yet so little, time had passed since that horrible, fateful night. It seemed so much had happened, yet so little had been accomplished since James was killed.

Darin…Darin…Darin…

She rubbed her forehead where she was staring at her notepad, but no matter how hard she tried, she couldn't mesh the man she knew with the one outlined in Harry's case files.

Harry...

That morning he'd taken her with him to follow up on a couple of items, one of them involving a visit to a mansion in Maryland where he'd left her sitting in the car. She didn't know the place and she didn't know who he was meeting with, but she got the impression it was important and it was something connected to her and James. But how, she couldn't be sure. And he wasn't sharing. Not even afterward during the ninety-minute drive out to Manchester.

Instead he'd asked her questions.

Aside from her checking and savings that had been emptied, did she have financial resources?

Yes, she'd told him. As she'd mentioned before, the bank book found on the kitchen floor beside Darin's body had been for an account at another institution. The account was where she held her parents' life insurance proceeds, monies she hadn't touched. There was also a safe deposit box, which held the few precious jewels her mother had owned along with the deeds to Kat's property and her own life insurance policy.

Did James have a life insurance policy?

That one had stumped her. Though they'd been engaged to get married, the topic of life insurance hadn't come up as far as she could remember. She did recall thinking about updating hers to include him. But did he have one that included her?

She honestly didn't know.

What she did know was that every McCoy man she knew was inside the house in the kitchen right now discussing things she wasn't privy to. She'd put up a fuss when Harry had first asked her to leave, but had quickly given in when she'd realized what kind of fight she would be in for against seven of the most stubborn men she'd ever met.

She caught herself scratching her right arm. All this exclusion was starting to make her itch.

She put her pad down on the bench next to her having accomplished little more than doodles down the right side of the page, then entered the house and went on to the kitchen.

Silence.

She stared into seven pairs of stony eyes.

"What? Can't a girl get a soda?"

She crossed the tile and opened the refrigerator, waiting for conversation to start back up. It didn't.

She closed the door then popped the can, discreetly trying to get a look over David's shoulder and the pad he had there. Connor reached to turn it over.

Kat gave an eye roll. "Come on, guys, I'm not some child incapable of keeping a secret. What's going on?"

Nothing but all of them looking at each other as if to make sure no one was near giving up the ghost.

"This does concern me most, you know."

"And we're just trying to protect you," Connor said.

"How can you do that without my knowing what you're doing?"

They obviously weren't convinced.

"Look, if your plan—"

"We're not planning anything," Marc said too quickly.

Kat stared at him. "As I was saying, if your plan calls for me to stay on the front porch and I walk around to the back because, of course, I don't know that your plan calls for me to stay on the porch, then my ignorance totally upsets things."

"You don't have to stay on the porch."

For the first time Kat caught sight of some sort of equipment on the counter. There was a low hiss so she knew it was on. Now what it did was another matter entirely.

"What's this?"

"Something you don't have to concern yourself with," Connor said, getting up and blocking her path to the counter.

Kat clenched her jaw, exasperation building up inside her to the point that she wanted to scream.

She made a small sound of frustration instead. "Fine. If you need anything, I'll be upstairs in my room."

She grabbed her briefcase where it was propped against the wall near the door. The whatchamajiggy on the counter made a louder sound and the green line on a small screen spiked.

She lifted her brows.

"I'm bugged?"

They were all looking at each other a little too closely.

Kat moved her briefcase and again got a response from the machine.

"Is someone going to answer me?"

"You're not bugged. And that's all I'm going to say," David said.

She looked at him. "Then what's that sound every time I move my bag?"

"A transmitter is somewhere inside there," Sean said.

"A transmitter? You guys put a transmitter in my bag?" That itchy sensation started to increase.

Harry's face was sober as he looked at her. "We didn't. It was already in there, Kat."

She blinked at him, trying to wrap her mind around his words. "What do you mean it was already in there?"

She stared at the careworn leather briefcase. She'd bought it for all its secret little compartments and many pockets.

"Who would put a transmitter in my bag?" she whispered.

Sean got up, touched a knob on the machine, then crossed to her. "That's what we're trying to figure out, Kathryn." He started walking her toward the doorway. "Now, why don't you go on outside or up-stairs so we can continue our conversation?"

She took in his earnest expression, his worried frown. She wanted to be in on the conversation. Wanted to discuss the possibilities of who might have bugged her briefcase. Wanted to be counted in on her own life, damn it.

And she would have told them that. But she trusted them implicitly.

She nodded slowly. "Okay. But I can't promise I'll stay away for long. And you have to swear a blood oath that once you guys have come to a con-clusion or have completed your plan you'll let me in on it."

They all shared another look.

"You have our word of honor," Connor said.

That was good enough for Kat. For now...

It would have to be. Because there was precious little else she could do about it.

HARRY FELT LIKE the biggest of all heels as he watched Kathryn reluctantly leave the room.

Truthfully, he hadn't had a problem with her stay-ing. It was the McCoys who questioned her emo-tional ability to handle the situation and the topics they were discussing. He'd tried to argue with them, but to little avail. They were living up to every last stubborn thing that had ever been said about them.

Sean wanted to protect his daughter, the others their sister. It was as simple and as complicated as that. Forget that she'd lived the past twenty-seven years taking care of herself. That she'd freed herself from her assailant the other night outside the safe house. That she was as capable as, if not more capable than, any guy to reason something out and to implement a plan.

Then they'd gotten down to the gritty details and he'd found himself glad they hadn't included Kathryn. Their talk was freaking *him* out.

"Okay," Connor said as soon as they were all sure Kathryn was out of earshot. "So we're agreed that Conrad Bowman—former partner of Darin Ichatious and Newton Granger—might be in on the murder."

They all agreed.

Harry leaned back and crossed his arms over his chest. "That doesn't explain why someone would empty Kathryn's bank accounts."

Marc waved that off. "A greedy someone who saw an opportunity and took it."

"And her being snatched the other night?"

"They wanted to find out how much she saw the night of the murder and how much she knew about her late fiancé," David answered. "Thus the reason for the transmitter you found in her briefcase."

It all made sense. Too much sense. Harry couldn't seem to shake the feeling that they were missing something here. Something big.

He rubbed his chin. "So Darin's murder was a revenge killing."

"Let's not forget that Kat was also set up to take the fall for it," Mitch said.

"There always has to be a fall guy. Or in this case, girl," Connor said, watching Harry closely.

Harry returned the scrutiny. He knew by Con's expression that they were on the same page. There was something missing. The question was, would they be able to figure out what before the murderer made his next move?

"WE KNEW they'd shut you out."

Kat looked up from her notes where she sat on the front porch. Liz, Bronte and Michelle smiled down at her. It was Michelle who had spoken.

Bronte waved something. "That's why we brought you this."

Kat accepted what looked like a kid's walkie talkie.

"It's a baby monitor," Liz explained.

Michelle winked, one hand unconsciously rubbing her distended belly. "And the other half is in the kitchen, taped under the table."

Kat looked more closely at the device. She rolled her finger along a switch and received an immediate buzz. Liz quickly reached out and flicked it back off. "No, don't do it here. Come on over to the office in the stables with us. We can listen in from there."

Kat laughed, not surprised the other McCoy women wanted in on this. And not surprised that they didn't bother going head-to-head with the stubborn men but instead found a way to outsmart them.

She reached for her briefcase then thought again. Better to leave it here in case it interfered with the monitor.

Michelle put her arm around her as the four of them walked toward the barn, taking a route that would keep them out of view of the men inside. "Then maybe later we all go for a ride, no? Give them all a shot of their own medicine."

Kat realized she probably meant "taste" but she was too busy thinking about what they would hear on the monitor.

CHAPTER TWENTY

SEAN STOOD at the doorway watching the McCoy women walk together toward the stables. He hid his grin from his sons and Harry. It was obvious the women were in cahoots. Which was just as well. While he wanted to protect Kathryn, he also understood her need to be involved in her own protection.

So he remained silent as he watched the women on their way to do Lord only knew what. But what he was sure of was that they weren't going to make chocolate chip cookies.

He began to turn away from the door to rejoin the guys at the table when a car slowed on the road near the driveway. He immediately recognized the older model sedan.

Wilhemenia.

His heart did a funny flip in his chest. After seeing her leave the shop last night with Walter Purdy, he'd come back out here and tossed and turned all night, unable to believe that she would be unfaithful to him. He would never dream of doing that to her. Yet the fact that she'd left with Walter had been undeniable.

Still, she was here now.

He walked out the screen door, letting it slap closed behind him. Wilhemenia parked but didn't immediately get out. Sean repressed the urge to go open the door for her, no matter how strong. Finally she got out, straightened her already neat skirt, patted her already smooth hair then opened the back door to get a bag.

Sean squinted at her.

"Hello, Sean," she said quietly, coming to stand in front of him.

For a woman as fussy as Wilhemenia was, there was something about her that struck him straight to the core. Something fundamental and, well, sexy.

"Hi, yourself," he said.

He waited for her to tell him why she'd come out. Did she want him back home? Had she come to apologize? Was she visiting to give him a chance to say he was sorry?

He told himself to wait for her to take the lead.

Then he forgot all that and asked if she wanted to come inside, if he could get her something to drink. The offer made him wince, remembering all the times she'd busied herself getting him tea he didn't want when all he'd wanted was her company.

"No, thank you."

She looked around at the cars, the stables then the house.

"You know, I've never really felt comfortable

here." She looked at him. "I know it's the house you grew up in. The house where you raised your kids. But somehow I...I don't know. I've always felt like an outsider."

Sean didn't know what to say. So he said nothing.

Wilhemenia held out the bag. "Anyway, you didn't take anything with you the other night. I thought you might need a few things. You know, clothes, toiletries."

Sean stared at the bag as if she were trying to hand him a snake. It was the one that had been sitting in the foyer when she'd told him she needed the space.

"Take it," she said.

He reluctantly accepted it.

A voice told him to say he'd seen her last night. Seen her leave the shop with Walter.

"Pops?"

He looked over his shoulder to find Connor in the doorway, his face stern as he considered the woman who was his stepmother.

"Wilhemenia," he greeted without much warmth.

"Connor," she said quietly, looking all the more uncomfortable.

It was then that Sean knew he was to blame for this. For this rift between his old life and his new. Only it hadn't really been a new life with Wilhemenia, had it? Because he hadn't given it his all.

He'd held something back. A very important something that he wasn't sure he knew how to give her now.

"Pops, we need you in here," Connor said.

Sean waved him away. "I'll be there in a minute."

He could tell his oldest son was still there without looking.

"Leave us alone, please," he told him.

He heard Connor finally step away from the door and Wilhemenia seemed to give a sigh of relief.

"Wilhemenia, I…"

"Please, Sean, don't say anything. I didn't come out here for any other reason than to bring you your things. I…I really must be getting going. I told Walter I'd be in the shop by one."

Sean's blood heated up. "The hell with Walter. You and I need to talk."

Wilhemenia blinked at him, surprised by the vehemence of his words. "I'm not ready to talk yet, Sean. And given your rude and disrespectful behavior, I can't say as when I will be ready."

"I don't owe Walter one ounce of respect," he said.

She seemed unsteady on her feet for a moment. "It's not Walter I was talking about."

Then with that she hurried back to her car, got in and drove away. And all Sean could do was watch her go, her words as stinging as if she'd slapped him.

"Pops?" Connor said again from the door.

He stood for a long moment, watching as Wilhemenia's sedan disappeared from sight. He'd already screwed up with one important woman in his life. He didn't intend to do it all over again with Kathryn.

He turned and went back inside the house.

"SHHH, they're plotting again," Liz said to the group gathered around the baby monitor. She checked the buttons. "Doesn't this thing go up any higher?"

Bronte waved away her hands. "You're interfering with the reception."

Over the small speaker came Harry's voice: *"So it's agreed then. Kathryn stays out here where she'll be watched twenty-four seven. We'll all take shifts so that there are two of us on at all times. And I'm willing to take the majority when I'm not in the city trying to track down the killer. The rest of you will trade off—"*

"I think we should all bunk here until this thing is over with," came Connor's voice.

Kathryn looked to Bronte who rolled her eyes. "Rambo hasn't got anything on Connor."

"How do we know the killer will come out here after her?" David's voice.

Silence, then Harry said, *"He's getting desperate. And if we act low-key enough, like we don't know about the transmitter in Kathryn's briefcase, he's sure to make his move."*

Kat shuddered down to her painted toenails.

"Transmitter?" Michelle asked.

Kat nodded.

They were using her as bait.

"No wonder they didn't want to let you in on this," Bronte said, crossing her arms. "They're dangling you out there like a nice big, fat worm."

"Bait? As in fishing, no?" Michelle said.

"As in fishing, yes," Liz said, looking around then grabbing a small box nearby. "So it looks like Mel was right. I guess I owe her five dollars."

"You bet on this?" Kat asked.

"Of course we bet on it. We all bet on everything. It's a Manchester tradition. Long story. Anyway, Marc once used Mel as bait to catch an assassin. She wasn't too happy about it and didn't think you would be either. So she gave me this for you."

Kat took the shoe-sized box and peeked inside. A can of professional grade mace, a stun gun, and a small baton were just a few of the many items.

Bronte took out the baton and snapped it so it extended to full size.

"Wow. Can I have that when you're done?" Liz asked.

Bronte stared at her.

"What am I supposed to do with all this?" Kat asked, picking up the stun gun and staring at it.

"Protect yourself, of course."

Michelle tsked. "You know, in case the guys in

there do—how do they say?—too much planning and aren't paying attention when…"

She trailed off, not needing to say the rest because they all were pretty much well versed on that.

There was a loud squeak from the speaker and all four of them covered their ears.

"What's this?" Mitch said.

Sean said, *"Well I'll be…"*

"That's our baby monitor." Connor sounded none too pleased. The sound cut off.

"Oh, great," Bronte said with a sigh, putting the baton back in the box. "I'm in big trouble."

The sound came back on. *"Bronte, I hope you girls got an earful,"* he said. *"And in case you're wondering, you're very definitely going to pay for this one."*

The sound went off again and Kat didn't think it was going to come back on.

The wide smile Bronte wore, however, was a bit puzzling. She wondered exactly what "paying for it" meant between the twosome. Then again, she didn't want to find out. That kind of information fell solidly into the too much information column.

"What do we do now?" Liz asked.

"We already found out what we wanted so I say we all go to the house en masse," Michelle said.

They all smiled at each other.

"Let's go," they said in unison.

HARRY COULDN'T BEGIN to express how much he admired the woman now helping her sisters-in-law fix a lunch the guys professed not to be interested in even though they all were eyeing the sandwiches like hungry hounds.

David leaned back on his chair legs and looked inside the refrigerator. "You wouldn't happen to have any of that paradise potato salad around anywhere, would you, Liz?"

That earned him an elbow to the stomach from Marc, reminding him that they weren't supposed to be consorting with the enemy. Harry scratched his head. How the McCoy women could be categorized as the enemy was beyond his understanding.

"What?" David said, rubbing his stomach. "I'm hungry."

"Actually, I could go for a bite myself," Harry said, getting up from the table.

Harry reached around Kathryn to pluck a piece of roast beef from the sandwich she was fixing. She slapped his hand away. He chuckled, then held the beef up to her mouth. She ate half and he the other.

The room had gone noticeably quiet. Harry and Kathryn simultaneously looked over their shoulders to find the room watching them, some with open interest, some with wary suspicion.

Harry cleared his throat, not liking the thought of another of Connor's fists being thrown in his direction.

"Can you get the chips, Harry?" Liz asked. "They're in the cupboard to your right."

"Got it." He grabbed the extra large bag and put it on the table.

And just like that the meeting was over and they were all at the table enjoying lunch.

Afterward Harry helped with the cleanup, although his intention was not to clear the table. Rather he wanted to get Kathryn alone.

"Got a minute?" he whispered into her ear where she loaded the dishwasher.

She looked at him questioningly.

"Meet me outside in five."

He turned, stole a few more chips from the bag Liz was putting away, then walked toward the door. "I'm going to get something out of my car. Be right back."

No one seemed to pay particular attention to his disappearance. Connor was calling Bronte on her earlier monitor prank, Michelle was wiping mayo from the corner of Jake's mouth, and Liz and Mitch were asking Sean about Wilhemenia who apparently had stopped by earlier without his realizing it.

With his remote, he popped the back of his SUV and pretended an interest in something inside.

"I think they suspect something's up," Kathryn said next to him.

Harry grasped her hand and led her around the other side of the car and to the far side of the stables. She gasped as he kissed her hard.

"Let them suspect," he said, pulling back to take in her flushed appearance. "I've been wanting to do that all day."

Her smile warmed him more than the sun on his back. "Well, all you had to do was ask."

"Not in front of your brothers and father. Not if I value my life."

She laughed as she smoothed her fingers down the front of his shirt like she'd been doing it all his life. "You sound like they'd get a shotgun and marry us on the spot."

"No, but they'd probably hang me from the nearest tree."

"You're joking."

"I'm joking."

He kissed her again, moving her until her back was flush with the side of the barn.

When they came up for air long minutes later he discovered that their kiss wasn't doing anything to lessen his need for her. If anything, it was increasing it.

"Wow. Who would have thought you'd have that in you after last night?"

Ah, yes, last night. From the minute he'd awakened her at dusk, until the sun broke the horizon in the morning, setting her blonde hair aflame, they'd made love. And even though they'd showered together, he swore he could still smell her unique musk on him.

In fact, he was coming to suspect that no matter how much they made love or how often, he'd never be able to get enough of this woman.

"Come on," he said, grasping her hand.

She looked over her shoulder toward the house. "They're going to see us."

"Not where I'm taking you, they won't."

"And where is that?"

"I'll show you."

When they'd arrived earlier, he'd found Mitch inside the new house on the other side of the stables. He'd been caulking the new tile in the master bathroom. Tile that Liz had changed her mind on at least twice.

One of the great things about living this far outside the city was that you didn't have to lock the doors. Not that there was anything to take from this particular house, unless you needed a couple of faucets and leftover tile, since it was unfurnished, but still, you'd never think of leaving a similar house unlocked in the city. He opened the back door and ushered a laughing Kathryn inside.

"This is…beautiful," she said, looking around the airy kitchen that held all the latest appliances and even had a large, old-fashioned brick fireplace where you could cook or warm yourself in the winter.

"Isn't it? Since it looks like Mitch and Liz aren't in any hurry to move in, I asked how much he wanted for it."

Harry felt Kathryn's gaze on him as he grabbed her hand again and led her into the dining room then the living room beyond.

"What did he say?" she asked quietly. Too quietly.

"That it wasn't for sale."

"Oh."

Harry didn't stop until they were upstairs in the front bedroom. When he turned to face her, he decided to ignore the questioning shadow in her eyes. He'd been joking at first when he'd asked Mitch how much he wanted for the place. But surprisingly once the words were out of his mouth he'd discovered maybe he'd been a little serious. More than a little.

"They just laid the carpet in here yesterday."

She looked around. "The master bedroom?"

"No. This is a guestroom. The master's in the back. But I like this one."

She took in the wall of windows overlooking the front of the McCoy spread then looked at Harry and smiled. "Me, too."

And just like that they were kissing again. Hungrily. Hotly. His hands sought her bra under her shirt while her fingers fumbled for the front of his pants. He backed her up until he could push the door shut with his foot then push in the lock.

"You can never be too sure," he said by way of explanation.

Together they sank down to the carpet, tugging and pulling at each other's clothes, the full light of day shining in through the windows. This room held a fireplace as well, but Harry didn't think either he or Kathryn needed any help getting warm. He was burning up as it was. And it had nothing to do with the room's temperature.

Finally she was bare to his gaze and his hands. He paused a moment to marvel at how utterly beautiful she was. And how awed he was that she was allowing him to touch her. Not only allowing him to touch her, but insistent about it. She took his right hand and pressed it against her breast.

"Impatient, aren't we?" he asked with a quirked brow.

"Excuse me if I don't think we have all the time in the world right now."

She was right, of course. It was only a matter of time before someone came looking for them.

There was something naughty about the situation. About knowing that nearby lurked six over-protective men determined to keep Kathryn's reputation intact. And willing to skin him alive if he so much as thought about sullying her honor.

"Oh, yes," she whispered as he dragged his fingers down the front of her stomach, his destination the thatch of soft curls at the apex of her thighs.

He'd no sooner burrowed through the glossy tangle and found her slick with need for him than she was pushing him back onto the carpet and straddling him.

"Wait," he said, reaching for his jeans.

He slid a condom out of his back pocket and she took it from him, tearing the packet open with her teeth then rolling the lubricated latex down the length of him. He gritted his teeth at the feel of cool against hot then groaned when she tightened her fingers around the root of his loins.

"I wouldn't do that if I were you," he murmured.

She gave another squeeze. "Oh? Why not?"

He grasped her hips until she was poised and ready then thrust upward, filling her instantly.

She gasped.

"That's why not."

The light from the windows so perfectly spotlighted her where she sat proud and upright on top of him. Her breasts were perfectly round. Her stomach perfectly toned. Her pubic hair perfectly trimmed and neat.

And her need for him perfectly naughty.

"Wait," he said.

She blinked open her eyes halfway.

"Here, put your knees here," he said, indicating she should put them on his wrists and he would grasp her shins.

"But I'll hurt you."

"The rug burn you get will hurt more."

She obeyed his request. Then she was rocking

on top of him…back and forth…her pink-tipped breasts swaying with her movements. Beads of sweat appeared near her carved collarbone. Her hair was tousled. Her skin rosy and heated.

Harry found it incredible that she would even give a guy like him the time of day, much less want him to the extent she apparently did. He wasn't sure what he'd done to deserve it, but as desire grew deep in his abdomen, he thanked his lucky stars.

The only problem was that the tomorrow he'd vowed not to think about was creeping closer and he could no longer ignore it. He wanted this woman, not just in this moment, but for however long she'd have him. And he was beginning to feel the fear that when this was over, once the real killer was arrested, her want of him would vanish leaving him pining after something he could never have.

She gasped and he realized he was grasping her legs too tightly, his conflicted emotions conveying themselves through his actions.

With a smooth sweep, he rolled her over and lay cradled between her hips, her beautiful eyes blinking at him.

"What about the rug?" she whispered as he thrust into her to the hilt, making her catch her breath.

"Let it burn," he growled.

CHAPTER TWENTY-ONE

LATER THAT AFTERNOON Harry rounded the original farmhouse after doing a sweep of the grounds. Kathryn was upstairs in her room, or rather Marc's old room, where she'd set up a laptop. When he'd checked on her a little while ago, she'd had her cell phone connected to her ear to check up on Greer's case. Sean and Mitch were there, Sean in the kitchen, Mitch in the barn office with Liz, who'd refused to be chased out of her own home, as she put it. The desire to take Kathryn again right there in her room had been nearly irresistible. Nearly. Now that there weren't so many McCoys running around the place, he had to keep on the alert. He knew it was only a matter of time before the killer made his move. And he couldn't afford any mistakes.

The sun was just beginning its rendezvous with the horizon. Harry squinted into the muted light, wondering what it would be like to grow up in a place like this. With nothing but land and air for as far as the eye could see. His knee-jerk reaction was that it was too open, made a person too vulnerable being so exposed. But his neighborhood in Brooklyn was deceptively safe. So many shadows and doorways to hide in. On its busy streets you could blend in, be anonymous. Here Sean could tell by the sound of a car engine which of his neighbors was passing. And the occasional unfamiliar car drew acute attention. Keeping on top of what was going on around you was probably second nature to Manchesterites. Not because crime was high. The last real crime had been one of the neighbor's teenaged girls taking another neighbor's tractor out for a spin one night.

At least since the McCoys had all grown up. He'd heard stories of their many exploits and guessed they'd been pretty much hell on wheels in Manchester.

The low crime rate was likely directly related to the vigilance of people like Sean. Do something illegal and you were sure to be caught.

He stopped near the window to Kathryn's bedroom and looked up at the square of warm yellow light. He heard her fingers tapping on her keyboard. Despite—or maybe because of—everything going on she was trying to keep on top of her cases. She'd already spoken of her associate's exasperation with her backseat driving but claimed it was all that was keeping her sane right now.

And him?

He scratched the back of his neck. Well, he supposed he wasn't really in a sane state of mind. How could he be now that Kathryn had become a real part of his life? He'd always considered his life full, satisfying. During the day he battled to make the world a safer place. Then at night he went home and read about fictional characters doing the same. Or scanned the newspaper. Or read a biography of someone else who'd made the most of his or her life. Which only inspired him to do more.

Then Kathryn had stepped into his apartment and made him see how very lonely his life was.

The revelation surprised him. As an only child, he'd been used to being on his own. After his mother had passed away a few years ago he'd been sorry to lose the pleasure of her company but he'd continued on, not seeing what was missing because it hadn't been there to begin with.

In all honesty, hadn't Kathryn's life been the same? Outside Darin, she'd been a workaholic who got most of her exercise on a treadmill at home while listening to depositions and reading legal briefs rather than walking outside or at a gym and possibly interacting with people.

Of course his relationship with Connor and the rest of the McCoys had helped to fill the void he'd been loath to acknowledge the past few years. And Kathryn also seemed to fit right in with them.

But what about how he and Kat connected?

He heard a sound.

Harry whipped around and came face-to-face with Connor.

"Whoa," his friend held up his hands. "Is that a gun in your hand or are you just glad to see me?"

He looked down to find that he had, indeed, drawn his pistol and had it pointed pointblank at Connor's chest.

He re-holstered the firearm. "You should know better than to sneak up on a guy like that." He glanced toward the drive. He hadn't heard a car drive up. There hadn't been any vehicles on the road for at least a half hour. "How'd you get here?"

"I walked."

Connor's place was at least a mile, two miles to the west. The way he'd said it made it sound like he'd just walked around the corner. "What's up? You're not on until tomorrow morning."

His friend frowned and stepped away from the house. "Bronte kicked me out."

"Oh."

Connor waved his hand. "Not permanently. Just until she can get the girls bathed and into bed. She says I...distract her."

Harry grinned. "That could be a good thing."

"What she means is that I distract the girls. I'm there, and they think playtime's been declared." He shook his head, his gaze aimed in the direction of his house. "Bronte says I have absolutely zero skills when it comes to discipline."

This made Harry raise his brows. Stern Connor no good at discipline?

"Truth is, I don't know how to deal with so many…girls."

"One's a woman."

Connor threw a grin his way. "How did you know I was including Bronte in the statement?"

Harry shrugged and continued his walking of the perimeter of the house, Connor following. "A good guess."

"What's your experience in that area?"

"What, with girls? Aside from wining and dining them, absolutely nil."

"Fat lot of help you can offer then."

"Never said I could help."

Connor's sigh filled the air. "I don't know. They're so…small, you know? And round and soft. And even when they're covered from head to toe in mud from their mother's flower garden and I'm supposed to be scolding them, all I can do is smile. Pisses Bronte off to no end."

"I can imagine."

"Trust me, you can't. A pissed off Bronte is not a pretty picture."

Harry found himself smiling at a mental image of Bronte facing off against a helpless Connor.

"Are you laughing at me?"

Harry shook his head. "No, sir, I'm not."

Connor gave him a nudge. "You are, aren't you? You're laughing at me."

"Okay, maybe just a little."

Connor gave him another nudge, swiped his thumb the length of his nose then put up his dukes as if to box. "Come on. Nobody laughs at me when I'm knee deep in dog do."

Harry laughed again.

Connor landed a punch on his right shoulder.

"Ow. Watch it, buster. That was a bit hard."

His friend landed another hit to his left shoulder. "What, is Harry a wuss?"

"Wuss?" Harry found himself putting his own fists up in mock challenge. "Did you just call me a wuss?"

"I calls 'em likes I sees 'em."

Harry landed a punch on Connor's right shoulder then followed to the left without missing a beat and without giving his friend a chance to recover from the first. Connor stumbled back a couple of steps but didn't lower his guard.

"Ah, a real comedian. You call that a punch?"

Before he knew it, the two of them were wrestling.

They heard a window open. "What are you two knuckleheads doing?"

Kathryn. She must have heard them and opened the window more so she could stick out her head.

Harry looked up at the same time Connor did. They both cleared their throats and stepped away from each other.

"Nothing," Connor said.

She made a sound of disbelief. "Yes, well, keep it down, will you? You wouldn't want to drown out the sound of any unexpected visitors."

Harry caught the humor in her voice and he and Connor shared a look.

"Yes, ma'am," Connor said.

Something hit him from the window. "That's 'miss' to you."

Harry bent and picked up the bobble head of a Patriots football player, waving it at Connor.

Kathryn's head disappeared from the window, apparently returning to her laptop.

Connor snatched the bobble head. "I can't wait until I'm laughing at you and Kat going head-to-head."

Harry raised his brows for the second time that night. Was Connor saying in an indirect way that he had his permission to date his sister? Yes, he realized, he was.

Now he had to convince himself that the scenario of him and Kathryn as a couple was feasible. Not to him. But to her.

A BRIEF KNOCK at the door.

Kat started to straighten her nightgown, then

changed her mind and tugged the sleeve down baring one shoulder. *Let's see what Harry does with that.*

"Come in."

Sean opened the door. "Oh, I'm sorry. You're ready for bed."

"No, that's okay," Kat said quickly, righting her sleeve and straightening her skirt. "I'm just following up on a few things on the laptop. Come in, come in."

She wondered if Sean could have looked any more awkward as he did as she bid, softly closing the door after him. She turned. "Do you want the chair?"

"No, no. I'm fine."

He crossed to the bed and sat opposite her, the bedsprings giving a muted squeak. He cleared his throat but seemed overly interested in his clasped hands.

"Is it true that Wilhemenia came by earlier?" she asked, hoping to break the ice.

His eyes lifted to hers. "Yes. Yes, it is."

Kat shifted in the chair, leaning her arm against the back. "Did she tell you I stopped by to see her yesterday?"

"You stopped by to see her?"

Obviously Wilhemenia hadn't chosen to say anything. Either that or she hadn't had a chance. "Yes, I did. I figured it was long past time that we'd met."

Sean's eyes warmed. "Thank you."

She smiled. "I didn't do it for you. I did it for me. And you're welcome."

He started staring at her in that way that he had when he'd first visited her at the county jail. The way that made her feel a little uncomfortable. He shook his head and glanced toward the window. "In the beginning whenever I looked at you, all I saw was your mother."

Kat's heart gave a tender squeeze. When she'd come into the room to put her precious few things away earlier in the day, she'd noticed a silver-framed picture of Kathryn McCoy sitting on the nightstand. She'd stood there staring at it for a long time, exploring how very much she resembled the other woman. Her mother. The woman she would never know except through the memories of Sean and her brothers.

"And now?" she asked quietly, realizing they were both looking at the picture in question.

"Now? Now I see only you."

Gratitude burst through her like fireworks.

"I never meant for any of this to happen," he said. "I'm so happy to have you in our lives. I just wish I could go back to before the murder and make you safe."

Kat swallowed hard, only now coming to understand why Sean had done what he had for so long. Why he had given her up for adoption. In his rough, roundabout way, it had been his way of demonstrating the ultimate love.

She'd be lying if she said she hadn't given the situation a lot of thought. Why had Sean given away his child? Based on what she'd heard from her brothers, about Sean not being there much after his wife had died, about his drinking, she'd thought maybe he'd done it for selfish reasons. That he couldn't handle one more child on top of the five he'd already had.

But what she was coming to see was that none of the McCoys did anything selfish. At least not knowingly. They were noble and honorable men in a time when those qualities didn't much exist anymore.

She now knew that when Sean had given her up, he had also given away what had remained of his broken heart.

She reached out and put her hands on top of his. "I understand how you feel. But let me tell you how I feel. I'm…glad this happened if only because I got the chance to meet you, meet my brothers. And even if tomorrow—"

He tightly grasped her hands. "Don't talk like that."

She searched his face. "I have to." She quietly cleared her throat. "Even if tomorrow something happens and I'm no longer…around, I'll be forever grateful for having had this time with you. Getting to know you." She held his gaze. "Coming to love you."

If asked what was one of the most beautiful things she'd ever seen, it would have to be watching the big bear of a man opposite her, her father, well up with tears. But rather than turn away, try to hide them, he held her gaze and allowed her to see how he felt, raw and undiluted.

"I keep thinking your mother would have hated what I did."

Kat smiled, tears blurring her own vision. "No, Dad. I think Mom understood. Not only that, I think she's smiling down on us right this minute."

CHAPTER TWENTY-TWO

THE FOLLOWING MORNING found all the McCoy men and a couple of McCoy women in the kitchen enjoying breakfast together. Kat shuffled in on the scene, her tangled hair in her face, her feet bare and her mood unclear.

"Whoa, sis, that's some look you've got going on there," David said good-naturedly.

Kat couldn't be sure, but she thought she heard a growl and she was pretty sure it had come from her.

"She's not much of a morning person," Harry said.

Everyone looked at him as if to ask how he knew that. Kat squeezed the last of the coffee from the nearly empty carafe. "I am too a morning person. But morning doesn't officially start until after I've had my first cup." She only got a half a cup out of the carafe.

"Here, let me make some more," Liz said, laughing.

Kat smiled her thanks and sat down. No sooner

had she taken her first sip than she found a plate full of scrambled eggs, two pieces of buttered toast, sausage links and a glass of orange juice in front of her. She blinked. "If I keep eating like this you're going to have to fix me a stall in the stables."

"You need to put some meat on your bones," her father said.

"Too skinny," Connor agreed.

"I hate you," Liz grumbled.

Kat eyed them then dug into her food.

A short while later she hoisted herself from the table. "I think I'm awake enough to find some clothes. The question is whether I'll still fit into them."

"I'll walk up with you," her father said.

Outside her bedroom door, he kissed her cheek and thanked her.

"For what?" she blinked, thinking she should have at least enough caffeine in her system to make sense out of a simple conversation.

"I've decided to go see Wilhemenia this morning, you know, after our talk last night."

He'd stayed in her room until well after midnight and the two of them had discussed everything under the sun. From stories of what each of her brothers had been like growing up, to her own stories of the mischief she'd gotten into as a kid. Finally the topic had turned to the here and now. He'd asked how she felt about Harry. She'd asked him about Wilhemenia.

She told him she thought it was sad that he couldn't voice his feelings to her, that he should learn how to tell Wilhemenia he loved her. And, yes, she knew that he loved her. One only had to mention her name and beyond the brief shadow of pain that passed over his face was a love that couldn't be denied.

"Break a leg," she told him. "And bring her back here for dinner."

"She doesn't like it out here. Says she doesn't feel comfortable."

"Well, we'll just have to make it our job to change that, won't we?" Kat said.

She went into her room and changed into a pair of cargo pants and a snug T-shirt Liz had loaned her. Maybe she'd go for a ride on one of the horses. It had been a long time since she'd ridden.

She made her way back down to the kitchen to find it empty but for Harry and Connor.

"Where'd everybody go?" she asked, refilling her coffee cup.

"Liz went home with Bronte to see about some kind of recipe or other," Connor offered.

"David's outside," Harry added.

"Jake's out in the barn."

"And Mitch is…around somewhere."

"Mmm. Quite a travelogue."

Connor got up. "I think I'm going to head home for a while, myself. I have some fertilizer to spread on the crops. I'll be back."

"See you later," Harry called from where he was loading the dishwasher.

"I can get that," Kat told him.

Harry looked over his shoulder. "What? Is my arm broken?"

The comment sounded so New York Kat laughed. "Fine. When you're done with that you can go make my bed for me."

"Now there you're on your own." He shook his head. "Never could get those hospital corners down."

"And, of course, if a job can't be done perfectly…"

"It's not worth doing at all," he finished with a wink.

He walked toward the door.

"Where are you going?" she asked.

"To walk the perimeter."

"Want some company?"

"No. You're the reason I'm walking it. Wouldn't make much sense to have you there should I run into somebody, would it?"

"Hmm. Guess not."

He let the screen door slap shut after him, passing David on his way inside.

"Where's Pops?" he asked Kat.

Grand Central Station. She'd heard the saying often enough but had really never understood it until this very minute. The constant coming and going.

Trains in the form of people intersecting and departing and arriving, asking questions, giving answers, and filling her head with so much activity she didn't have a thought to herself.

What was David's question? Oh, yes. Dad. "Gone. He went into the city."

"Wilhemenia?"

Kat nodded.

"Good. It's about time they patched things up."

"Too bad Connor doesn't feel the same way."

"Connor's got a chip on his shoulder the size of Virginia. Always has. Always will. You just have to learn to ignore him."

"Either that or buy a really big crane."

David grinned. "I hadn't thought of that, although I may have tried to knock it off a time or two myself without any luck. Anyway, I'm going into the city for a while myself. Kelly wanted to move some boxes. Something about exchanging winter stuff for summer stuff, or something like that."

Well, that was one chore she wouldn't have to worry about, wasn't it?

"Have fun," she told him.

"Yeah, see you later."

And just like that she was alone in the house.

Kat looked around. Okay, she wasn't completely, entirely alone. Harry and Jake and Mitch were around somewhere. If not inside the house, then outside. She was safe.

A shudder ran down the length of her back.

Stop it. Everything's fine.

Why, then, didn't it feel that way?

HARRY TRIED to concentrate on the job at hand. Which wasn't easy considering he'd rather be inside the house with Kathryn lingering over the last of the coffee, perhaps talking about things in the paper. Anything other than dealing with the predicament he wished Kat had never been placed in.

He'd walked the perimeter of the McCoy place so often he'd swear he'd worn a groove through the grass. First he skirted the house, checking for anything out of place, scanning the surrounding shrubs, and then he went farther out, making sure there were no cars in sight, anyone who wasn't supposed to be there. After that he crossed in front of the stables and then the new construction.

He paused there, at the new house. He'd never been one for the whole white picket fence thing. Then again, neither had any of the McCoys a short time ago and look what had happened to them. All of them married, and happily at that.

Harry hadn't given marriage much thought before because there hadn't been much reason to. He always thought it strange that people would approach life like that. Twenty-five? Time to get married.

Now he understood the desire to stake a claim on someone, make her his. Not just now, but forever.

He recognized the need to wake up to the same person every morning, go to bed holding the same person every night. He even realized that not a moment went by that this same person wasn't on his mind.

More specifically, Kathryn.

He looked up at the front bedroom where he and Kathryn had made love the day before. What they'd done seemed incredible to him now, when he wasn't caught up in the heat of passion. All the McCoys had been nearby. There had been a long list of other matters to address. And all he'd been able to focus on was his overwhelming need to feel her flesh filling his hands. To sink deep into her sleek wetness.

He released the porch hand railing and rounded the other side of the house, thinking it would be better if he were a little more on his guard. While the McCoy place was remote, it wasn't untouchable. Until the killer was caught, no place was. And he'd have to remember that if he was going to protect Kathryn.

"Hey, Harry," Mitch's head popped around the corner of the stables when Harry reached them. "I need to make a run into the next town over for some feed. I'm bringing Jake with me to help. Can you spare us?"

He waved him off. "Sure. David and Sean are still inside. We're covered."

"Great. Be back in forty-five. Hour at the most."

As Harry finished his sweep of the area behind

the stables he heard Mitch's truck start up and drive down the road. He rounded the barn, coming to a halt as something struck him as odd. More specifically, certain missing somethings.

The only car in the drive was his.

Shit.

He hurried for the house even as he fumbled for his cell. Where in the hell had everybody gone?

KAT CLEANED UP the rest of the kitchen, you know, those parts men always either conveniently forgot or didn't much pay attention to. She wiped the counters down, mopped up some spilled milk in the fridge…then stood staring at the machine in the corner that monitored the transmitter planted in her briefcase.

She crossed her arms over her chest and squinted at the mystifying piece of machinery. She forgot for a moment who would want to follow her, and how they'd put the electronic into her briefcase and focused instead on how the machine worked. On a small television-like monitor a steady green line indicated that the transmitter was nearby. She could tell that by looking near the door where she'd propped her briefcase against the wall.

She shook her head as if to clear it then thought to go upstairs and make her bed. She took a step and the steady line arced high indicating that whoever had planted the transmitter in her briefcase was not only tracking her, he was very nearby.

Kat stood stock still, her heart feeling like it had lodged in her throat. Through the corner of her eye she considered the machine. Maybe it was something she'd done. Maybe there was something on her person that had caused the machine to react. She moved slightly back to where she'd been and the spike went down.

Okay. That was creepy.

She moved forward again and the line arced upward.

Yikes.

She wildly looked around. Should she call out for Harry? For her brothers? Incredibly, she seemed incapable of all but the smallest sound just then, a noise not unlike a squeak.

When she'd initially spotted the machine, she actually hadn't thought it would come to use. Maybe she'd allowed herself the luxury of thinking she was safe because the ranch was so isolated or because there was so much testosterone around.

She realized how very, very wrong she'd been....

CHAPTER TWENTY-THREE

SEAN PULLED IN FRONT of the flower shop. Since it was closed on Sunday, he'd fully expected to find Wilhemenia at home. When she wasn't, and since it was too early for church, he'd decided to drive by the shop. And there parked right in front was her car...and Walter Purdy's.

He gripped and released the steering wheel several times. He'd never known her to go into work on a Sunday.

Maybe it's not work she's doing, a voice whispered.

Before he'd known that was what he was going to do, he was standing outside the shop, trying the door handle. Locked. And the Closed sign was turned to face out. He looked inside, not seeing anyone, then knocked.

Walter's was the first face he saw. And he looked about as happy to see him as Sean felt seeing Walter.

The other man turned and went into the back. Was he ignoring him?

Sean knocked again, this time more insistently.

Finally Wilhemenia appeared and hurried across the shop floor to unlock the door.

"Sean," she said, obviously surprised.

"Wilhemenia. I stopped by the house. When you weren't there, I tried here."

"Oh. Yes. Walter asked that I come in and help with arrangements for the Hopkins funeral."

I bet, Sean thought, not liking the green-eyed monster that was rapidly growing in size inside him.

"Sean," Walter said, coming back out, looking far too dapper in his tweed jacket, pressed slacks and bowtie.

"Walter," he said back.

"Look, since Wilhemenia's not ready to tell you, I will. Your marriage is over. Has been for some time. So why don't you just make it easy on all of us and move on?"

"Walter!" Wilhemenia gasped.

Sean's blood level rose. He looked back and forth from his wife to this man who was telling him the state of his marital relationship. He opened his mouth when his cell phone gave a shrill chirp.

Wilhemenia stared at him, her expression going from shock to disappointment.

Sean tilted his phone so he could read the display. The screen read 911 with five exclamations behind it.

Kathryn…

"I've got to go," he said.

"I hope you'll finally come to your senses and make it for good," Walter said.

Sean continued to the door, then at the last minute turned and strode purposefully toward the too pretty florist. Sean grabbed a handful of expensive shirt in his hand and yanked Walter so they were face-to-face.

"The next time you speak to me, buster, it will be with respect. And never again will you speak to me about my wife and the status of my relationship with her, do you hear me?"

"Is that a threat?" Walter asked, although he was clearly concerned for his physical well-being.

"You're damn right it is. And next time it won't be my hand in your shirt, it will be my fist in your face, you got it?"

He heard Wilhemenia's gasp and turned to face her.

"And you. I want you to go home—to our home—now and wait for me. When I call later, you'd better be there."

When he walked through the door it was with a great deal more pride than he'd had when he'd entered.

HARRY BURST INSIDE the kitchen, his heart hammering out an ominous rhythm in his chest. The first thing he became aware of was the whine of the transponder on the counter.

The killer is here...

The next thing he became aware of was that Kathryn was nowhere to be seen.

"Kathryn?" he called out, striding through the first floor.

How had this happened? How had it turned out that he'd left Kathryn alone and no one was around for backup?

He took his pistol out of his shoulder holster and flipped off the safety. Everything over the past half hour played out in his mind. They'd all allowed themselves to be lulled into a false sense of safety. Just the window of opportunity the killer had been looking for.

He climbed the old wood stairs, careful to stay to the side and make as little noise as possible while still moving quickly. He checked the first three bedrooms. At the fourth, he readjusted his grip on his pistol then pushed open the door with his left hand.

Kathryn's surprised gasp suffused his tense muscles.

"Oh, thank God!" she cried. "I thought it was..."

She didn't have to say who she'd thought it was. They'd both known.

She threw herself into his arms. "I heard the alarm on that stupid machine in the kitchen and I freaked and ran up here."

Harry allowed himself a moment to enjoy the

feel of her body pressed against his, relieved to find her safe and sound.

"Put the gun down. Now."

Harry turned toward the door, automatically tucking Kathryn behind him. Rather than putting his gun down, he turned on a masked man of about his height, dressed completely in black who was pointing an equally lethal weapon at him.

"You shoot me, I shoot you and Kathryn goes free. Is that part of the plan?" Harry asked.

"No. I shoot you, you drop, and I take Kat is more how I see things going down."

Harry heard Kathryn's gasp from behind him where she held the back of his shirt in her fists.

"We're not alone," Harry said.

The masked man chuckled. "You couldn't be more alone. I've been watching this place for three days. I know exactly where everyone is. And they're not here."

"James?"

Harry could hear the shock in Kathryn's voice, as if she was seeing a ghost.

And perhaps she was.

The gunman reached up and took off his mask.

Darin Ichatious aka James Smith.

Jesus.

He'd never stopped to consider that all this had been a ruse. That Darin hadn't been killed at all but had masterminded his own demise. His own personal, specialized brand of witness relocation. Kill off James Smith and Darin Ichatious could assume another identity somewhere else. Or maybe not even somewhere else, but in DC.

"Hello, Kat," he said in a soft way Harry didn't like at all.

Kathryn didn't appear to know how to process the information she was presented with. And Harry couldn't blame her.

"Why?" Kathryn whispered, appearing unaware of her movements as she shifted from behind Harry and into the line of fire.

Harry jerked her back. "Stay here," he ordered.

She didn't appear to register his words. Instead her attention was focused on the man who had been her fiancé. A man who had died in front of her eyes. A man she had been arrested for killing.

"Why?" she asked again.

"I'm sorry, Kat. I never meant to hurt you," Darin said, tucking his mask into the waist of his dark slacks, his gun trained on them. "You were never supposed to know I didn't die that night in your kitchen. The emptying of your bank accounts was supposed to have been blamed on identity theft. Still…I'm a little surprised that after all this, you didn't have an inkling I was still alive."

"My fiancé was murdered. Why would I have believed any differently?" she whispered.

Harry cursed himself for not seeing the signs.

He'd been so distracted by the subject he'd been protecting he hadn't been paying enough attention to the person he was protecting her from.

"The gun," Darin said again.

Harry felt Kathryn's fists in the back of his shirt again.

In that one moment he knew he'd do anything to protect her. Even if that meant giving up his firearm.

He released the clip, dropped it to the floor, then bent down to put the gun down as well.

"Good. Very good." Darin said. "You know, you surprise me, Kincaid. Seducing the grieving fiancée only days after the death of her groom. Isn't there an agency rule against that? If not, surely your own moral code should have stopped you from doing something so low."

Having his and Kathryn's relationship referred to in that way made Harry want to pick his gun back up and shoot Darin in the head. But he didn't like the setup in this room. In here, if he didn't hit his target then a retaliating bullet meant for him might hit Kathryn. And he couldn't take that chance.

"Move," Darin said, stepping out into the hall and motioning with his gun for them to follow.

Keeping Kathryn behind him, Harry edged toward the door, then pulled her to precede him down the hall, her at his front, Darin at his back.

"When I say run, run," he whispered into her ear.

He was rewarded with the gun sharply pushed into his back. "You forget, I did what I did to a woman I loved. So just imagine how expendable *you* are to me," Darin told him.

Harry knew Darin was here for Kathryn, although for what purpose he couldn't be entirely sure. Although he felt the pieces were hovering around him waiting to be grabbed.

Down the stairs they went. Just short of the bottom, Harry shoved Kathryn, "Run!"

She did.

As expected, Darin raised the gun to shoot at her and Harry took full advantage, grabbing his arm and aiming it for the ceiling. The resulting tussle caused Darin to lose his footing and Harry tried to compensate. They both tumbled the rest of the way down the stairs, Harry's hands tightly holding Darin's gun arm out of the way.

"Let me go!" he heard Kathryn shout from the direction of the kitchen.

He looked that way, giving Darin the opportunity to gain the upper hand.

"Drop the gun," he heard for the second time in so many minutes. Only this time it wasn't Darin saying the words.

He became aware of the change in atmosphere when Darin slumped in defeat. He looked to see four black-clad men, well-armed, filing into the room from the kitchen, surrounding them. The last one held Kathryn hostage.

Darin dropped the gun. At their bidding, he slid it across the floor until one of the men stopped it with his foot.

Harry got to his feet. "Which agency are you with?" he asked the unfamiliar men.

They looked at each other, then back at him.

Harry reached for his own ID to the sound of the arming of automatic weapons.

"Whoa. Just getting my wallet. I'm U.S. Marshal Harry Kincaid. The woman you're holding is a witness under the protection of the U.S. justice department."

One of the men faded back into the kitchen, speaking quietly into a hand-held radio.

Darin stood up as well. "I'm the protected witness, not her."

Harry stared at him. "No, James Smith was the one under protection. James Smith is dead."

And Harry wished he'd stayed that way.

Kathryn looked more afraid than he'd ever seen her. And there was nothing he could do to help her. That hurt him more than any bullet.

"What…what's going on?" she asked.

The man tightened his grip and she gasped.

"Which agency are you with?" Harry demanded again, his palms itching with the need to hit the guy who was causing Kathryn pain.

"We're not with any agency."

It was then the pieces swarming around coalesced into a clear picture.

He turned to where Darin was rubbing his jaw and eyeing the gun one of the men still had his foot on.

Harry said, "You were blackmailing Conrad Bowman, weren't you? The three of you—you, Bowman and Newton Granger—were in on the Russian campaign money scam together but you made a deal three years ago not to include Bowman in your testimony. Just so long as he kept giving you the money you wanted. Money you used to feed your expensive gambling habits."

Darin wiped his mouth with the back of a gloved hand. "Have it all figured out, do you, Kincaid?"

"I know that when Newton Granger was released, that made the equation two against one; rather than turning on Bowman for allowing you to convict him, he reunited with his old cohort against you. What's the saying? Your enemy's enemy is your friend?"

"Is that why you emptied my bank accounts?" Kathryn asked quietly. "You needed money?"

She didn't have to say it, but lingering there in the air was that she would have given him money if he'd only asked.

"Oh, he needed money, all right," Harry said. "Not for gambling debts, but to disappear because he knew Granger and Bowman would come after him, make sure he never testified against anyone again. Only he hadn't planned on dropping the passbook to the account that held the big money. He left it lying next to the already dead body he'd arranged to disfigure so it would be mistaken for him. A ploy guaranteed to work when some well-placed money resulted in the body in question being cremated before an identifying autopsy could be performed." He shook his head, gazing into Kathryn's stricken eyes. "All along we'd thought the passbook was left purposely to frame you."

Kathryn's voice sounded reedy. "Is that why you tried to kidnap me? It was you, wasn't it? You tried to take me so I'd have to give you the money when the authorities unfroze the account?" Tears were bright in her eyes.

Harry cursed that Darin was still capable of hurting her.

"Why? Why did you choose to use me as a front?" she whispered.

Darin had the good graces to look reluctant. "In the beginning you were an easy target. A train stop along the way. You had money. You were low profile. And you were easy to manipulate."

Harry watched Kathryn flinch at his words.

"Only I never planned on falling for you," Darin continued.

Kathryn's swallow was loud in the quiet room.

"But that didn't matter, did it? Not in the end. You already had your plan made and you were going to follow it through no matter what."

Peripherally Harry caught movement.

He finished what Darin hadn't. "It's my guess he targeted you because you didn't have any family to interfere."

There was the sound of several guns being cocked in addition to the guns already present as each and every one of the McCoy men stepped out of the shadows, every gunman and Darin covered.

"Meet the family," Connor said, looking more dangerous than any other man in the room.

CHAPTER TWENTY-FOUR

KAT'S HEAD SPUN. The metallic sound of guns being cocked filled her ears, the smell of gun oil and gunpowder assaulted her nose, and the arms holding her tightened until she couldn't breathe.

"Let the woman go," her father said from where he aimed a gun of his own at the man behind her.

"We're not interested in the woman," came the response.

"Then you wouldn't mind releasing her now, would you?" Jake said, stepping further forward and aiming his weapon at the temple of one of the other armed gunmen.

Kat was shoved toward Harry and he easily caught her. Her heart beat so hard in her chest she was half surprised it didn't explode altogether.

"No one needs to get hurt," said what appeared to be the lead gunman. He was the one who'd grabbed her in the kitchen. "Just let us have Ichatious and we'll leave. We were never even here."

"No can do," Connor ground out. "No one breaks into our house."

Sean touched Connor's shoulder. "Listen to what the man is saying."

"No!" Kathryn said. "If you let them take James—Darin—they'll kill him."

Harry's fingers tightened on her arms.

"And your point would be?" Connor asked.

Kat stared at him as if seeing him for the first time. And in a sense she was. Never had she witnessed such sheer violence on his face. She had little doubt that he meant what he was saying. He didn't care if these men shot James in cold blood right here in the living room.

A part of her told her he was doing it for her. That by putting her at risk James had brought this anger and need for revenge on himself.

Another part of her knew she'd do what she had to to save James's life.

"Faking his own death and stealing my money isn't a capital offense, Connor," she said strongly, trying to shrug off Harry's grip no matter how much she'd like to melt into his arms and pretend none of this was happening. "You let them take him and you're playing judge, jury and executioner."

"You don't let us take him and we kill you all," the gunman said.

"Says who?" Marc asked. He'd moved behind the man in question and was pressing his firearm against the side of his neck.

Sudden movement.

Kat found herself being pushed into Harry again as James brushed past and made a run for it.

"No!" she shouted as he used the distraction to dive for the kitchen and freedom.

The gunmen turned all their guns on her.

"At ease," Sean said.

And just like that the McCoys dropped their firearms to their sides.

The gunmen went after James.

"No!" Kat shouted, trying to run after them.

A lone gunshot outside froze her in midstep.

MUCH LATER that night Sean turned into his driveway in Bedford. A single light shone in the window. He stared at it, his mind filled with the image of Kathryn's face when she'd realized James Smith aka Darin Ichatious had been shot. Never in his life had he witnessed such an expression of horror. And if he could have changed what had happened, he would have in an instant, if only to spare her.

After she'd gotten a hold of herself, she'd packed her things and asked to borrow Liz's car. Nothing anyone could say to her could stop her from leaving. Could get her to talk about what she was feeling. Could urge her to forgive him.

They'd all had no choice but to let her go. Harry included. After all, her life was no longer at risk. The man who had placed her in jeopardy was dead, his body removed by the men who had shot him. Then the black-clad figures had all disappeared into the shadows as quickly as they'd appeared.

Sean dry washed his face with his hands. Had he made a mistake? Should he have done as his daughter wished and insisted the men leave without Ichatious? But with what outcome?

He supposed what he could be thankful for was that the plan he and the boys put together had worked. It seemed a shame they had left Harry out of this particular ruse, but it had worked the way they'd thought. While Sean had really left the house that morning to drive into Bedford, his five boys hadn't done the things they'd said they were leaving to do. Instead they'd dropped back, never more than a minute away from the house. They'd known their apparent absence would tempt the killer from the shadows. And they'd been right.

Movement caught his attention and he looked to see Wilhemenia had opened the front door and stood silhouetted by the light within. He blinked then absently reached for the handle, in some strange way her appearance a beacon he felt desperate to reach despite the problems that plagued their marriage.

He climbed the two porch steps and she opened the door for him. They stood like that staring at each other for long moments.

"Are you all right?" she asked, her gaze taking him in.

He nodded. He was as right as he was going to be. "Thanks for being home."

Was he imagining things or was she smiling at him? "I wouldn't have dared not be home."

He remembered the scene at the shop earlier. Yanking Walter by his shirtfront and threatening him. Demanding that his wife be home when he returned.

He made a move to apologize for his behavior, then changed his mind when he saw the warm expression on his wife's face.

"I've never seen you so jealous before," she said quietly.

Sean grimaced.

"I…in a strange sort of way, I liked it."

He looked at her long and hard.

He'd been just going through the motions for so long that he realized it had been a good long time since he'd shown his wife any genuine emotion. His display of anger earlier must have driven something home for her.

He realized that part of their problem had stemmed from him thinking he needed to be the type of man a woman like Wilhemenia would want. The type of man who went to church on Sunday, who didn't sweat when asked to wear a tie, who was appropriate for a woman of her standing in the community.

The type of man like Walter Purdy.

Who knew that Walter wasn't what she wanted at all? That it would turn out she wanted him?

"Come here you ole he-man you," she whispered and grabbed him by the front of his shirt and tugged him inside.

KAT SAT IN THE MIDDLE of the king-size bed in a downtown hotel room, her knees folded to her chest, her eyes unfocused on the television, the images flashing from CNN providing nothing but a blur of color.

James had been alive…

She remembered his bloodied face that night a week ago. She recalled every tear she'd shed for him. The nights she'd spent in a county jail arrested for his murder. And he'd been alive all along…

She knew her thoughts were both an attempt at self-preservation and distraction. She didn't want to think about her family standing back and allowing a man to be killed in exchange for her own life. She didn't want to think about her watching him die twice.

She pressed the heels of her hands against her temples to try to stem her tears and began rocking back and forth.

Was the price of a human life so tiny? Worth little more than a rabid dog taken out back and shot?

She winced at her choice of words.

While she hadn't seen James's body this second

time around, she had little doubt that he was now truly gone.

And what was sadder still was that she was the only one in the entire world who seemed to care.

Harry had tried to keep her from leaving the McCoy house. Had attempted to plead with her, to get her to look at him, gaze into his eyes, but she couldn't. He'd been part of what had happened. And she didn't know if she could forgive him for that.

And that's what hurt the most.

A soft knock sounded at the door.

Kat's head snapped up and she scrubbed at the tears flooding her cheeks. She couldn't be sure if it was actually the door or if the sound had come from the television.

Another knock.

"Kathryn?"

Harry.

Her heart squeezed so hard in her chest it took her breath away.

"Kathryn, I know you're in there. I'm not going anywhere until you let me in."

She tried to make sense out of the images flickering on the screen, put the voices with the faces.

"I'll stay here all night if I have to."

She got up, opened the door, then went back to sit in the middle of the bed.

She didn't look at him. Couldn't. But she couldn't let him stand in the hall waiting, either.

For a moment she thought maybe he'd stayed out in the hall and let the door close on him. Then he moved into blurry sight between her and the television.

"Are you all right?" he asked softly.

She didn't say anything. Didn't have anything to say.

He sat on the bed in front of her, putting his face at eye level. She dropped her gaze to the bedspread.

"Kathryn, I just want to say how sorry—"

She made a soft sound. "Don't. Don't try telling me you're sorry James is dead. Because we both know you'd be lying."

"That's not what I was going to say."

She waited.

"What I was going to say is that I'm sorry you're hurting so much. I'm sorry I couldn't protect you today, that I couldn't stop you from having to watch that happen."

Her chest burned from the inside out.

Neither of them said anything for what seemed like a long time. She vaguely registered that the show that had been on had ended and another had come on. She listened to Harry breathing. She wiped away tears that she couldn't seem to stop.

He got up from the bed, clearly agitated. "Damn it, Kat, haven't you cried enough for that no-good son of a bitch?" He grasped her shoulders, pulling her to the side of the bed and forcing her to look up at him. "What is it about him that you're grieving for him all over again?"

She blinked at him, steadily holding his angry gaze. "You don't get it, do you? No, no. Of course you wouldn't." She swallowed back the emotion in her throat. "This…my crying…it isn't about James…Darin. It's about me. It's about my having to watch him die…twice. About knowing there was something I could have said, something I could have done, to stop it from happening the second time."

"Jesus—"

She grasped his powerful forearms, pleading with him to listen. "It's about my valuing life apparently more than any of you do. It doesn't matter how much money James took or how much he hurt me. He didn't deserve to die."

She watched his face shutter.

"It's about me not knowing how to love with conditions. When I love, Harry, I love all the way." She let him go. "The same way I love you."

MUCH LATER that night Harry lay wide awake in his own bed, marveling at what had happened at the hotel earlier. "I love you" usually meant the beginning of a relationship.

With him and Kathryn it had marked the end.

He pushed from the mattress, nearly stepping on Bob where he lay sprawled across the floor.

"Sorry, buddy," he muttered and stepped over him.

He stalked to the kitchen where he took a long swig from the water bottle he kept in the fridge. But the cold liquid did little to cool his body temperature or clear his mind. If anything it woke him up and made him feel everything even more intensely.

Bottle in hand, he leaned his forearm against the freezer door and stood there for long moments, concentrating on little more than his breathing.

The sharp memory of Kathryn's broken voice made it seem like she stood right next to him as she said, "I can't explain what happened between us over the past week, Harry. And I won't ignore that it happened. But I can't…I mean where…what do we do now?"

He hadn't had an answer. Not then. Not now.

"Everything I knew before is gone," she'd said. "And I've been dropped into this…parallel universe where nothing seems to make sense. Nothing but the way I feel." She seemed to plead with him with her eyes. "But I can't trust that, can I? I loved James. And obviously that was so very, very wrong."

"Kathryn, I…"

"No, please don't. I…I can't. Not now." Her swallow had sounded loud in the quiet hotel room. "Maybe not ever."

Harry knocked his forehead against his forearm. *Maybe not ever…*

The words reverberated through his mind, driving him mad with the possibility.

No, he hadn't planned to fall for Kathryn. It wasn't as if he'd been glad when he'd thought her fiancé had been murdered. Like he'd cheered when he'd learned she was free. Then when he'd taken her into protective custody, it wasn't as if he'd purposely set out to take advantage of her vulnerability.

It had just happened.

"Oh, that's a hell of an explanation," he said harshly to himself.

Bob meowed where he was winding around and around Harry's ankles, his coarse fur scratching his bare skin. The cat's battle scars came from having spent so much time on the streets before. Harry had taken him, every scratch and missing patch of hair a testament to his experiences. But where you could see his scars, Harry's weren't as apparent. They were buried deep within him.

He wasn't used to this. Wasn't familiar with this…aching. Who would have thought that emotional pain could manifest itself in such a physical way? Sometimes it seemed as if the mere act of drawing a breath was too much of a burden. His chest stung in a way that had he not been in such good shape, he would have feared he was at risk of coronary failure.

He'd come into the kitchen to get a drink of water and here he was, long minutes later not having moved from in front of the refrigerator. He forced himself to open the door and put the water away.

Bob meowed at him but all he could do was stare at the tom.

When his mother had died five years ago, a victim of pneumonia when she'd thought all it had been was a chest cold, he'd mourned. What surprised him was how very similar the emotions he was feeling now were to the grief he had experienced then.

But Kathryn hadn't died. Kathryn was alive if not completely well and a short ways across town in a hotel room. She'd looked tiny and vulnerable in the middle of that huge king-size bed when he'd gone to see her. And even though he could physically touch her, he hadn't been able to reach her.

"Please, leave," she'd said to him when they couldn't seem to connect. Nothing of what she was saying made sense to him and nothing he had to say moved her.

"I can't do that, Kathryn," he'd told her, afraid if he walked out that door, left her like that, he'd never be able to make his way back.

"You don't have a choice. I want you to leave and so you'll leave."

And he had left. Reluctantly. Hoping against hope that she'd change her mind. That perhaps they could try to work this out. That he could spend the night there holding her in the way he yearned to hold her. Soothe her pain although he couldn't understand it.

Only he understood it now, didn't he? At least a bit of it. She had lost everything. Had been yanked from her moorings and set afloat on a sea that would never let her find homeport again.

And he had tried to tempt her into anchoring next to him.

But what did he have to offer her? At best he was a workaholic with no life outside his career. At worst, he was a loner who'd rather read about the opera than go to one.

He remembered her final words as he held the hotel room door open, about to exit.

"Thank you," she'd whispered.

At first he'd thought he'd misheard her, imagined the words.

"Thank you for saving my life. In more ways than you'll ever know."

But it had been she who had saved his life, hadn't it? She who had reached inside him and grabbed his heart tightly, forcing life and color into his listless and gray world. She who had showed him what it meant to love. Truly love.

And then she had taken it all away from him.

CHAPTER TWENTY-FIVE

THE FOLLOWING MORNING Sean lingered in bed, his wife resting in the crook of his arm. Her hair smelled fresh. Her body felt supple and warm next to his.

Hell, if he'd known that showing a little jealousy could have accomplished this, he'd have done it years ago when he'd first caught Walter Purdy looking at Wilhemenia in a way he hadn't particularly liked.

On the nightstand his cell phone vibrated. He lazily reached for it and read the text message from Mitch. "Can't get thru 2 Kat."

He put the phone back down and drew a deep breath, the memory of his daughter's face the day before weighing heavily on him.

Wilhemenia shifted. "Penny for your thoughts."

"A penny is more than they're worth," he said.

Her gaze was steady on him.

Damn she was beautiful. He found it difficult to believe that he'd nearly let her slip through his fingers.

She laid her head back down on his shoulder and was quiet for a long moment before she said, "You're going to have to start sharing things with me, Sean."

He raised his eyebrows.

She gestured slowly with her hand. "I feel like these last four years we've been leading separate lives. You with your job and me with mine. You with your family and…well, my family is part of your family," she said referring to the fact that her daughter Melanie and his son Marc were married with kids.

He knew she was right, but he didn't know how to change it.

He didn't realize he'd said the words aloud until she was looking at him again.

"You can start by telling me what you were just thinking when I offered you a penny."

How could he? "It was more of a feeling than a thought.

"What was the feeling?"

He stretched his neck then burrowed his chin back into his chest to meet her gaze again. "Fear."

She blinked. "Of what?"

"That my daughter will never forgive me. That I'll never be able to get this…sharing thing right. That if I don't learn how to share with you I'll lose you forever."

He'd only meant to tell her about Kathryn. So he

was more surprised than she was that he'd said all he had.

The moisture in her eyes took his breath away.

"Aw, hell. If I'd have known it would make you cry, I would never have said anything."

She laughed. "I'm not crying because I'm sad, Sean. I'm crying because I'm happy."

He didn't get it. And he was afraid he never would.

"Have you never cried?" she asked.

"Of course I have."

She shifted away from him and began getting out of bed.

"Where do you think you're going?" he grumbled, tugging her back into his arms.

She giggled. Giggled. He remembered her doing it a few times in the beginning. But not in a long, long time. He realized he'd missed hearing the sound.

"I've got to get to the shop."

"You mean Purdy hasn't fired you?"

"Fired me? He's probably afraid you'll…beat him up, or whatever you want to call it, if he so much as dares say an off-color word in my presence."

Sean grinned and pulled her even closer. "Good. Then he and my superiors won't mind if we take a much needed day off, will they?"

KAT FOUND IT hard to believe five days had passed since she'd last seen any of her family...and Harry. It seemed like just yesterday. Yet a lifetime ago.

She sat stiffly in the back of the hired car in a simple black dress, watching as rain soaked the view through her window of the Capitol building. After a day of being holed up in her hotel room with the curtains drawn, she'd forced herself to start moving again. And move she had. Without the help of her brothers or Harry she'd found out that James's... Darin's body had been found washed up on the shores of the Potomac. She'd agreed to identify the remains, but only through carefully taken photos.

She'd also agreed to see to his burial arrangements.

The contractors had made significant improvements on her townhouse and had told her that while work wouldn't be finished for a while she could move back in by the end of the week. But she didn't know if she wanted to go back to a place that...well, a place that no longer reflected her as a person. So she'd rented a furnished apartment in a more ethnically mixed area of the city on a month-by-month basis until she figured out what would suit her.

She'd also put in her resignation at the law firm, the thought of eighty-hour workweeks also no longer appealing to her. She was already in the opening stages of starting her own practice, taking with her a good half of her clients.

She'd acquired a new client who was facing the death penalty for grabbing a gun and killing her husband and his best friend when they'd been chasing her down to rape her, apparently something they'd been doing for years. If a small part of the reason she'd taken it on was because despite her efforts she hadn't been able to save Joseph Alan Greer, well, she wasn't saying anything. All she could hope was that this case would have a better outcome.

She was thankful her brothers had given her some much-needed time alone. Well, at least a little. Starting that first night they'd taken turns calling the cell phone she'd bought. She had no idea how they'd tracked the number. Scratch that. Any one of them probably could have easily gotten the number given their connections. At any rate, she hadn't started returning the calls until two days had passed. And only then because Connor had shown up on her doorstep, arms crossed over his impressive chest, demanding to know why she was shutting her family out.

Her family…

Even now the mere idea gave her cause for hope.

Yesterday she'd even gone out to lunch with her father. She smiled softly as her fingers played with the necklace she wore. She wasn't sure when she'd begun to think of him as "Dad" or "her father," but she was glad she had. He'd given her a plain cardboard box full of items.

"Some of your mother's things I thought you might like to have," he'd explained. "Wilhemenia came out to the house and helped me put them together for you."

She'd been touched beyond words. Even now she wore the small cameo that held a wedding picture of Kathryn and Sean McCoy, and pearl earrings she'd found in a handmade jewelry case.

But that was yesterday. Today…today she was going to bury James.

She'd contacted James's…Darin's mother again twice, once by phone, once by telegram, letting her know of the funeral arrangements should she want to attend. She'd received pretty much the same response she'd gotten the first time around. Which meant that on this rainy May day it would be her and James's casket and a pastor she'd arranged to read the final rites.

The cemetery lay on the outskirts of the city. Nothing fancy. A small plot behind a small church. She'd arranged for only the burial, seeing no point in going any farther than that given everything that had happened. She had received a small, handwritten card from James's one-time secretary, Janet Talbert, offering condolences and apologizing for not being able to attend today.

The car pulled into the narrow road that wound through the cemetery. Here the rain had stopped but a fine mist filled the air, making it thick and milky.

She indicated where the car should go and it stopped next to where a small tent had been erected over the casket bearing a modest floral arrangement that had been sent over by Wilhemenia.

The driver opened the door for her and provided an umbrella. She thanked him and walked over to meet the pastor who was standing alone off to the side of the site.

"Miss Buckingham," he said.

"Actually, it's McCoy," she corrected. Something else she'd done over the past few days was officially change her name to Kathryn Buckingham McCoy.

He smiled at her kindly. "Miss McCoy. Will anyone else be joining us?"

She shook her head. "No. This is it."

"Very well. We'll begin in a moment then."

She nodded, glad that he'd not registered surprise at her pronouncement that she was the only one who'd be attending.

Moments later, he began reading from his Bible.

Kat stood numbly staring at the casket, listening to the pastor's words, when she realized she was no longer alone.

The pastor paused, looking over her shoulder. Perhaps a visitor to one of the other sites.

"Pastor," she heard the unmistakable sound of her father's voice as he stepped next to her and took her arm.

"'Morning," Connor said, coming to stand on her other side.

And just like that, she was no longer alone. Her father and every last one of her brothers were with her.

For the first time that day she felt moved to tears. Not for the lone man lying in the casket but for the men that had come to the funeral dressed in their Sunday best just for her.

The pastor finished and shook hands with each of her family members as Connor began leading her away.

"The women are back at the house cooking up a storm, you know, for a memorial dinner," he said, his chin coming up. She wasn't sure if it was because his tie was too tight or if the words "memorial dinner" had been stuck in his throat—probably a mixture of both—it didn't matter. She responded by hugging him and kissing him on the cheek.

"Hey, where's mine?" David asked.

And then she was in the arms of all of her brothers.

As they led her to her father's car—apparently someone had paid off her hired car and sent it away—she caught sight of another man standing a few rows on the other side of James's plot and slightly behind a tree.

Harry.

"Are you coming, sis?" Mitch asked as he held the car door open for her.

"Huh? Oh, yes." She smiled at him as he handed her in.

The door closed and they drove away, Harry's silhouette growing farther and farther away.

A COUPLE OF DAYS LATER Harry stood outside Kathryn's law offices. He knew she only had a few days left at the firm. Even knew where she was shopping for her new office. It was just after five. He looked at his watch. Kathryn would be coming out just about…

Now.

She didn't see him. Which wasn't surprising because he was concealed behind a large stone column. But every time he was this close he half-expected her to sense his presence. Look his way.

But she never did.

He'd been following her ever since the night she'd asked him to leave her hotel room. He hadn't been able to sleep so he'd driven to her hotel and sat outside until she'd finally emerged the following day. And since then he'd barely left her presence. He told himself he was doing it just in case the hired gunmen who had taken Darin out had a change of heart and came after her. But he knew that was a lie.

He found it ironic that he'd come full circle. From watching her because of her connection to

Darin Ichatious, to watching her now because he couldn't bear to go without watching her.

The most difficult part had been seeing her standing alone at Ichatious's burial plot while the pastor read from his Bible. He'd been about to join her when the McCoys had surprised him by pulling up.

He hadn't tried to approach her since.

He rounded the column as she walked toward the parking garage across the street where she would get in her Lexus then drive to her new apartment a short ways away. He headed to where his SUV was parked up the block and got behind the wheel, waiting.

She pulled out of the garage and he let a couple of cars separate them before he fell into place behind her.

Every day he expected his ache for her to lessen. And every day he was disappointed when the ache merely grew stronger. Even Bob had seemed to become disgusted with Harry's constant absences and moping and had taken up residence with Mrs. Steinhaufer across the hall.

A few traffic lights and a couple of turns and he stopped two blocks up from Kathryn's four-story walkup. It wasn't Georgetown, but neither was it the slums. The apartment buildings were old but not historic, neat but not stylish. He was surprised she was still living there when her townhouse appeared to be coming along nicely and was surely livable by now.

He'd been even more surprised still when he'd driven by her house after she'd gone to bed last night to find a discreet realtor's For Sale sign in the front window.

Kathryn parked her car and walked to her building door. Shrubs and trees blocked his view so Harry pulled closer. The instant he stopped he heard a knock on his passenger-side window.

Kathryn.

He pushed the door lock even though the doors were already unlocked, pushed it again, then reached over to open it rather than just the window.

"Hi," he said, as if he hadn't been caught sitting outside her apartment.

"Hi, yourself." She wore a crisp navy blue business suit with slacks, her blond hair loose and soft, a cameo at the hollow of her throat. "You know, I've been wondering if you were ever going to get up the guts to say something to me."

He stared at her.

"I know you've been following me for the past week."

Jeez. He'd thought he'd been careful. What did it say about his prowess as a marshal if he couldn't even trail a civilian?

"At first I more sensed you than saw you. Then a few days ago I made a couple of maneuvers to force you out."

The supermarket. He'd had a feeling she'd seen him.

She seemed to be studying him, her face sober, her beautiful eyes full of pain. "At first I thought you were trying to find the courage to approach me. But I just now realized that you weren't, were you? You've just been following me."

Harry felt awkward sitting inside the car the way he was while she stood outside. He pushed open his door and climbed out only to find her walking toward her apartment.

Damn.

She turned near the front steps. "Are you coming?"

He hesitated. He'd crossed this line once. He didn't want to cross it again with the same results.

Kathryn wrapped her arms around her waist as if to ward off a shiver.

"I don't know if it's a good idea," he said.

A good ten feet separated them. Ten feet and the entire world.

"I see," she said quietly, glancing down at the sidewalk.

Neither of them said anything for a long time. Then finally she looked up at him again.

"You know, I'm still not really ready for…this. For you."

Harry grimaced. This was why she'd forced his hand? To tell him to get lost again?

"I wasn't ready for you before either," she continued, "but I couldn't help myself."

Obviously she'd gotten over that.

Harry looked up and down the street, anywhere but at her, as he tried to find the strength to weather another rejection.

"We'll have to take things slow."

He stared at her. "What?"

A soft smile warmed her face. "I said we'll have to take things slow. You know. Maybe a dinner here. A movie there."

His throat felt so tight he thought he might choke. So he nodded.

"Yes," she said, as if to herself. "Maybe it's finally time."

She turned to walk up the stairs.

Harry wanted to call out to her. To grab her and kiss her.

She turned again, wearing a sexily suggestive grin. "What are you doing tonight?"

Screw taking things slow...

As soon as she disappeared inside the door, he took the steps two at a time, grinning when he found her holding the door for him. He gathered her up into his arms, this angel of a woman who had transformed his life, taken over his heart, and kissed her with the intensity of every emotion he'd ever felt for her.

EPILOGUE

Four months later...

"BACK! FARTHER! Go, go, go!" Connor shouted.

Kat watched her oldest brother fake a couple of throws then launch the football to David who was waiting for it at the far end of the front yard. She and the women were sitting on the farmhouse porch watching the men play tackle football. They were divided into two teams of three with Harry playing on the side opposing Connor and David. The women heckled them and sometimes cheered them on but mostly tried to keep all the children out of the way of the action. On the other side of the porch on a swing made for two, her father and Wilhemenia sat, chatting like young lovers.

Kat tugged her gaze away from the lovebirds and watched as Harry took David down like he was a sack of feathers. The football tumbled from her brother's hands and Harry picked it up and ran in the opposite direction for the winning touchdown.

Harry, Marc and Mitch celebrated with some

hearty high fives and back patting as Connor led David and Jake to the porch, grumbling all the way. Bronte put her arms around Connor's waist. "Oh, don't worry, baby. You'll get 'em back next time."

Kat noticed the way her oldest brother's ears reddened at the special attention.

She was coming to realize that no matter how rough and tumble her brothers and Harry were, once you chipped away at their hard exteriors with sweet words they were putty in your hand.

Kat walked up to Harry and put her own arms around him.

Slow. That's what she'd said four months ago when she'd been ready to let him back into her heart. What that meant was that they spent one night a week apart if just to prove that they could. Of course, that one night would become history tonight. They were scheduled on a red-eye out of DC to Vegas.

She tried to prevent the smile that threatened, but realized she was fighting a losing battle. No, this time there wasn't to be any long engagement or hall rental or elaborate wedding. Last week over morning coffee at Harry's place he'd asked her to marry him and she'd said yes. No ring. No sappy promises. Just an agreement that they would spend the rest of their lives with each other.

Of course, she knew their elopement would upset and disappoint her family, all of whom were already ribbing Harry about monkey suits and rehearsal dinners. And they didn't even know about the proposal. But they would first thing tomorrow morning when she and Harry called from Vegas to tell them the news of their elopement.

"Enjoy your win while you can, Kincaid," Connor grumbled. "That won't be happening again."

The children were gathered around the couple on the opposite side of the porch, Wilhemenia holding the latest addition to the McCoy family, Jake and Michelle's third baby girl.

Kat patted Harry's stomach. "Think you guys are up for another round?"

Connor put his arm around her shoulders. "I'm up for kicking Harry's butt any day of the week."

"Ah, but I'm not talking about a rematch. I'm talking about guys versus girls."

Bronte, Michelle, Liz, Melanie and Kelly all looked at her.

"Well, maybe not Liz," she said with a wink.

She'd learned that morning that she wasn't the only one good at keeping secrets. All those kids Mitch had been begging Liz to have? Well, she was pregnant with the first of them. Only she hadn't told him yet.

Mitch homed in on Kat's words. "What? Why? What's the matter?" Mitch asked.

Liz took the football from Harry's hands. "There's not a thing wrong with me. And a girls versus guys game of tackle football sounds perfect."

"Tackle, what does she mean tackle?" Marc asked. "Tag. We'll play tag football."

Melanie poked him in the stomach. "Okay, you guys play tag, we'll play tackle. How does that sound?"

Judging by the look in Marc's eyes he was all for the idea.

Mitch was still stuck on what Kat had said. "What do you mean 'maybe not Liz'?"

Kat winked at him. "You'll have to ask her, big brother."

She gave Harry a kiss and a secretive glance before running out into the yard, motioning for Liz to throw her the ball.

Ah, yes. In a few short hours she would be Mrs. Harry Kincaid. But it was definitely McCoy blood that ran in her veins

*Everything you love about romance...**and more!***

Please turn the page for Signature Select™
Bonus Features.

Bonus Features:

A REAL McCOY

The Writing Life...
A day in the life of Lori and Tony
(aka Tori Carrington)

6:00 a.m.
Wake up five minutes before the alarm goes off to the smell of Tony's brewing coffee downstairs. I join him on the back deck where big steaming cuppas and glasses of orange juice and the morning papers await. I get the comics, the entertainment sections, the store flyers and read our daily horoscope; Tony gets the rest. A story about a sixty-five-year-old man in New York City shooting at hawks from his second-story roof with a twelve-gauge because they're bothering his pigeons provides our morning chuckle...and also gets the creative juices flowing.

7:00 a.m.
We feed the animals—three indoor cats, countless outdoor cats, a blue jay and squirrels—then go up to our shared office. Via the Internet Tony switches on a Greek radio station that stays on all day (think opa Zorba music) and we both check e-mail on our separate computers. Then while Tony meticulously maps out the plot for our next book, I compile all the

Post-it notes and little pieces of paper with snippets of dialogue and ideas one or the other of us jotted down the day before and decide which stand the test of time and which are tossed. We're both in deep immersion mode now, living in worlds that aren't ours but are of our making, spending time with characters that are as dear to us as family.

12:00 p.m.
Fifteen brilliant new pages in the can, our next story coming to exciting, vivid life, we knock off to make dinner. Today it's dolmathakia (stuffed grape leaves), feta, fresh bread and a nice boutari (red wine).

2:00 p.m.
After dinner we take our daily siesta, snuggling up together and allowing ourselves to dream about what we've accomplished so far that day, and what we hope to accomplish yet.

5:00 p.m.
We go for a brisk long walk through a nature preserve, hoping to glimpse deer, beavers and chipmunks and watching the old groundskeeper chat with the rose specialist. There's love there, we think, which reminds us of our own love.

6:15 p.m.
Our boys, Tony Jr. and Tim (adults now but they'll always be our "boys"), come by and we snack on salami and an array of cheeses and black olives on the back deck, all of us sharing details of our day and

talking about books we've read, movies we've seen and discussing questions that confound us or delight us.

8:00 p.m.
Tony and I head back up to the office. Deadline looming, so I write five more pages while Tony follows up on e-mail.

10:00 p.m.
Conversation sparks. I put my feet up on my desk, Tony leans back in his chair and we start talking. Just talking. Sometimes about our work in progress. Sometimes about our family. Always about life.

12:00 a.m.
We power down our computers, close the office door and head downstairs to catch a bit of Letterman and local and international news before switching to a favorite DVD or broadcast movie and losing ourselves in worlds of other writers' making. We both fall asleep during the best part, then I wake Tony at a little after one. We both make sure all the animals are fed and tucked in for the night, lock up the house and head up to bed, happy and tired and looking forward to making tomorrow even better than today.

Tips and Tricks
Writing Tips

Ask an editor, any editor, what they're looking for and they'll invariably tell you "a good book." And when all is said and done, that's really what we're all looking for, isn't it? We want to laugh, cry, be surprised and touched. We want to immerse ourselves in familiar or different worlds and live lives that reach beyond the everyday, yet share a fundamental theme that bonds us with the characters, lets us into their hearts and their minds for a short while, seduces us to understand the problems they're facing and the decisions they make and—especially in romance—cheer and rejoice in the happily-ever-afters they find. We want each story we read or movie we watch to linger with us beyond the last page or the closing credits. And if the writer is really good, well, maybe we've also learned a little something along the way. Something that perhaps alters our own lives, makes them that much better, or provides a glimpse of something we may not have considered before. Gives us cause to say, "ah" or "oh" or hopefully both.

We're of the belief that everybody has at least one book in them. A good one. The key is in the telling, the sharing. Dig deep. You can't merely crank out pages, marvel at how the words snap, crackle and pop, and how they're just as good if not better than those published by other authors you've read. That's not what a good book is about. What it is about is the heart of the story and the storytelling. You can't be the outsider looking in, recording external details; you must live the story, be the characters, feel their angst, their humiliation, their pain, their love. You must laugh out loud at the passages you want to be funny, sob at the black moment when it appears all is lost. Do this and what will come shining through is your own unique voice—your way of telling a story as no one else can. Oh, sure, there are no truly new ideas out there. But what is different about your story is that it's yours, colored with your beliefs, your experiences, your distinctive take on life. And in the end, that's what all stories are: reflections of life...reflections of you.

We also subscribe to the "plotting is better" school of thought. Think of plot as a rough map of the road you want to travel, a guide that keeps you on track but doesn't prevent you from breathing in the unexpected scents you come across, appreciating the panoramic scenes you encounter or stop you from taking that fork in the road that's not even on the map. To provide an example, with our McCoy miniseries we brainstormed a very detailed personal outline for the first five books. One that—based on the characters and their own perspectives—defined the roles they played in each other's lives, created something special among all of them, as well as between two or three of them, experiences only they would understand. And by extension, we hope it created an intimacy not only between each of the characters, but between the reader and the characters, as well. This road map was something we were also able to refer to as we wrote Kat's book. It allowed us to help shape a bond between the brothers and their baby sister that was shaded with all that came before, and colored with everything that is new and fresh and about promise for the future.

So, that said, the best possible tip we can give you is to write a good book. Everything else—the list of Top Ten Ways To Make Your Book a New York Times Best-seller, how to edit, what other authors/reviewers/editors/agents have to say on the subject—well, they're all excuses not to write, really. And all topics you can take in after you've written that good book.

A good book we're out here dying to read.

Here are a few online links to resources if you find yourself in need of those excuses, or have your good book in hand and are ready for the next step:

eHarlequin.com is an excellent resource for writers
Romance Writers of America's home page: www.rwanational.com
In the NW Ohio/SE Michigan area? Check out Maumee Valley Romance Writers of America (MVRWA) at www.members.aol.com/mvrwa
www.fictionfactor.com/articles.html
www.forwriters.com
www.publishersmarketplace.com

We wish you joy in your own personal journey...
For more information on the authors, their advice and their books, visit www.toricarrington.com.

10

In Too Deep
by Tori Carrington

SHE WAS BACK. Hot, fleecy-soft and magnificently naked in his bed.

Ben Edwards knew instantly that the figure stretched out beside him wasn't his pet potbellied pig, Elvis, or, worse, his longtime butler, Newerth. Nor was the woman a figment of his imagination, a ghostly image from the past, or a manifestation of his dreams. No. It was spring, and beautiful, free-spirited Alannah White had returned in her unique way by slipping into his bed while he slept. If he had any doubt it was her, he had but to look at the single *Aspidistra elatior* in the clay pot sitting on the ledge of the multipaned bedroom window, backlit by the coming dawn. Over the past four years the plant had grown taller, the pot it was in bigger. And every year Alannah took the plant—called the cast-iron plant—with her when she left, along with a huge chunk of Ben's heart.

Ben drew in a deep breath, filling his nose with the sweet scent of Alannah's skin. He barely dared to budge the hand that lay against her curvy hip for fear that he'd wake her. Afraid that the move would force him to face his own demons. Right then, he merely wanted to relish her gypsy spirit, touch her warm skin and forget that he'd determined to refuse her; had told himself that this time he'd be strong enough to turn her away.

Only, he hadn't planned to wake up with her already in his bed.

Giving himself over to his baser instincts, he melded his fingers to her supple flesh, oh, so gently pressing her more tightly against his aroused body. He closed his eyes and groaned softly. Every year he told himself this was it, this was the time he was going to give Alannah an ultimatum: stay forever, or don't come back. If he didn't pull away now, he knew that strength would surrender to his fundamental need of her in his life, even if only for a few hours, days, or weeks.

Alannah shifted in her sleep, wriggling her bottom tantalizingly against him.

Sweet mercy.

Four years had passed since she'd swept into his life. He'd hired her to transform the plain, grass-covered lawn of his vast estate outside Providence, Rhode Island, into an English garden reminiscent of the home he had just transferred from to expand his financial consulting business across the pond. Four years since he'd first laid eyes on her, transplanting a buddleia that had been placed in the shade to a spot with full sunlight in front of his house. Her spiraling black hair had shone blue in the warm light, her long tanned legs bent under her while her breasts pressed invitingly against the soft white material of her T-shirt. Then she had turned her electric-blue eyes on him. Ben had felt as though she had somehow managed to turn the sun so it shone solely on him, setting him on fire and making England seem very far way.

And stirring in him a yearning to possess something that could never be his: her.

With agonizing care Ben circled his hand around her slender hip, over her smooth stomach and up to cup a small breast. The peak instantly stiffened, although her breathing indicated that she was still asleep. Heat, sure and swift, filled his groin and he arched into her. Within a few hours of first meeting Alannah she'd been in this very bed. And within those same few hours, that's where he'd wanted to keep her, always. But the only certainty in their sometimes relationship was that she would leave.

Ben moved to retract his hand. Alannah stirred and caught the limb, pressing it between her breasts. "You're awake," he said, his heart thundering in his chest.

She shifted until she was facing him, predawn shadows softening her features and turning her eyes to liquid black. She reached up and curved her fingers along his cheek, then walked the tips along the line of his jaw. "Hi."

The greeting was simple and direct and filled Ben with a need that transcended the mere physical. He longed to possess her, inside and out. Make love with her until she begged for mercy. Hold her to him until they ceased being two separate entities and instead became one.

"Hi, yourself."

Her plump lips bowed into a smile. "Did you miss me?"

Had he missed her? Every bloody moment of every single day. He brushed a silky black coil of hair away from her mouth. "Oh. Were you gone? I hadn't noticed."

She laughed softly, then laid her head against his chest. Intense emotion seared Ben's insides, rendering him incapable of doing anything more than hold her tightly to him, his hand hot against her sleek back. Raised an only child in a family devoid of affection, he had never known that a simple touch could communicate so much. The writer Anaïs Nin once said that ecstasy was born of the melding of physical need and deep love. When he'd first touched Alannah he had discovered the truth in those words. He craved her when she was here, and when she was gone, leaving him an emotional wreck, he couldn't cope with any more.

He shifted until his chin rested against the top of her fragrant curls and stared at the plant in the window and the splashes of color beyond it heralding the coming dawn. The son of a factory worker, he'd accomplished more than he'd ever dreamed of financially. Now his personal life was in dire need of attention. He found himself craving a wife. Wanting kids. He looked out over his hulking estate and longed to turn it into a home. And nowhere in that picture did wildly sexy Alannah fit in, no matter how much he tried to make it so.

"I missed you," Alannah whispered against the hair on his chest, the touch of her breath making him shudder.

"You miss nothing."

She rubbed her cheek against his skin. "Maybe."

Her fingers swept lightly over one of his flat nipples, then trailed down the middle of his abdomen, leaving flames licking in their wake. Ben drew a ragged breath.

"Alannah. There's something you and I need to discuss."

He trapped her fingers against his stomach, holding tight.

"Sounds ominous."

Perhaps that's because it was.

Ben closed his eyes, calling on every ounce of resolve he had. If this was to be done, it had to be done now. Before he caved and gave in to his need for her this one last time. Before he lost himself in the feel, taste and smell of her and forgot himself. The problem was he feared it was already too late….

During the weeklong bus trip it had taken her to get from Tacoma, Washington, and her last job as a horticulturist to Providence, Rhode Island, and Ben, Alannah had been afraid that this would be the time Ben would refuse her. She had seen it in his eyes the last time she'd left. That expression that said more than words could, but if the words could be spoken, they would have ended their longstanding spring fling forever. For the past eleven months she'd worried that he might find the woman who could give him what he wanted, what he needed. That elusive something that she could not provide: permanence, marriage, family.

She reasoned that it was that same fear that had compelled her to slip into his house in the middle of the night, strip out of her clothes, then climb into his bed while he slept. She'd sensed that while emotionally Ben might have erected barriers, physically he wouldn't be able to refuse her. But as she lay there still as the waning night, her hand ensnared by his, she feared that the situation was worse than she'd imagined. He meant to refuse her attentions. Refuse her need to be with him this one last time.

Longing blended with anguish and pulsed through her so strongly it took her breath away. She couldn't imagine her life without knowing that Ben was out there somewhere, wanting her as much as she wanted him.

"Alannah, you and I need to talk." Ben's voice reflected the pain she felt, calling out to something in her she couldn't resist.

"Shhh," she said, responding to the pain rather than the words. Emotion she could handle. It was always the words that got to her. She languidly slid her leg over his. She nearly cried out in relief when she found his arousal thick and pulsing. No matter how hard he tried, he couldn't hide his physical desire for her.

Ben groaned. But rather than move away from her, he pushed her hand toward its original destination. Alannah's blood thickened as he curled her fingers around his erection and squeezed both their hands around the hard proof of his desire for her. A need that couldn't be denied by any amount of mental argument. A want that not even she could stop herself from wanting.

16

Up, then down, he worked her hand against his hot flesh. She flicked her thumb over the silken dome, coming away with a bead of moisture that told her how close he was to crisis. If she had any doubt, his actions did away with them. In one smooth move he pinned her flat against the sheets, spreading her thighs with a quick nudge of his knee, then resting the knob of his arousal against her slick flesh. Alannah gasped, straining upward against him, trying to coax him inside. But he compensated for the move, staying put as he reached for a foil packet in the bedside drawer and began to sheathe himself.

He surged forward, filling her to overflowing. Her back came off the bed as she took him in, inch by inch, wanting him with a ferocity that erased coherent thought from her mind. Flames licked over her skin, then exploded inside her body, igniting a fathomless yearning she feared might not ever be satisfied. He surged forward again, forcing a low moan from her throat.

If his lovemaking was a little more thoughtful, gentler than she remembered, she chose not to acknowledge it. Instead she curved her fingers down his spine and grasped his firm rear. Ben muttered something under his breath then bucked against her, teasing the pearl of her arousal until he pulled back and swelled into her again…and again…and again. Alannah threw her head back and clutched him harder, her back shifting against the sheet, her heels finding and digging into his calves as she tilted her hips up to take him deeper.

This is what she'd been working toward. This total, complete abandonment. These sweet few moments when she forgot she was a dirt-poor girl from a small town outside Memphis whose parents had died when she was ten, leaving her to raise her little sister as best she could until child welfare caught up with them. All she could concentrate on was her desire for the man joining with her, and his need to possess her. The swell of emotion as their bodies melded, then parted, only to meld again. The overwhelming sense of being outside herself as her soul reached out for something she wouldn't dare hope for at any other time.

Ben's hands grasped her hips almost roughly, holding her still as he bucked against her once, twice, then toppled her over the other side of the swirling wash of color, following shortly thereafter. Giving them both what they'd been after.

BEN SAT ACROSS from Alannah at the large rough-hewn pine table, watching as she pulled apart a piece of cheese, then slipped a sliver between her lips. She wore one of his crisp business shirts, the whiteness contrasting with her tanned skin in the dim light of the kitchen. One button held it together and the flaps bowed open as she reached down and fed a piece of apple to Elvis, who was all too happy to see his mistress return.

Ben ran his hands through his tangled hair several times, trying to ignore the calling of his body even as he came to terms with the details of his plans. Nowhere had he allowed for making love to Alannah. His hormones raged, his heart beat an uneven staccato against his rib cage and he was afraid if he couldn't have her again within the next five minutes, he'd go mad.

"He looks good," Alannah said, jarring him from his thoughts.

18   Ben looked at the hundred-pound potbellied pig shimmying against her bare leg. Neither he nor the pig seemed able to forget that he'd been a gift from Alannah. A gift that constantly reminded Ben of her. And a ceaseless source of companionship, although a sore replacement for the woman Ben had always wanted but could never capture.

"Look, Alannah…"

He noticed her movements slow at the tone of his voice, but she didn't meet his gaze. Instead she seemed to concentrate on feeding Elvis, although she'd stopped matching him bite for bite, as though her appetite had up and left her.

"There's something you and I need to talk about." Ben hated the fact that he couldn't just come right out and say what was on his mind. The last thing he wanted to do was hurt her. And he wasn't sure how, but he knew that his turning her away would hurt her, even though their flings never lasted more than a couple of weeks. And even though she would always eventually leave of her own volition.

"What I'm trying to say here is…" What was he trying to say? "I mean…" *Oh, just be out with it, man.* "How long are you going to stay this time?"

Ben had broken Rule Number One. Although it had never been outlined as such, he knew that asking Alannah how long she was going to stay was forbidden territory. He'd never asked over the course of the past four years. Partly because he'd been afraid she wouldn't answer. But mostly because he hadn't wanted to face the truth that she would eventually be leaving. He hadn't wanted to acknowledge that small, hapless part of him that always hoped she might stay forever this time. It had happened that way over the past four years of their sometimes relationship. And it was now up to him to break that hurtful cycle.

THE GREAT THING about plants was that they always knew where they belonged. Unlike Alannah, who had never known where home lay. She funneled her fingers into the warm, rich Rhode Island earth, settling the soil around the roots of a transplanted *Anemone blanda*, then running the back of her hand across her forehead. In the four years since she'd initially transformed Ben's backyard into an English garden, the plants had flourished. The tulips and daffodils and bluebells were blooming. The vines of the *Clematis tangutica* climbed the trellis and the foxglove and aconite looked hearty and healthy. The cherub fountain she'd found at an estate sale gurgled.

She'd purposely designed the garden with self-sufficiency in mind. Which left her with very little to do other than prune, weed and fertilize come springtime.

Something cold and wet pressed against the arch of her bare foot. She glanced down to find Elvis prodding her, likely hoping that she had produced a treat from the warm earth. Alannah wiped her hand on her shorts, then rubbed his bristly haired snout, smiling at his soft, animated snorts of approval.

"I missed you, too, baby," she said quietly, wondering why her emotions hovered so close to the surface lately. But she didn't have to dig far for the answer. It was becoming increasingly clear that this would be her last trip to the land that had captured her affection four years ago. And to the only man who made her wonder what her life might have been like had circumstances been different.

20

Alannah produced a slice of apple from her pocket. Elvis noisily approved of the unexpected treat. So easy to please. Every year the potbellied pig greeted her as if she'd left the day before. She'd brought Elvis to the estate three years ago. She'd been drawn to the black-and-brown porker while on a job in Savannah and had meant him as a gag gift. Ben was so anally neat and organized she'd figured he needed the opposite in a pet. Nobody had been more surprised than her when he'd kept the squealing piglet rather than shipping it off to a neighboring farm. Newerth, Ben's uptight butler, had even confided that he'd caught Elvis sleeping in Ben's bed on occasion, a sight Alannah had a hard time imagining.

"Maybe you needed each other, huh, Elvis?" she said softly.

The pig burrowed his snout into her midriff in search of another treat, tickling her in the process. It seemed no one had bothered to tell the hundred-and-some-pound animal that he was no longer a piglet. Alannah smiled, her gaze drawn to movement in a nearby window. She met Ben's gaze where he stood on the other side of the beveled pane, a portable phone to his ear.

Their positions had been pretty much the same the first time she'd laid eyes on him, except then she'd been transplanting a buddleia in the front of the house to a sunnier location and he'd been watching her from the living room. She was surprised that not much had changed since that long-ago day. Her stomach still pitched to her feet. Her mouth went dry. And her heart felt as though it had been claimed by an outside source she was helpless to stop.

Ben had been unlike any other man she'd met before. His crisp, English accent teased her ears. His hot gaze made her open like a daylily under the warm rays of the sun. His self-possessed nature compelled her to make him lose all control. His unconditional acceptance of her made her want to plant her own roots in the soil of his love and stay forever, even though they both knew that she couldn't.

How long are you going to stay this time?

His words from a few hours ago echoed through her mind, causing her muscles to clench and her skin to itch. He'd never asked her before, lending credence to her fear that this time he meant to put an end to her annual visits.

Alannah broke the visual connection and dropped her gaze to the ground. She'd always known that this day would come. Sensed that one day Ben would want more than she was able to give him. Only, she hadn't expected it to come soon. She stabbed her trowel into the soil. "What did you think? That he'd wait for you forever?" she scolded herself. She repeatedly told herself that Ben deserved more. Knew that somewhere out there was a woman without her emotional baggage, who could put her own past aside and devote her life to him. Make his house a home. Give him children. The children she could never have for fear that they'd inherit her father's illness.

"I think you should take Elvis with you this time when you go."

The words caused Alannah's hand to still. Judging by the shadow falling across the garden, Ben stood directly behind her. A part of her was startled by how quickly he had moved from the upstairs to the garden. Another was bowled over by his words.

22

"The neighborhood has a rule about keeping animals. And they don't classify swine as pets."

She looked up to find him rubbing his neck and looking toward the house next door.

"So far I've been able to convince Mrs. Kindridge that Elvis is a rare breed of dog. But one of these days she's going to have those cataracts removed and get a closer look. I don't want to be responsible for her having a coronary."

First he'd asked how long she planned to stay; now he was telling her to take Elvis. Alannah felt the ground shift beneath her. And it didn't still when Ben finally met her gaze, the somber shadow there contrasting with the lightness of his words. If she'd been talking to anyone else she might have thought this a ploy to get her to stay, a deliberate attempt to hurt her, or even a type of reverse psychology to get her to rethink her actions. But this was

Ben. And Ben didn't play games. He said what he thought and did what he said. His integrity was one of the many qualities that had drawn her to him. He was everything and more than her alcoholic father had never been. And his lovemaking skills far surpassed anything she'd ever dreamed of.

"I...can't," she said softly, unable to rise to her feet. "I just...can't."

His eyes narrowed. "Can't what, Alannah? Take Elvis?" She watched his thick throat work around a swallow. "Or leave?"

It was over. Ben should just come out and say it. Save both him and Alannah the pain that was sure to come by continuing a charade that was up the moment it had begun. But as he stood there surrounded by the magnificent garden she had created with her slender hands, a garden that brought England home to him here in Rhode Island, the sunlight turning her hair a glossy blue-black, he could do little more than stare at her, the words in his throat jumbling. He'd been surprised he'd said what he had. Surprised he'd told her to take Elvis with her this time when she left.

"I...can't," she whispered again, her lips a plump red against her tanned skin.

"You can't take Elvis? Or you can't leave?" he repeated before he could stop himself.

Of course she'd meant that she couldn't take Elvis. The only thing she could make a commitment to was the plant she'd moved from the bedroom window this morning to the kitchen window. And then only because it was portable. He stood waiting for an answer to his question, ignoring the part of himself that wanted to take it back, pretend he'd never asked it.

Instead she ignored it. She got to her feet, gathered her gardening tools and then headed toward the gazebo where the landscaping equipment was kept in the bench inside. Elvis wandered toward his mud hole at the side of the steps, an ingenious invention he and Alannah had put together when she'd first brought the noisy porker to his house. Ben followed Alannah.

"Damn it, woman," he said, his words harsher than he'd intended. "Talk to me. Say something."

She carefully put her tools away, then secured the slat back down, turning the compartment back into a bench. The morning sun filtered through the lattice wall, playing hide-and-seek with her features. "What do you want me to say?"

"I'd like you to say what's on your mind, for starters." He stepped into the gazebo with her, noticing when she took an automatic step back. He was caught off guard. She'd flinched, as if afraid he meant to physically assault her.

"Okay, then," she said, her gaze flitting everywhere but to his face. "I can't take Elvis. You know that."

"Do I?" he asked, careful not to make another move for fear that he'd startle her again. "There seems to be a whole lot I don't know about you, Alannah. Aside from the fact that you have a magical way with plants. And that every year around this time you pop up for a visit that only leaves me wanting more." He stared at the ceiling. "I don't even know where you're from, for God's sake. If you have a home there that you go back to when you leave here. A family. Kids." He met her gaze meaningfully. "Or why you just flinched when I made a quick move."

She made a small, strangled sound that dived deep inside him, making him regret having said anything. Putting together bits and pieces over the years, he'd already surmised that she hadn't had an easy upbringing. Tinges of a Southern accent colored her honeyed voice, but she never mentioned anything about the South. Jagged scars marred her perfect skin. Marks that couldn't be explained away by a bike mishap or even a car accident, but he feared were from another person.

"Johnsontown."

Ben strained to hear what she'd said.

"Johnsontown, Tennessee. That's where I'm from."

The South.

"I don't go back there. I haven't been back there since—for a long time."

It was the most she'd voluntarily revealed about herself since they'd met. That she was doing so now caused hope to swell in Ben's chest. He stood quietly, waiting for her to offer more. Outside, the gentle spring breeze rustled the new leaves. Birds chirped. And the water from the fountain burbled. But Alannah remained silent.

"Tell me, Alannah. Tell me what it is you're keeping from me." Ben recognized the pleading in his voice, but couldn't help himself. He gently grasped her arms. "Tell me what it is that prevents you from loving me."

Her eyes widened as she looked at him and her throat made a clicking sound as she swallowed. She opened her mouth as if to say something, then pressed her lips tentatively against his. Ben stood completely still, watching her. She snaked her hands up and around his neck and brought her body flush with his, the tips of her breasts teasing his chest as she took a deep breath and launched another attack.

Ben didn't doubt that her desire was real. But he knew a diversionary tactic when he saw one. They were a daily occurrence in the world of financing. Clients trying to hide losses, or explain away a bad investment. But dealing with it in his professional life was one thing. Encountering it in the woman he wanted more than anything else quite another. He felt her fingers on his bare stomach where she'd pulled his oxford shirt from his pants. Then she was tunneling the same fingers between his skin and jeans, too impatient to undo the snaps as she sought his erection.

Need, pure and intoxicating, steamrolled over Ben. The only thing Alannah had ever been willing to share of herself was her body. And at one time that had been enough. No. Now he realized that it had never been enough. But he hadn't known how to go about getting more. Couldn't figure out how to break through her emotional barriers to the woman beyond. And it frustrated him beyond reason to know that he probably never would.

A few moves left her without shorts and panties. She pushed him back until he sat down on one of the cushioned gazebo benches. He'd always wanted her more than was wise, and right now it wasn't hard to understand why. She pulled her T-shirt up and over her head, leaving her black curls in wild disarray and framing her heart-shaped face and blue, blue eyes as she straddled him. When Alannah visited, Ben knew to always be prepared, and now wasn't an exception. He handed her a condom. She took it and kissed him. Soulfully, her tongue lapping, her teeth biting. Ben lost himself in her attentions. Then she was taking him inside her, slowly, torturously, her pink-tipped breasts heaving merely inches away as she drew in ragged breaths of air. He pulled one of the stiff peaks into his mouth and sucked, reveling in her low moan of pleasure.

Then two things happened at once: his butler, Newerth, called out for him, apparently having shown up earlier than expected after his weekend break; and he realized she had never put the condom on him. Nothing separated him from her slick, tight flesh. He groaned and recklessly surged up into her....

AFTER THEIR sexy interlude in the gazebo, Ben couldn't run far enough, fast enough from Alannah. He'd pulled his clothes together and jogged toward the house to answer Newerth's page. If she had been the sensitive type, she would have been stung by what amounted to his rejection after being so intimate. But nothing seemed to be as it once was. And she was slowly coming to realize that soon she'd have to go. This time forever.

Alannah affectionately hosed down Elvis then dried him off, her stomach squeezing at the thought that she'd never see the obnoxious potbellied pig or his master again. She stepped into the kitchen to find Ben gone and his very English butler seeing to lunch. Or dinner, as he preferred to call it.

"Master Edwards was called away to an important meeting," Newerth informed her in his clipped accent.

Alannah told herself she wasn't upset that he hadn't said goodbye himself before leaving, but her heart wasn't having any of it. "Did he say when he might be back?"

Newerth indicated that no, he hadn't. But his somber expression told Alannah more than his words. It seemed that everyone but her knew the score.

"I see," she said quietly.

"Here," Newerth said, pouring a cup of tea. "Have a seat."

Alannah did as he bid, drawing warmth from the antique cup. "Join me?"

The stodgy butler had always reminded her of the role Sir John Gielgud had played in the movie *Arthur.* Tall and gangly, he'd seemed barely able to tolerate her presence on previous visits, turning his nose up at what he undoubtedly saw as unacceptable behavior. A widower in his fifties with two grown children back in Liverpool, he'd been with Ben for seven years and was more companion than hired help. Just like the garden she had nurtured for Ben, Newerth was another piece of the home that he had left behind.

"Don't mind if I do," Newerth said, surprising her. He grabbed something from the cupboard, poured himself a splash of tea, then sat adjacent to her. "Something to liven things up?" he asked, holding up a bottle of rye whiskey.

Alannah held her cup out and summoned up a smile. Newerth poured until there was more rye than tea in her cup. Two hours later Alannah felt as though she had a new best friend.

"I don't know what I'm going to do, Newerth," Alannah said, having long since forgone the tea and pouring straight rye into her cup. She poured the butler a dollop, as well. "I know I should go, but I can't seem to make my feet move toward the door, you know?"

The older man nodded his head, his eyes glassy, his

words revealing a bit more of his own upbringing. "I have the same problem meself. I do so miss home, you know. My youngest just had my first grandchild. A boy. Named after me, of all things."

Alannah patted Elvis on the head where he sat next to her chair and Newerth fed the pig a bit of the salad he'd fixed. "You know, I don't think you've ever told me your first name."

The butler smirked. "Newerth is my Christian name."

"Oh."

They stared at each other, then began laughing, the whiskey having broken down all class barriers.

"Oh, my," Newerth said, glancing at the clock. "Dinner's already a half hour late." He pushed from his chair. "I'd better go clean up. I don't think Master Edwards would approve."

Alannah stifled the desire to ask him to sit with her a little longer. "Yes, well, I think a cup or two of this would do Master Edwards some good. Don't you?"

Newerth smiled at her, then shuffled from the room, his neat black suit rumpled. Alannah screwed the top back on the rye, then eyed the nearly empty bottle, her gaze drifting toward the phone on the opposite wall. Her thoughts wandered to her sister. And the instant they did, guilt coated her insides. Like her, Kyra had left their hometown when she was very young. But unlike her, she had stayed put in the first place she'd gone to: Tampa, Florida. Uncapping the bottle again, Alannah poured the remaining contents into her cup, then retrieved the cordless receiver and brought it back to the table. Within moments, the line was ringing.

"Al!" her younger sister practically shouted. "How

are you doing? Where are you? God, it's good to hear from you."

Alannah pressed her chin against the receiver and smiled. "It's good to hear your voice, too, sweet pea."

"You sound funny. Have you been drinking?"

Alannah shrugged. "Maybe a little."

The next five minutes were spent catching up. Alannah told Kyra all the places she'd visited and worked over the past four months, and Kyra told her about her latest boyfriend and her bookkeeping job at an architectural firm. But obviously Alannah had told her little sister a little too much over the years. Because Kyra knew exactly where she was just then, despite Alannah's careful avoidance of the topic.

"So…are you going to give the gorgeous Brit more than a couple of weeks this time around?"

Alannah nearly choked. "How did you…"

"It's springtime, isn't it?"

Silence.

"Al? Are you still there?"

Yes, she was still there. In Ben's house. Waiting for Ben to come home. So she could leave him again.

"What would you think about my coming by for a visit?" she asked her little sister.

BEN RETURNED from the meeting that could have waited until another time, his ears automatically alert, listening for sounds of Alannah's presence. If the house seemed a little brighter somehow, he tried to tell himself it wasn't because she was there. Soft laughter drew him toward the kitchen. He stopped in the doorway, eyebrows raised, looking at where Alannah and Newerth were tying one on.

"Sir." Newerth instantly got to his feet, grabbing for the two bottles littering the table. "Al...I mean Mistress White and I were just passing the time with some conversation until you got back."

Al? "Looks like you and Mistress White have been doing a bit more than conversing."

Alannah's soft, musical laughter filled the bright kitchen. Elvis charged Ben's knees, nearly knocking him off his feet. Alannah tested the bottles, then picked up the one that still held rye. "Care for a nip?"

Newerth immediately made himself scarce, leaving Ben facing a thoroughly sloshed Alannah. He nearly groaned. Even half in the bag she was still the most incredible creature he'd ever laid eyes on.

"I think I'll pass," he murmured. "Come on. I think it would be best if you had a little nap."

He helped her up from the chair. She swayed against him, smiling up at him. "Only if you promise to come with me."

Fire blazed a trail down his abdomen. "I'll tuck you in. How's that?"

She made a face at him.

In the upstairs hall she lost her footing. Ben steadied her against the wall, where she stood silently for long moments, staring at him. She was going to be the end of him, this spirited beauty who drifted in and out of his life like a real-life Persephone emerging from the underworld. He watched her lick her lips, and then before he knew he was going to do it, he was kissing her. No, he wasn't merely kissing her. He was devouring her. As if he kissed her long enough, hard enough, she'd agree to his every demand. Moments later he came up for air, lost in the desire and darkness of her eyes.

"Stay, Alannah," Ben whispered, holding her hair back from her face so he might kiss her again. "Please stay."

"STAY...PLEASE STAY."

Alannah floated on a sea of bright sunlight, Ben's strikingly handsome face smiling down at her. She reached out to scratch her palm against his stubble-covered cheek and the image receded. She shakily drew her hand back, another image taking its place as she watched. Dark hair was replaced by light, brown eyes were traded for hazel, and Ben's smile for a hateful scowl. Ben had become her father.

"Stay put, or I'll kill you."

Alannah tried to fold in on herself as she traveled in a time warp back to the two-room shack that had been her home for much of her early life. She was crouched in the corner holding her little sister, Kyra, and her father was beating her mother again. Only, now a shotgun had replaced his fist, and her father was holding the barrel against the side of her mother's battered head. "I warned you, didn't I? I told you that if you sassed me again I'd make sure you never said another word."

A blast deafened Alannah, then something wet and sticky speckled her face even as she pressed her sister's head into her stomach. Another blast and both her parents were dead on the dirty linoleum floor, leaving her and her sister alone.

"No!"

Alannah emerged from the nightmare gasping for air, wiping feverishly at the sweat on her face.

"It's all right, love. It's okay now. It was just a dream."

Alannah fought against Ben when he tried to hold her as the world slowly shifted back into focus. She finally gave in and collapsed against Ben's broad chest in a sobbing mass. It had been years since she'd had the nightmare. Since she'd thought about that time at all, even though it was always with her, stuck to her like a tattoo. She reasoned that Ben's passionate request earlier that day had brought the terrible memories back, reminding her why she had never returned home. Reminding her why she had to keep moving. Reminding her why she had to say goodbye to Ben one final time...

Ben held Alannah so tightly he was afraid he might snap her in two. Never had he been so alarmed about another's well-being. But when she'd frantically called out in her sleep, then wilted against him and wept, he knew that he didn't have a real clue about the woman he held. He'd always guessed she had demons snapping at her heels. He was afraid he'd underestimated the size and viciousness of those demons. Easy to do, considering Alannah's own free-spirited attitude toward life. Her ability to drift in and out of his like the season she represented. He'd never imagined she was actually running from someone or something.

Ben repositioned her limp body against his, his fingers splayed against her silky hair, his chin resting against the top of her head. He'd give anything to know what she'd seen in her dream. What she was running from. But he had the terrible sense that he would never learn either. If there was one thing he'd come to know about Alannah, it was that she was self-sufficient, not given to depending on anyone for anything. When he'd tried to give her more than the agreed-upon amount for taking care of his garden after their first encounter, she'd staunchly refused. And whatever money he managed to slip into her bag before she left during her next two visits was mailed back to him with a note bearing a simple smiley face.

Dusk settled around the manor, filling the bedroom with purple light and casting the single plant in the bedroom window in shadow. He suspected that Newerth must have brought the plant up when he'd been otherwise occupied.

Of course, he didn't expect an answer to his earlier question. He'd been out of his mind with need when he'd asked her to stay. Although his desire for her to do just that was doubly strong now. Didn't she see that they could help one another? He could help her face down her demons with a united front. And she could give him springtime all year round. She shifted against him restlessly. Ben's throat tightened as he smoothed her hair back from her face. "Shhh. Rest, my love. Everything's going to be all right." He only wished he could make it so....

BEN SNAPPED AWAKE. He must have drifted off while soothing Alannah after her dream. His gaze swept instantly to the window. The plant was gone. Bloody hell.

He'd determined not to fall asleep. When she'd looked at him with such sorrow on her face, he'd known she planned to leave as soon as she was able to. But he'd wanted to talk to her first. Lay all his cards on the table. Make one last-ditch effort to try to get her to stay.

Yes, his pride demanded that he just let her go, let her walk out of his life without a fight. But there was a part of him that kept repeating, What if. What if he did let her leave without giving it, her, everything he had? Would he spend the remaining days of his life wondering if things could have worked out differently? That if he had said this, or done that, she might have stayed?

He catapulted from the bed. It took him mere seconds to determine that her things were gone. He was halfway down the stairs before he even realized that he was only half-dressed, having taken off his shirt before lying down with her.

"Alannah?"

The plaintive sound of his voice caused his heartbeat to kick up another few notches. His fear was that she was already long gone. Vanished from his life forever with nothing more than a town name to use to look her up. A town he suspected she would never return to.

"Alannah—"

He halted in the doorway to the kitchen, his skin slick with sweat, his breathing labored. There, standing in the middle of the kitchen with tears in her blue, blue eyes, was Alannah.

Alannah stared at Ben. He looked irresistibly rumpled from having just gotten out of bed. But she had to resist him. No matter how hard that was to do. Her heart dipped into her stomach. She felt as if her entire world was being ripped apart at the seams. She should have been gone by now. That had been the plan. If she'd briefly entertained any thoughts of staying on at Ben's manor, even for an extended visit, they'd been chased away by the memories of her parents' deaths.

How could Ben understand—how could anyone but Kyra possibly understand—that the only way she could battle the demons was by keeping ceaselessly on the move? That the challenge of finding a place to stay, designing new landscapes, digging her fingers into the rich earth provided her a sense of peace she couldn't find elsewhere?

"Elvis is gone," she found herself whispering.

"Elvis?" Ben looked as if a hundred-pound flat rock had been lifted from his chest. "Good Lord, Alannah, I thought you had left."

In two long-legged strides he stood in front of her, grasping her arms, his sexy brown eyes intense as he looked down at her. Alannah absently allowed the duffel that held all her belongings to slide to the floor, but held tightly to her potted plant.

"Damn it, Alannah. Don't go."

She swallowed hard, the sound seeming to echo in the large, silent room.

"Stay here with me. Whatever it is you're running from, whatever haunts you, we can work it out together. Give me a chance. Give us a chance."

She wavered on her feet.

"You're everything in this world that I hold dear," he whispered, his mouth tempting her gaze, her touch. "Marry me, Alannah."

The back door opened and closed and Newerth said, "He isn't out back…oh."

The butler came to an awkward stop mere feet from them.

"Elvis," Alannah whispered, incapable of saying anything more.

"Newerth?" Ben said in an even voice. "Leave us."

"Leave…oh. Yes, sir."

The butler shuffled from the room and once again they were alone.

Biting emotion assaulted Alannah from every direction. The loneliness of the past ten years spent out on the road, roaming from place to place, job to job. Her love for the man gazing at her, his huge heart in his eyes, looking as if he'd give, do absolutely anything if she'd just stay there with him.

"I…I can't," she said, her voice breaking.

They stood there like that for what seemed an eternity. Then slowly Ben's gaze changed. The warmth that had filled his eyes moments before cooled to a dark ember. The hope that had animated his features vanished, leaving behind a cold mask. "I see."

No, he didn't see. Couldn't. Didn't he understand that she loved him more than her own life? Didn't he know that leaving him after every visit was the most difficult thing she'd ever had to do?

He released her and stepped back. "Very well, then." His gaze scanned her from head to toe, lingering on the plant she still held on to for dear life. "Then it ends right here." She thought she saw him wince even as he said the words, but couldn't be sure because of her own flinch. "No more spring visits, Alannah. This is it. I won't be here when you come back next time."

Alannah's heart beat so loudly she barely heard him, but the meaning of his words was very clear.

Newerth appeared in the kitchen doorway and quietly cleared his throat. "I just received a call from the neighbor Mrs. Kindridge. It seems Elvis has made his way over there."

"Thank God," Alannah whispered. At least one thing in this whole mess would turn out all right.

Newerth smiled. "Mrs. Kindridge's eyesight must be worse than we thought. Even up close and personal, she swears Elvis is the nicest dog she's ever come across."

Alannah couldn't seem to pull her gaze from Ben's somber features. She secured the strap of her bag over her shoulder. "I, um, better be going."

"Don't you want to take Elvis with you?"

She bit her lip, then shook her head. "No. This is the only home he's ever known. He belongs here. With you."

Ben cursed under his breath. "And you, Alannah? Where is your home?"

She looked at him long and hard, then turned away.

His feet cemented to the kitchen floor, Ben watched Alannah walk out the door with that cursed plant. Another man would rush out after her. Do anything, say anything to get her to stay. Another woman would have stayed.

He'd expected to feel a sense of release once he'd reached closure in his on-again, off-again relationship with Alannah White. But as he stood there in his hulking excuse for a house, his butler hiding in the shadows somewhere waiting to do his bidding, and his "dog" having run away to the neighbor's, he felt a sense of grief so overpowering it nearly brought him to his knees.

He'd never felt about one person the way he felt about Alannah. Her gypsy spirit, her lust for life and love, had cast a spell over him he was helpless to break. He'd thought finally ending things would allow him to move

38

on. Free him to live life the way he thought it should be lived.

Only, he couldn't imagine his life without Alannah in it. Even if it was only for the few days every year when she showed up on his doorstep, bringing the sun with her.

"Sir?" Newerth said quietly. "Is there anything I can do to help?"

"Get out of my way, man. I'm going after her." But when he reached the door and rushed out to the street, she was nowhere to be seen.

ALANNAH HAD ALWAYS BEEN alone. But until now she hadn't known what true loneliness was. It had been four hours since she'd told Ben goodbye one last time. And every tick of the clock made the pain more palpable, more biting.

"Anything else, miss?" the truck stop diner waitress asked.

Alannah glanced out to where the passengers were re-boarding the bus. "No. No, thank you." She drank the remaining coffee in her cup, dug change for a tip out of her pocket, then slid out of the booth. Denver. That was the sign on the front of the bus. She hadn't realized that's where she was heading until just then. When she'd arrived at the bus station she'd gotten on the first bus heading out.

She stood at the diner door, waiting for hope to blossom in her chest. She'd never been to Denver, but she'd always wanted to go. Different setting, different indigenous plants. And now was the perfect time to go. She'd have her pick of landscaping jobs. But instead of hope, she felt nothing but desolation. Instead of jagged, snow-capped mountains, she saw Ben's loving gaze, virtually felt his knowing touch.

The cowbell above the door rang.

"Excuse me?" someone said in a small, reedy voice.

Alannah blinked and found herself face-to-face with a woman—not much older than she was—standing in the open doorway clutching a young girl's hand. She looked cold and scared and as alone as Alannah felt. The woman glanced behind her, as if expecting to find the devil on her heels. Alannah's heart squeezed so painfully it took her breath away. She moved to allow the woman and her daughter to pass.

What would have happened had her mother left her father? Had she packed up their meager belongings and taken off with her and Kyra? Would things have turned out differently? Or ended up the same?

The woman helped the girl up onto a stool, then took off her threadbare red jacket. The girl immediately started chattering on about what she wanted as her mother counted the handful of change she'd scrounged from her purse. Alannah felt suddenly dizzy. Could her own actions, moving from place to place, be a manifestation of what she hoped her mother would have done? That even if the three of them had to be constantly on the move, at least her mother would still be alive? That they could have been still a family?

She glanced toward the bus to Denver waiting outside, then back at the woman. The stranger had had the strength to face down her demons. Did she have the same strength? Or would she live out the remainder of her life constantly running from the past? The woman told her daughter she had to have oatmeal instead of pancakes. Rather than protesting, the girl quietly accepted the cheaper meal, her eyes draining of laughter.

Alannah dug in her pockets, then her wallet, pulling together every dollar she had.

"Get her the pancakes," she told the waitress. She turned toward the woman, took her hand, then placed the money in it. "Do whatever it takes. And…good luck."

Alannah hurried for the bus.

THE PLANT WAS in the window.

Ben blinked several times to determine that he wasn't seeing things. Then someone shifted next to him, and a warm, bare bottom was pressed against his burgeoning arousal. Dear Lord, Alannah had come back.

He groaned and pulled her flush against him, restlessly stroking her back and her arms, seeking her mouth for a more meaningful welcome. He hadn't stopped to think that she might be sleeping. Her tongue sought access to his mouth, then swirled inside, revealing that she wasn't only not asleep, she was as hungry for him as he was for her.

Minutes later they finally came up for air. Alannah's breath filled his ear as she clung to him almost desperately. "I got as far as Scranton. I just couldn't go on."

He pulled back to stare into her beautiful face. "Why?"

Her smile was happy and sad all at once. "Because I love you," she whispered so quietly he nearly didn't hear her. "Because you're right. I need to stop running. Because when you asked me where home was for me, I wanted to say here."

Ben pulled her back into his arms, holding her as if he was afraid she'd disappear if he didn't.

"Is this for good?"

She went still in his arms. Then he felt her mouth on his shoulder. Soft, wet flicks of her tongue that started a fire in his groin. He thought she was embarking on another diversionary expedition and moved to object. "Yes," she said. "This is for good."

THE FOLLOWING DAY Ben drove like a madman to get home after a meeting he'd been unable to reschedule. His heart beat an anxious rhythm against his rib cage, his hands were slick against the steering wheel.

"Face it, man, you're afraid she's not going to be there," he told himself. As the car tires squealed against the asphalt, he knew that the words were true. He'd awakened this morning believing last night a dream. But with Alannah pressing against one side of him and Elvis against the other, he'd known what had happened was very real.

He ran his fingers through his hair as he turned onto his street. Damn it. Was this how it was going to be? Every time he left the house, would he be afraid she'd change her mind and wouldn't be there when he got back? He realized that yes, it probably was. Too much had happened between the two of them for things to go differently. Yes, he believed she loved him. But that hadn't stopped her from leaving before. And it wouldn't stop her from leaving again.

He raced into the driveway, parked, then catapulted from the car. He was halfway to the door when he caught a flash of white near the front water fountain. His steps slowed as he spotted Alannah bent over the fresh earth, Elvis frolicking by her side. His breath caught in his throat. She was still there. *This time,* a little voice told him. He ignored it and crept up behind her.

"What are you doing?" he asked, pleased when he startled her.

She turned and sat down on her delectable rump while Elvis charged his knees.

"Hi," she said, giving him a smile as bright as the spring sunlight.

"Hi, yourself."

"Elvis, um, and I were just seeing to a little overdue gardening."

Overdue gardening? Alannah never left without making sure every last thing was seen to.

She moved to stand, revealing what she'd been working on. The plant she'd dragged with her all the way to hell and back was packed in the brown earth, the pot discarded beside it. Doubt, insecurity and uncertainty drifted from Ben's body on the light breeze. Alannah slipped her arm around his waist and squeezed.

"Are you all right?" she asked.

He looked at her. Really looked at her. Taking in her vivid blue eyes. Her smooth, tanned skin. Her red, red mouth. And knew that he'd never worry about her again.

"I am now," he whispered, and kissed her.

Then he led the way to the house that had been turned into a home, Elvis galloping around them.

THE END

Originally published as an online read.

TOP TEN

Signs He's Going To Propose
by Andrea Kerr

Ah, spring. The season when a young man's fancy turns to love and marriage? If you're wondering whether or not your sweetie is ready to pop the question, ask yourself if he's exhibiting any of the top 10 signs, listed here in no particular order. But remember, men are fickle creatures, and the romance experts here at eHarlequin.com can't be held responsible if your finger remains ringless despite indications to the contrary!

1 He takes you jewelry shopping.

If accompanying him to the jewelers isn't obvious enough for you, then nothing we say will convince you that yes, this man is planning to pop the question. He thinks he's being sneaky about scoping out your preferences for white versus yellow gold, round versus pear-shaped diamond. Maybe it's not the most romantic of tactics, but at least you won't have to love what's in the little velvet box if you pick it out yourself.

Warning: Knowing how much or how little he spent on your ring can be dangerous territory.

2   His ex gave him the "marry me or else" ultimatum. And lost.

It may sound harsh, but men are often "loosened up" to the idea of marriage by a previous girlfriend. Although your guy never got around to popping the question to his marriage-minded ex (lucky for you!), she probably dropped a lot of hints before finally dropping him.

Warning: If you suspect this is the case with your man, before saying yes, be sure he isn't just trying to make his ex-girlfriend jealous.

3   He gets all goo-goo-eyed around children.

Men have biological clocks, too, and your guy may be starting to hear the alarm now that all his buddies are too busy with diapers, Little League practices and dance recitals to go golfing with him.

Warning: This guy is ready to be a dad, and as his current girlfriend, you may seem like the obvious choice for the role of Mommy. Before you say yes, make sure it's you he's marrying, not your ovaries.

4   He's added lunges into his exercise routine.

He may be concerned that, having gotten to his age without ever going down on one knee, he may not be able to get back up once he finally assumes the position.

Warning: Okay, we're making this up. He's probably just added lunges to his exercise routine to tighten up those gluts.

5   He talks to himself.

A lot of guys need to practice the big speech, and they want to know they're going to look good when the time comes. What better way than to do a dress rehearsal in front of his toughest critic, himself! Maybe that's what you witnessed when you saw him nervously muttering to himself the other day?

Warning: Or maybe not. Maybe he has an equally nerve-wrecking presentation scheduled at work. Maybe he just talks to himself, and this is the first time you've noticed.

6   He takes your hand, looks deep into your eyes and whispers your name before asking you what you'd like on your pizza.

He's bought the ring, he wants to ask the question; in fact, he's about to ask the question when it suddenly hits him there could be a better time or place, or that he just needs a few more practice runs in front of his mirror. Be patient. He'll find the right moment.

Warning: The "right moment" may never come if he is, in fact, just too afraid of commitment to actually get to the point. And that's okay; you don't want to marry a guy who can't ask you a simple question.

7   He's uncharacteristically concerned with making things "perfect."

True story; friends of mine almost didn't get engaged on a kayaking trip because the fianceé-to-be was so irritated that her boyfriend was wasting time trying to track down a camera before they set out for the day.

The before picture: a very impatient girlfriend. The after picture: a very happy but slightly ashamed bride-to-be.

Warning: It's hard to keep yourself camera-ready at all times.

8 He's planning a romantic evening or getaway.

Has he made reservations at your favorite restaurant or asked you to go away with him for the weekend? Is your anniversary coming up? If so, he may be reflecting on the very special relationship you two share and be planning to make it permanent.

Warning: While proposals do happen under these circumstances, many a bridal hopeful's dreams have been dashed by assuming too much about a night out. Your guy may, in fact, just be flexing the muscles of his romantic heart. Either way, just relax and enjoy.

9 He wants to introduce you to his family.

If you've had Sunday dinner with his parents for the past five years and still don't have a ring, then this one doesn't apply to you. But if he invites you to another city, state or country to meet his parents at long last or decides it's time his children from a previous relationship met the woman in his life, chances are he's pretty serious about you.

Warning: It's great that he wants you to be part of his family, but if his intentions are subject to their approval—watch out!

10 You're expecting.

Planning for the surprise arrival of a mutual relative some time in the next nine months? Pregnancy can inspire even the most confirmed bachelor to propose. And while we certainly don't suggest or condone "accidentally" getting pregnant to inspire a proposal, if you were already planning on being together forever, well, now you have a really good reason to get started on those plans.

Warning: Before you say yes, consider whether you would have married this man if the stick hadn't turned pink. Then consider is he merely proposing because he thinks he has to?

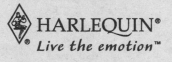

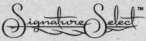

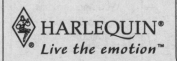

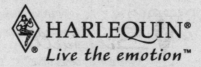

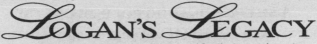

LOGAN'S LEGACY

Because birthright has its privileges and family ties run deep.

The long-awaited Logan's Legacy conclusion is here!

THE HOMECOMING

by *USA TODAY* bestselling author

ANNE MARIE WINSTON

Sydney Aston is determined to reunite Danny Crosby with his long-lost son. But she soon finds herself falling totally in love with this tormented man—and realizes that this could be a homecoming for all three of them.

Where love comes alive™

Blaze™

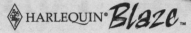